I started working in nightclubs and pubs at the age of 16. Anything from promoter, bouncer, DJ, barman, manager, and owner. I retired from the hospitality industry on 31 December 2022. I have two sons who are my pride and joy, and a German shepherd called Spike.

For Alex and Max.

J. C. Jones

CLUBLAND

AUSTIN MACAULEY PUBLISHERS
LONDON * CAMBRIDGE * NEW YORK * SHARJAH

Copyright © J. C. Jones 2025

The right of J. C. Jones to be identified as author of this work has been asserted by the author in accordance with sections 77 and 78 of the Copyright, Designs and Patents Act 1988.

All rights reserved. No part of this publication may be reproduced, stored in a retrieval system, or transmitted in any form or by any means, electronic, mechanical, photocopying, recording, or otherwise, without the prior permission of the publishers.

Any person who commits any unauthorised act in relation to this publication may be liable to criminal prosecution and civil claims for damages.

This is a work of fiction. Names, characters, businesses, places, events, locales, and incidents are either the products of the author's imagination or used in a fictitious manner. Any resemblance to actual persons, living or dead, or actual events is purely coincidental.

A CIP catalogue record for this title is available from the British Library.

ISBN 9781035824496 (Paperback)
ISBN 9781035824502 (ePub e-book)

www.austinmacauley.com

First Published 2025
Austin Macauley Publishers Ltd®
1 Canada Square
Canary Wharf
London
E14 5AA

Fran, Mum, Dad, and Leebob, and the gang.

Cover by Max Jones.

Chapter 1
Goodbye

Opening the blue steel front door for the last time, Jimmy wasn't sure what sort of reception he was going to get. The old lock clunked as it always did. It had needed replacing for years but it was one of those jobs that no one ever got round to doing. He closed the door behind himself, and it became apparent that he would not be getting a reception of any kind. The whole club was deserted.

Jimmy stood alone in the foyer in the dark. After over 10 years, he was not even going to get a handshake. Jimmy walked through to the bar and turned off the alarm. As he walked, he was putting the lights on as he went. After so many years, it was second nature and he probably could've done it blindfolded.

For the last time, he powered up the old girl and got ready for his final Saturday afternoon shift. Jimmy stood there before he turned the jukebox on and just listened to the hum of the fridges and the lights.

He, of course, had half-expected no one to be here. Ever since he had announced, just over a month ago, that he was leaving, the shoulder had been so cold he nearly caught frost bite on several occasions. Removed as manager, busted down to afternoon bar shifts and general menial tasks. Owners ignoring he even existed, the other manager lording it like he'd won the lottery, but he had nearly finished working his notice period. Just six hours to navigate and it would all be over.

It had been a sad series of events that had led to this point but here he was, he couldn't change them, not now, even if he had wanted to it was just too late.

He approached the long main bar downstairs in Parkers' nightclub. On it was a bottle of champagne and a card. He opened the card and found it had £100 in it and very brief 'Thank you for 10 years' service and all that you have done' written inside. He felt a wave of relief that anything was there but a distinct feeling that it was very little when compared with what he deserved.

10 years previously, he'd come in and turned the dive bar into *the* alternative bar to be at. Live bands, rock nights and not just galvanised a scene, he'd created one. He was determined to make them pay. He told himself to just breathe, it was nearly over.

The shift passed by relatively quick with no dramas. A few people popping in to say goodbye and the usual few who popped in for a few games of pool and a pint or three. The last month had made him feel he was going out with a whimper when it should've been a bang.

Exactly at 6pm, David, the now sole manager, walked in. He strutted up to the bar; he was wearing that godawful cologne that always made Jimmy sneeze.

"Keys."

David held his hand out. Jimmy had most of his keys taken away over the last month under various guises and excuses already so they weren't many left. Jimmy handed him the key ring with the remaining few keys on it. David smirked at him; he was having great trouble controlling his emotions at this point. Jimmy was quite worried that if David got any more excited, he'd piss himself but he managed to keep his bladder under control. Jimmy turned to the bar and picked up his card and the bottle then he started stepping away.

"Jimmy, you are about to find out exactly what it takes to run a nightclub!"

Jimmy spun on the spot, walked the six or seven yards between them very quickly and purposefully. In his haste and belying his feelings, he ended up standing no less than ten centimetres from David's face.

"No, David, *you* are about to find out what it takes to run a club."

Jimmy didn't raise his voice, there was no need, the weasel was terrified of him anyway. He turned and strode outside into the sunshine. His heart was racing and he could feel his pulse in his fingers that held the bottle of champagne. He would only return into that club once—but we'll get to that later.

Saturday, 1 August, and he was finished at the club. A project he'd poured his heart and soul into over the previous 10 years. He had worked tirelessly, made the owners a fortune, and now he was on his own. Jimmy didn't want to destroy it though, he just wanted to show them the error of their ways and he was hell bent on making David eat his words.

Jimmy had one week to get his new club ready to open. There was no other option; he'd already invited everyone and God, did he do to take some money. It had cost a fortune so far. Friday, 7 August, it was all systems go. It had to happen.

He had leased an old derelict nightclub in an industrial area of the city. The building containing the club was pretty big. It was a two-storey building and had several empty shops and an abandoned restaurant. Jimmy could see the potential in the area though. Set just far away from the main streets, lots of quirky buildings around and Jimmy could see how it could become a very Bohemian independent area. The rents were cheap, and if just a few businesses opened, the footfall would increase dramatically.

The lease had been agreed back in January to initially open as a youth centre. When he'd gone in, it was just a shell. It had no working electrics; the floor was warped, and there were some interesting plants growing where the roof leaked. Those problems were put right as swiftly as possible and then he had to confront the toilets, which had no actual toilets or sinks. It made him laugh a bit that the previous tenants had taken the old stinking toilets but left the condom machine with £150 in it on the wall.

The whole building had crazy murals on the wall of film scenes and action heroes. They had unfortunately flaked over the years due to the damp and had to be painted over, some required four or five coats as they kept showing through every layer of paint that Jimmy applied.

Outside had been jet washed down to remove all the cobwebs, debris and road dirt that had accumulated in the previous few years of being empty. It was then painted in black gloss. Jimmy hoped that not only would this be very visible, but it would also be easy to keep clean and repaint as, and when, necessary.

It was all coming on well. Electrics were in, toilets had toilets with working sinks and overall; Jimmy was beginning to take a real sense of pride in it. It was quite hard with work to find the time to keep the refurbishment going at a good pace, but he found going in at three or four in the morning both therapeutic and rewarding. His productivity had always been much better at night. He was definitely not a morning person.

Soon he felt he was getting a real handle on it all but then February, March and April happened. First, his eldest son was born in the February which was amazing, then came March and the council pulled the funding for the youth centre. They cited government cuts and how it was a national problem, but Jimmy noted their offices had been recarpeted and were being keep at a very high standard. Then, the final nail in the coffin happened in April.

The powers that be at his beloved alternative club gave him a pay cut citing the current economic situation. He was now between a rock and a hard place.

Youth clubs don't make any money but bills still needed to be paid and he had responsibilities to his growing family. The wage he was now on was simply not enough to support them all and he was finding out the hard way just how expensive babies were.

He spoke with the owners of the club, Tom and Anne, about his wage cut but they said it the only way and that for Parker's to survive there had to be savings made. How they were all in it together. They themselves then jetted to Ibiza for a month which was another kick in the teeth. He loved them both very much, he saw them as family almost, but they weren't allowed to treat him like this.

Also knowing he'd spend the next month carrying David was the final straw. He had no option but to reassess his current situation and work out a plan of action.

May was a weird month. Without telling a soul, Jimmy decided to turn the near complete youth club into a nightclub. He didn't even tell Isabelle, his partner and mother to his eldest son. They'd been a couple for several years, having met at a comedy night at a local pub. Isabelle was a beautiful woman. Strawberry blonde hair three quarters of the way down her back, fine freckles, five foot eight, and very athletic in appearance. They had hit it off from day one.

She was a feisty lady which wasn't a surprise as her mum was French and her dad was from Cornwall. A fantastic mix of genetics.

Jimmy had made the decision and now all he had to do was make it happen. He started buying lots of things on eBay to upgrade everything from the light rigs to the sound system. It didn't matter that a lot of it would be second hand, they were all new to him. It also meant he could stretch his budget further. He had a clandestine meeting with the head of a brewery about installing the pumps and he knew there was no turning back.

At the end of May, the owners returned from Ibiza, and just when he thought things could get no worse, he was proven wrong, very wrong. Whilst there on his holiday, Tom had decided that they were no longer an alternative rock club, and he was going to bring Ibiza's dance scene to the city and right into Parker's. Tom was going to target a completely new audience. Just what was needed but it reaffirmed the position Jimmy had found himself in was now totally untenable and his only option was the one he had taken for himself.

Jimmy went home that night and filled in the application for a premises licence on the new club. He would submit it that week and at that point, he knew everyone would know what was afoot as the notice would be in the local newspaper. He sat on his leather chair in his office checking and then rechecking the forms for errors until he was completely satisfied they were right.

Clutching the filled in forms, he arrived at the council office and paid the £180 fee for the application. He found it quite ironic that one of the main reasons he was back at that building was due to a decision made somewhere within the same building.

The lady in reception checked his forms and after doing so told him he should put his official blue notices up tomorrow morning on the club's doors. At that moment, the process would begin and he would learn his fate in 28 days. Leaving the council offices, he walked the short distance to the local Journal Newspaper offices and put the advert in the paper for next week's edition. He was utterly filled with dread; it came over him like a wave and he couldn't stop sweating.

The guilt he had been supressing had fully manifested itself. Jimmy closed his eyes and pictured his little boy. He would not want for anything if he could help it. Returning to his car, he knew that those tasks had been the easy bit of his mission today. The engine started and he began driving to Tom and Anne's house.

Their house was set slightly out of the city on a hill overlooking the valley below. Normally, he would've found the drive out quite pleasurable and he genuinely enjoyed going to their house, having been many times before, but not today. Today, he was not to be the usual welcome guest popping by for a chat and to put the world to rights.

He turned left at the natural spring that spouted out of the base of the hill that their house was situated on; he noted how it was not running very fast but still looked very refreshing to his increasingly dry mouth. Jimmy's car pulled into their drive. He swapped his sunglasses for his normal glasses and he got out. A deep breath, stand up straight, a quick internal pep talk, and he was as ready for this as he ever would be.

His legs felt as if his boots had lead weights in as he walked across the gravel. It seemed so quiet with just the crunch of the gravel underfoot with every stride that he took. Standing on the doorstep, he reached out and rang the bell. A short time passed before Anne answered it.

"Jimmy! How are you? Come on in."

She closed the door behind him and showing him through into the kitchen.

"TOM, Jimmy's here. Can I get you a drink?"

Before he could even think, he had replied, "Coffee please, Anne."

Outside he had told himself don't have a drink. Make this so he can exit super quick without embarrassment, if necessary, but his mind was now pure mush. *Just great,* he thought to himself sarcastically.

Tom came into the kitchen and sat down at the big old farmhouse style table where Jimmy was sitting.

"Jimmy, good to see you. What can I do for you?"

Swallowing deeply, he got ready to begin the speech he'd practised 100 times.

"Well, you see…"

"Do you want sugar, Jim?"

"Oh err, no thanks. See the thing is…with everything that's been happening and going on, I've had to make some choices."

Tom eyed him very suspiciously, rubbing his hands together on the table as Anne placed his coffee in front of him and put one down for Tom as well.

"Thank you. I've applied for a licence to turn the err…umm youth club into a nightclub."

Jimmy paused briefly and looked at his audience. Tom was sat bolt upright now with his hands stationary as Anne sat herself down beside him. It suddenly felt like an interview.

"I'm here to tender my resignation to you. I thought I should do it in person."

He breathed out and he thought about picking up his coffee but knowing his hands were trembling as the adrenaline surged around his body, he thought better of it.

Silence had descended in the kitchen and you could hear the TV talking to itself in their front room. Tom sat swilling his coffee around, thinking carefully about his response. Jimmy, well, he was now trying to drink a boiling hot coffee as fast as he could.

"I wasn't expecting you to say that. That's a big step; have you thought it through?"

Tom was clearly trying to fish for any extra information he could get from Jimmy.

"I don't feel that I have a choice, I have a family to think of."

Jimmy sat looking at the table, not wanting to look at them anymore. As betrayed as he felt by their actions, it didn't mean he had stopped caring.

"Well, I guess we have no choice but to accept your resignation. Bit of a conflict of interest otherwise. Anne and I will talk tonight and work out your notice period."

Jimmy hadn't noticed Tom was now standing until he tucked his chair under the table and left the room abruptly without looking back. He'd left so quickly he had even left his freshly brewed coffee behind.

"He'll be ok, he'll come around eventually, Jim."

Jimmy tried to finish his coffee as he sat there quietly with Anne, both of them trying to think of something to say just so they could change the subject. They'd all been through so much together but Jimmy had changed the whole dynamic in one short visit.

"Thank you for the coffee."

Jimmy stood up and pushed the chair back under the table.

"I'll see myself out."

He walked down the hallway and opened the front door. Feeling a palpable sense of relief that he'd told them, that everyone knew, and he was no longer carrying the burden of the secret. The mass of adrenaline was now free flowing through him. He'd geared himself up for an argument, perhaps even a fight and it had petered out into just downbeat disappointment.

Jimmy felt he understood how they were feeling. They had watched him grow from a firebrand 18-year-old into the 28-year-old man they saw before them, and now he was flying the nest.

Jimmy had incredibly mixed feelings as he drove away. It was like breaking up with a lover you adore but treats you wrong. Sometimes you have to look out for you no matter how good a lover they were.

It was agreed that Jimmy would work a month's notice period. This would give everyone time to adjust and get everything in order. The month was spent with everyone tiptoeing around the subject. Or more honestly, it was spent avoiding Jimmy and taking away parts of his role.

Jimmy, for his part, just kept his head down and worked whatever they wanted. He didn't want bad feeling or animosity, but it was hard to avoid. He had nights he'd run for years taken off him, no promoting them, no DJing at them and he certainly wasn't allowed to attend them. He even had to turn over all the social media accounts that he had built up over the years with passwords being changed immediately, keys were removed as they were apparently needed, and overall, it was quite an unhappy period in there for him.

Towards the end of June, the licence was granted for his new club with no objections. Jimmy had to agree to certain conditions which almost all premises did. It was a major relief, though when it came through as he had put all his eggs in one basket. Without the licence being granted, he would've had big problems.

The club he was building was really starting to take shape and gave him solace. Isabelle was nervous because of it all but understood where he was at. She was being as supportive as she could be and offered him lots of encouragement and reassurances. Jimmy tried with all his might to be as professional at work and overall he did. All logs were kept, reports written, CCTV logged and orders maintained. And that is how we got to the 2 August.

For the first time in his adult life, he was unemployed; he had no boss and no job. He'd always worked. He had a job of some sort since he was 13-years-old. Jimmy had always liked the feel of having money he had earned in his pocket. The pressure he felt in that week was more than he had experienced before or since. Jimmy was scared, excited, nervous and full of bravado. Or at least putting on a face to the world that everything was alright and going as planned.

The Wednesday before the new club opened, he took in his first beer delivery. It felt very real now that it had arrived at the club. Taking it in was a bit surreal. The barrels weren't stock for other people they were his and that meant they were also his responsibility to sell.

The bar was ready to go. The new anti-slip floor had been laid, the spirits sorted, fridges stocked, and now the beer had arrived. He had even found the time to put the hand towel dispensers up in the toilets. All he needed was the pumps installed but that was Thursday's job. It was only at this point he realised it was truly happening. He wasn't the manager anymore; he was the boss. To bring him back to earth, he was also the cleaner, the bar man and the odd job man.

Jimmy had painted the club's walls white with a black trim for all the ledges and wooden edges. It looked pretty damn good. He'd hidden lights in the wooden panels around the building and installed grills for the light to shine through. This meant he could alter the colour schemes in the seating areas. Friday couldn't come quickly enough as far as he was concerned. Jimmy just wanted to get it out of the way.

He knew the first weekend would be ok, but it was trying to get people in regularly that would be the real challenge. After the pumps were installed on

Thursday, it was finally time to put the sign up and introduce the whole city to Jumping Jacks.

Chapter 2
Jumping Jacks

Come 7:30pm on 7 August, everything was set; everything was as ready as it possibly could be. Bar staff was in place. DJ was sorted and all, Jimmy was just waiting for were the door staff. His friend had promised two door staff. Reputable, reliable and well versed in the job. 7:45pm, they still weren't there and he was getting worried. 7:50pm, still no sign and it was getting into twitchy bum time.

As he stood on the doorstep outside hoping they would turn up, he heard, before he could see, a clapped out 1996 Ford Escort van. Christ, his inner monologue said as the two oldest swingers in town got out of the vehicle. This was Martin and Pete. True to form, they were well versed; in fact they were so well versed, they should've been pensioned off 10 years ago.

Fuck my life, Jimmy thought to himself as he watched them pry themselves out of the car. Over to the front doors they both hobbled, both obviously in need of new hips or knees, or more probably both.

"Hi, we're from Hardaker Security."

"Good evening, guys."

"I'm Pete and this is Martin."

Noticing they both had SIA badges on that were in date and at this point, keeping a civil tongue and reminding himself that beggars can't be choosers, he decided he would proceed with them on the door that night.

"Welcome to Jumping Jacks, I'm Jimmy. If you sign in on the door sheet, I'll be back in 2 mins to give you your instructions for the evening, gentlemen."

Jimmy returned into the club and turned the main house lights down. Now just disco lights pulsated around. He felt a slight smugness at just how good the lasers were that he'd bought off eBay. The DJ, Andy, had a compilation of modern hits blaring away and looked ready for the evening. The bar staff were checking the optics and the glasses. They too were ready. It was now time for game face. Doors open and here we go. Too late to change anything now.

Jimmy made his way back to the front door. He checked his jacket for his gumshield and his SIA badge, having seen the door staff, he figured he might need them tonight.

"Right, gentleman, tonight is ticket only."

Jimmy reached into his jacket pocket.

"The tickets look like this."

He handed Pete the ticket that he had kept in his pocket for the door staff.

"Keep that for reference. Remember no ticket means no entry."

He ducked into the cloakroom and returned with two radios.

"These are your radios, guys. They'll put you through to me or the bar. Any issues, call me."

Martin, the other doorman, who had thus far remained quiet, looked at him a bit sheepishly.

"I can't use that; I have hearing aids."

He pointed to his ears. Jimmy smiled, although inside he wasn't happy.

"Ok, you two share the one and I'll take the other inside with me."

As he closed the internal door behind himself, he wondered if the old timers would still be awake at 3am, let alone able to use a walkie talkie. He'd just have to keep a strict eye on them and make sure they were coping ok, or at least awake.

He walked back through the club. Although, all the checks were done, he was still double-checking things he had double checked already. He saw Isabelle sat at table near the bar. Jimmy could see she had a made a real effort that evening and had dressed to impress. She had already got him a drink and he sat down on a stool opposite her.

"Nervous?"

Taking back the double vodka red bull in one gulp, he looked at her.

"Of course, but everything that could be done has been. So now we just have to wait."

Standing up, he walked to the bar and ordered another drink. He was determined not to have too many but he knew he needed something to calm his nerves and quick.

Time moves slowly when you start clock watching but still Jimmy checked his watch for the 10th time in 20 minutes. 8:05pm it read. The first few people were coming in. Taking in the interior and talking amongst themselves. Jimmy watched them move around as they got a feel for the venue. As he was watching the first customers arrive, Hannah, the new bar supervisor, approached him.

"Jimmy, could we get some change for the tills and the card machine please?"

Jimmy immediately felt the panic rise inside him. In his haste to get everything ready, he had totally forgotten to get change for the tills.

"Shit! Give me 2 minutes."

He was telling himself to think. How the hell had he managed to overlook the change? He'd had all week to sort it. He'd met the manager of the Ferrers pub which was two hundred yards away about a week ago. Can I ask him? He thought. He had no choice. He had to.

"Right, the card machine is in the office if you could grab it please and I'll be back in 2-3 mins. Tell everyone the first drinks are on me as a welcome gift for coming."

Although, bar staff were standing around with complimentary champagne greeting everyone at the door, he now had to give the bar away too, which was a pain. He necked his drink, set the glass down, and hurriedly stormed out of the club and up the road to the Ferrers.

Jimmy had always liked the look of the Ferrers. It was a proper old school boozer, even down to the hops hanging from the exposed rafters. The pub was quite busy with a lady on karaoke intent on destroying a Cher song. He made his way through the pub and spotted the landlord.

"Good evening. Can I have a quick word please?"

Jimmy hustled his way into the landlord's conversation. Those around the landlord clearly wondered who on earth he was to interrupt their conversation but the landlord was obliging of his request.

Jimmy returned to Jumping Jacks with enough change to see him through the night but knew he now owed the Ferrers a favour which didn't please him. He walked through the club and handed Hannah the change.

"Here you go. It can go straight in the till. Can I get the city radio please?"

"Of course, I'll bring it over to you."

Hannah had impressed him so far and seemed to be on the ball. It was her first job since finishing university, and she was very keen to make a good impression and learn the ways of nightlife. He was initially a bit apprehensive that she was a bit too refined for this sort of work but so far nothing had proved too much.

Taking his seat again opposite Isabelle, he finally relaxed a bit. Looking round the club, which was starting to get quite busy, he was very pleased to see people taking selfies. He hoped he was going to see a few of them on Facebook very soon. He had surmised that if at least half the people he'd invited turned up, even just to be nosey, they would have a solid opening.

Hannah put the radio and earpiece down. Jimmy attached it to his belt, put the head piece on and signed on.

"Echo Alpha, Jumping Jacks signing on."

He had used the one in Parker's 100s of times, thousands probably, but he felt nerves at using his own for the first time.

"Hearing you loud and clear, Jumping Jacks."

Jimmy felt great relief as the response came back over the air waves. The radio linked all the pubs and the city CCTV in the hope of reducing trouble in the city. Jimmy had been one of the driving forces behind it over 5 years before when the system had been trialled. Until then, the pubs did a ring round to warn one another of trouble or troublemakers, but it had been appalling at best and only actually effective on quiet nights when you could hear the telephone at the bar ringing.

The first part of the evening went really smoothly. Jimmy was mingling with the people he'd invited. Introducing Isabelle to everyone, sometimes if they'd even met before which annoyed Isabelle quite a lot. The people were inquisitive and of course, asked lots of question; in fact it was a lot of the same questions. What clientele are you aiming at? What's the music policy?

Jimmy took the time with all of them to explain that Fridays would be alternative night and Saturdays would be the Dirty Disco, a mixture of old and new. The tunes that you love but don't admit to. You turn them up in the car when they come on, but that guilty pleasure remains your secret. It also meant he could be the DJ on a Saturday as it was his forte.

He loved alternative music but had long argued that over 25s were not catered to in the city. A fun night for people aged 30 plus was the way forward. Now he was quite literally putting his money where his mouth was.

"Jimmy, can you come to the front door please?"

The internal radios all crackled into life; that was the first call ever on the internal radio but Jimmy was just pleased they worked. He couldn't tell whether that was Pete or Martin but at least they'd grasped the radio. Excusing himself from the conversation he was in, he made his way to the front doors. As he opened the internal doors, he saw Tom stood there, quite clearly very drunk.

"This man says he knows you and wants to come in."

"Jimmy, what the fuck is this? They say I'm not invited."

Jimmy stood looking at a swaying Tom who was slurring his words, he noted he had two or three of his drinking buddies with him as well and no designated driver in sight to reign in their excesses.

Taking a deep breath and ignoring what his gut was telling him, he said, "Tom, good evening. How many are with you?"

"Two…no three." Tom slurred his response and followed it up with a wheezing laugh come cough.

"Give them all a wristband. They're ok."

Jimmy motioned to Pete to let them in. After Tom had given him a few hard pats on the shoulder and made his way into the club, Jimmy shut the internal door.

"Don't worry, I'll keep an eye on them."

Jimmy tried reassuring the door staff, but he was more trying to reassure himself. The door staff were looking at him very sceptically and he was now hoping, and praying, Tom wouldn't make a complete ass of himself but when he was drunk that was an unlikely thing. He didn't want the door staff questioning his judgement on the first night.

By 1am, the opening night was in full swing. Andy was reading the room well and the people in were having a great time. It probably helped that the club could hold 350 people, but Jimmy had limited it to a maximum of 200 on the opening night. People could get served quickly, they could move around without feeling crushed in, and most importantly, there was no queuing for the toilets.

Jimmy continued working the room with Isabelle. He was enjoying hearing all the compliments from his new customers. Someone once said that satisfaction is the highest form of happiness. Jimmy was certainly feeling satisfied. His train of thought though was very rudely interrupted.

"RATS! ALL FUCKING RATS!"

Jimmy recognised Tom's voice bellowing over the music. He instinctively spun around and spotted him holding court at a tall round table between the bar and the rear fire exit. Leaving the conversation he was having, he strode directly over to the table.

"Is everything ok?"

Jimmy noticed that the tall round table that Tom was at with his three friends had quite a few empty glasses on it. This would have to be addressed with the glass collectors but now was not the time. It was a bit late for that and he would have to deal with things as they were.

"Fuck you, Jimmy."

An age seemed to pass as Jimmy stood there looking at Tom. He was angry and drunk but his slumping shoulders also told Jimmy he was upset.

"What's up, Tom?"

"This, they're my customers and you've fucking stole them."

Tom was gesticulating around with arms at all the people he could see.

"Bollocks, Tom, you're just drunk…"

"Rats, all fucking rats."

As Tom was becoming more irate pointing at customers without care who they were, Jimmy knew this had to be dealt with immediately before he created an even bigger scene, and that was the last thing he needed on his opening night.

"Think you'd best go, Tom. Call me tomorrow and we can talk about it."

Tom looked at Jimmy with menace in his eyes for a second before he grabbed his jumper and stormed straight out of the rear fire exit. Jimmy was left at the table with Tom's three friends. They could hear Tom yelling in the street. No one said a word as they gathered their belongings and followed Tom out of the fire exit. They hadn't even finished their drinks.

Jimmy beckoned a glass collector to come over and they cleared the table very quickly.

"Make sure you're clearing these tables a bit quicker."

The glass collector gave a nod of agreement. As Jimmy turned back to the club, he saw a lot of people looking in his direction and then turn their heads away quickly. *Suppose everyone loves a bit of rubbernecking*, Jimmy thought to himself. Inside he was pleased it hadn't escalated into anything more serious.

The rest of the evening passed without another incident and Tom's outburst had quickly been forgotten by all. The lights went up at 3am and everyone who was left filed out. Jimmy, who had been stood on the front door since 2am, shook everyone's hand as they left, thanking them for coming and saying he hoped to see them all again soon. Hannah came out from behind the bar.

"Club's clear, boss."

"Have the toilets been checked?"

He'd been paranoid about checking toilets for years. Many years ago at Parker's as he sat drinking and playing pool after hours with his original boss, TJ, at around 4am they'd heard a door squeak open and a very drunk woman had come stumbling into the bar area. After they had finished that evening, they'd locked the club, not checked the ladies toilets properly and she had been fast asleep in a cubicle until she woke up and gave them both a heart attack.

"Yes, the toilets have all been checked."

"Cool, just gave them a quick tidy up and mop the floors and we'll all have a little drink and a debrief."

"There is one little issue, Jimmy."

Jimmy looked at her over the top of his glasses.

"Isabelle is asleep on the sofa."

Jimmy sighed. He was quite used to it.

"No worries; if she's asleep, she can't drink anymore."

He walked over to Isabelle and could she see was quite comfy on the sofa. He still had plenty to do so decided to leave her there whilst he finished up. He shut the large double doors, turned off the external lights and headed into the club wondering what tomorrow night would bring.

As it happened, he needn't have worried too much about the Saturday. Total count through the door was less than 100 people. The reality of the situation set in and he knew how much work he would have to do. He needed people popping in during the weekday evenings for a few pints and a couple of games of pool and he needed Friday and Saturday to be busy with people out looking for a good time. He had loads of advertising to go out and had set up all the social media accounts.

He was still trying to gather a following to the posts and the tweets. He was currently followed by 62 people on Twitter and as the club he was following 1600 but he knew it would get better numbers eventually. What was needed was a new take on advertising in the city. Something different none of the other clubs were doing.

During the week after the club opened, Jimmy received a phone call from a mobile phone number is didn't recognise.

"Hello, Jimmy Harris here."

"Good morning, Mr Harris."

It was a lady's voice and quite possibly the poshest accent Jimmy had heard since he watched The Queens Christmas Day speech.

"It's Mrs Borrick-Sykes here. I wish to talk to you about my daughter and the conditions with which you are making her work."

Jimmy was slightly taken aback by this and who the hell was her daughter? He thought as wracked his brain for answers.

"Please continue, Mrs Borrick-Sykes, and I'll see if I can help."

"My daughter is Hannah and from what I have been told, you have her scrubbing toilets in all the filth at the end of every evening. Do you realise what sort of diseases she could catch?"

Mrs Borrick-Skyes was clearly very angry with this situation and her daughter's working conditions as she perceived them. Jimmy inadvertently laughed.

"It's not a laughing matter, Mr Harris. If she catches something, then she could die!"

"Mrs Borrick-Sykes, I'm not quite sure what you've heard but I can assure you she's quite safe…"

"Mr Harris, who knows what filth is in there. I won't have her treated this way."

"Mrs Borrick-Sykes, all she, or any member of staff, has to do at the end of an evening is mop the toilets…."

"She has a *MOP?*"

"She has a mop and a bucket and gloves."

The phone went very quiet. Jimmy was determined not to interrupt this pause in conversation, he enjoying not having his ear chewed.

"I'm sorry, Mr Harris, I was under the impression she was on her hands and knees scrubbing the toilets."

"No, Mrs Borrick-Sykes, that's my job in the morning."

"Oh well, thank you for clearing that up. Have a good day, Mr Harris."

With that, the phone went dead. Jimmy decided not to mention it to Hannah who had prewarned him her mother was a little posh and just a bit protective. Although, Jimmy was still shocked to find out her mother sounded posher than the Queen. Even when she was embarrassed.

The next few weeks fell into a distinct pattern. The only day the club was shut was a Monday night. He worked all the others. It meant he was living in a bit a twilight zone. Constantly getting home at 3am or 4am, sometimes even later if something needed fixing. He knew it was necessary as they couldn't afford to waste money on wages. The weekend numbers weren't great. They were picking up but not quickly enough and he knew this had to alter, and quickly.

As August became September, he was still trying to think of a gimmick or a way in, whilst at the same time being very aware he was running out of money.

One September evening, as he was closing down at the end of a Friday night, his mobile phone started ringing in his pocket. He took it out and saw it was David calling. *What does he want?* Jimmy thought to himself. It wasn't as if their last conversation had ended well. Jimmy decided to answer even though it was late.

"Evening, David, what can I do for you?"

"Jim, no, it's Tom here. Can you come to the club as quick as possible?"

"I'm just shutting down, Tom, it's nearly 4am. Can it wait until tomorrow?"

Jimmy was trying to as polite as possible but he was feeling pretty tired and not in the mood for games.

"No, Jim, it's got to be now. There's been a serious fight in the beer garden and a lad has been stabbed."

Tom was obviously very panicked; Jimmy could hear that very clearly in his voice.

"We can't use the CCTV system and the police need footage as soon as possible."

"Ok, I'll be there in a quarter of an hour, Tom, put the kettle on, I've just got to lock up."

Jimmy shut the safe, turned the lights off, checked the fire doors were locked and turned all the lights off as quickly as he could. As he walked through the deserted city to Parker's, a part of his brain thought this might all be hoax but he couldn't risk it being real and him ignoring it.

As he got near Parker's he could see it was real and definitely not a hoax. He couldn't see Parker's yet but he could see the blue emergency lights bouncing off the buildings in front of him. He turned right into Bakers Lane and could see that Parker's was completely cordoned off with police tape. There were police vehicles everywhere and officers milling about. Whatever had happened had to be very serious. As he neared the police barriers, an officer approached him.

"You'll have to find another way home, Sir. This area is cordoned off for police business."

"Hi, I'm Jimmy Harris, I've been called down by the owners to work the CCTV."

Jimmy was hoping she didn't think he was one of the many drunks she'd probably already had to deal with that evening.

"Wait there, Sir, and I'll check."

She walked off towards Parker's and left Jimmy stood on his own by the police tape. A minute later, the officer returned. This time she was glowering a lot less at him.

"Follow me, Sir."

She lifted up the tape for him and Jimmy ducked underneath. It felt a bit weird to him walking into Parker's. He had been in there every day practically for 10 years and then not been in for two whole months.

"Jimmy, thank God you're here."

Tom greeted Jimmy very enthusiastically as he shook Jimmy's hand and gave him a slight hug; very different from their last interaction on the opening night of Jimmy's club. He was being welcomed like a long-lost son.

"Come to the office and I'll explain what's happened."

Jimmy followed Tom into the office. It still looked the same as the last time he'd seen it but Jimmy felt it was all very different somehow. He sat down in front of the CCTV units in his old chair. David was lurking at the back of the office.

"Make yourself useful, David, go and brew some coffee."

David scurried out of the office without a word and Tom preceded to explain what they needed as an officer stood and nodded in agreement. Parker's had a lot of cameras covering both floors and the smoking area. Jimmy knew them all very well as he had installed them all. Jimmy set to work immediately. The police wanted the incident from as many angles as possible.

As Jimmy watched through, he found himself being impressed at the speed of the response from all the staff. He might have been gone but they had not forgotten the training that was instilled in them.

Within two hours, everything was sorted and Jimmy could leave. As Jimmy stood in the doorway to leave, Tom thanked him for coming and getting the required CCTV. As they shook hands early that morning with sun already up in the sky and parted ways, neither of them knew that that would be Jimmy's last ever visit to Parker's as it was to shut permanently at the end of October. The negative press over this incident coupled with the change in musical direction had taken them down. For all he'd wanted them to see the error of their ways, he felt great sadness that they had shut, perhaps even a morsel of guilt.

It was a Monday at the end of September when Jimmy took his dog, Sammy, for a walk to the Anchor pub. It was a lovely evening for a pint one evening. He knew TJ would be working. TJ had left Parker's nightclub to run the Anchor about 3 years ago and Jimmy would often pop in to see his friend. They had grown very close over their 7 years working together.

First with Jimmy as just a DJ and promotor, then as his assistant manager, and finally as joint managers together. TJ had always been a great listener and sounding board. Often reigning in the more ridiculous of Jimmy's marketing ideas. Tonight, though Jimmy had a question for him.

Entering via the courtyard at the back of the pub that served as the beer garden, Jimmy found a table under cover and latched Sammy to it with her lead whilst he went to the bar and ordered himself a pint and one for TJ as well.

"Evening, Jimmy."

TJ was clearly pleased to see him. He was leaning round from the deepest recesses of the cavernous old oak bar just to say hello.

"I'll be over in a few minutes."

The smell in the Anchor always intrigued Jimmy. A cross between wet dog and harvested hops that seemed to seep out the very pores of the building and it didn't make the slightest bit of difference if it was a dreary winter's day or a blazing hot summer's day. That smell was always there.

"I'm just outside with Sammy. I've got you a drink."

Sitting himself at the table, he opened the bag of pork scratchings and put them down on the floor for Sammy to enjoy. He then lit himself a cigarette and just for a moment, enjoyed the peace and quiet of a cool Monday evening. Sammy had finished her scratchings and Jimmy half his pint by the time TJ managed to join them.

TJ was originally from Northern England and still retained a distinct Northern twang to his accent even after over 20 years in the south. Nearly 40 and quite thickly set, his tough exterior hid the artist inside.

After catching up on all the gossip and rumours of the city, especially those regarding Parker's, Jimmy had something to ask his friend.

"TJ, I've had an idea I want to run by you."

Jimmy lit another cigarette.

"I would like to be able to come here at closing time and hand all your customers a free entry wristband for the club."

TJ sat and listened as Jimmy explained his idea. Jimmy knew as he talked that TJ was already mulling it over.

"I figure this will help us both out. If I put a time limit on them then they've got to leave here so it'll help you clear the pub, and I will get customers."

Jimmy leant back on the bench. TJ took a sip of his pint. He was clearly still thinking about it. Jimmy waited, he wanted to speak but he knew silence was his friend here.

"What time?"

"Well, you call last orders at 11 so I figured 11:15ish?"

The silence continued for at least another 30 seconds as TJ looked at him.

"You want another drink?"

"Yeah, go on then."

TJ got up and went to the bar. 10 minutes later, he returned to their table. Jimmy had seen him inside the pub on the phone behind the bar, but he couldn't lip read so had no clue who he was talking to or what about. TJ set the pints down and smiled at Jimmy.

"The owner said yes."

Inside Jimmy was jumping for joy but managed to keep his calm on the surface; he didn't want TJ, or anyone else for that matter, knowing that this was literally the last roll of the dice.

"That's great news. I might even come and do it myself. Sneak a pint or two in."

Jimmy repeated the same request to over 12 pubs in the city. 4 were kind enough to say yes. Due to licensing requirements, the club had to have a door entry price on Fridays and Saturdays, but he could negate it this way. He was banking on a few things. Firstly, customers wanting something for nothing.

Secondly, his competitors being slow in their response and finally people coming in making the club busy and others wanting to go somewhere that was busy. That Friday would be the acid test and it would soon come round.

As he got himself ready for work, Isabelle walked into their bedroom. She'd got a lovely black dress on with a shawl around her shoulders. She was making a real effort this evening and it showed. She could tell it was important for Jimmy and that there was more riding on it than he was letting on.

"I thought I'd come in with you tonight. Mum said she'd stay over and baby sit."

"That would be nice, I'd like that."

"I feel like we hardly see one another at the moment. I'd like some time with you."

Jimmy finished putting his cuff links on. He'd heard this a lot over the last few months and it was starting to grate a bit. He had explained so many times that once it was going well things would change, but like his own personal Groundhog Day they were back at this point. He also knew that she'd probably agreed to meet a few friends at the club who would happily keep her company and drink the profits.

"We're getting there. I've got a new advertising plan this week that I hope will take it all up a gear. We will get more time together but it takes time to get these things running smoothly."

"I know you have. You've mentioned it possibly 100 times today alone. Well, until you have more time at home, I will just have to come in and keep you company as you work. And if that's what it takes so be it. We're in this together, Jimmy."

He adjusted his tie and put his jacket on. Isabelle promptly readjusted his tie and straightened his jacket out. Tonight, was going to be a very important night. They were at least dressed well for the occasion.

Chapter 3
Jumping Jacks Angels

Standing in the club with the bar staff, all sat before him Jimmy explained about the wristbanding to them all. Which pubs they could go to, the time frames and what he expected of them. He told Alice, the cloakroom girl, how to log them down so licensing couldn't get annoyed. Then finally, he reached into a large bag on the table and started handing out black hoodies with 'Jumping Jacks' emblazoned on the back in white. With four staff going out at any point in time, he'd figured they'd need to stay warm and be noticeable.

Everyone put the hoodies on and they were busy inspecting one another.

"We look like a bike club."

George, one of the bar staff, who was getting louder every week, was now busy impersonating a biker much to the laughter of his colleagues.

"Jumping Jacks Angels."

A throw away comment by Hannah, at the time everyone laughed, but the name stuck.

As 10pm came round, Jimmy went and collected the wristbands. He decided before hitting the pubs that they could all stand in High Town and wristband people milling around in the city centre. Jimmy walked over to Isabelle's table.

"I'm heading out wristbanding. Would you like to come with me? We could get a drink together in the Anchor."

Isabelle looked up at Jimmy, but he could already see she was set for the night.

"I'll wait here. These heels are killer to walk in and I've got a few friends coming in to see me. Plus if it gets busy, I can help out here."

Jimmy gave her a kiss on the cheek and smiled. She didn't even know how the till worked or how to change a barrel. How is she going to help? Jimmy thought to himself but he bit his tongue. He turned and motioned for the staff to join him. As the flyer team made their way out, Jimmy headed over to Hannah by the corner of the bar.

"Whilst I'm gone, keep an eye on her."

Hannah just gave a knowing smile and a little nod. That was code for all drinks to be singles and don't serve her quickly. She knew the drill; all the staff knew the drill.

Walking into the city centre, Jimmy scanned around. All the shops were closed and the coffee stands locked up for the night. A few seagulls were fighting one another over half a bag of discarded chips and a few groups of party goers were bristling to and fro. The guys knew what was expected of them and scampered off in all directions attempting to drum up new business. Jimmy waited until 10:40pm and then made his way to the Anchor.

Cheekily, he texted TJ on his way. 'Incoming' was all he sent, it was all he needed to. When he arrived at the back gate of the courtyard, there was TJ watching proceedings with a couple of pints sat on the struts of the giant iron gates that guarded the back of the pub when the pub was shut. He liked standing there. You could look down on the oval courtyard and people watch but as the gates were set to one side, hardly anyone would notice you.

"How's the wrist band idea going?"

"I'll find out later."

Last orders were soon called and customers started milling around to get another drink or three. Jimmy always likened it to a well organised colony of ants. He stood there shooting the breeze with TJ regaling him with stories of some of the drunks he'd dealt with during the course of the night.

Just after 11:10pm, the first of the Jumping Jacks Angels turned up. Jimmy watched them mingling through the crowds. He could see them explaining about the club, where it was and what was on offer tonight. Some refused, some agreed, and were having wristbands attached to their wrists. Jimmy hoped inside that a fair few of them would actually turn up and weren't just taking them to be polite.

Having decided he'd seen enough for one evening, Jimmy finished his pint and made his excuses to leave. Walking the back streets to the club, he was alone with his thoughts. *Would this work? What would the reaction be? What was he going to do if this didn't work?*

As he approached the club, he noticed a queue of people waiting to get in and his mood lightened considerably. Then he spotted Martin's van wasn't outside where it normally was and Pete was alone on the door. As he got closer,

Martin's van appeared around the corner and stopped opposite the front doors. Jimmy hurried his pace a bit, skipping past the queue and he managed to get to the door just as Martin did. Jimmy couldn't believe his eyes as Martin stood there clutching a bag of fish and chips.

"What the fuck are you doing?"

Martin looked at Jimmy and could see the younger man was clearly enraged. If only that lady hadn't taken so long in front of him in the chip shop, he would have got away with it.

"I was hungry and I nipped to get some tea. I've been working all day."

In some crazy world, Martin seemed to think this was a fine reason to leave the door with just one man on it. Jimmy could feel his blood starting to boil.

"Are you for real? I don't pay you to eat."

By now, Pete had stepped back sensing this was not going well for his colleague. In a mistaken attempt at a peace offering, Martin offered Jimmy a chip but unfortunately for him, that was not the wisest thing he could've done.

"You're finished. Get your things and fuck off."

"What? Are you being serious?"

"Yes. End of story, gather your things and leave."

Jimmy, on the other hand, couldn't believe there was any part of Martin's brain actually thinking what he had done was acceptable! He reached into his pocket and retrieved his SIA badge. He fixed it on his arm and turned round. Pete was handling the queue very well and the flow of customers into the club was moving very steadily. Jimmy saw Martin was still stood there, fish and chips in hand, just staring at him.

"Was there anything else?"

Jimmy stared at Martin who could feel Jimmy's eyes boring through him. He'd never seen Jimmy this angry. Martin shook his head and walked back to his van muttering under his breath.

Jimmy breathed slowly through his nose to regain his composure. As quickly as he'd started to regain his composure, he felt the bag of chips land perfectly on the back of his head as he heard Martin yelling expletives at him and speed off down the road. Jimmy picked up most of the chips and Pete handed him a dustpan and brush for the rest. As Jimmy dusted himself down, he thought to himself that at least the wristbanding was working, and thank God, Martin hadn't ordered beans or curry sauce with his chips.

It was just before 8am the next morning when Jimmy's phone rang. Craig Hardaker, the boss of Hardaker Security, calling at this hour could only mean he'd already heard about Jimmy firing Martin.

"Good morning, Jimmy here."

He put his glasses on and sat up in bed.

"Jimmy, it's Craig Hardaker here. Martin has been on the phone saying you've fired him for no reason. He's pretty angry."

Taking his time, Jimmy fully explained what had happened to Craig including the fact he had ended up wearing a bag of chips.

"Ahh you see, Martin didn't tell me that bit. Don't worry, Jimmy, I'll get you another man this evening. I'll call you back with the details."

Jimmy ended the call and lay there staring at the ceiling. If Pete and Martin were the first choice, what on earth would he come up with to replace one of them. Jimmy didn't have to wait long to find out.

Jimmy and Hannah had nearly finished setting for the evening when the door to the club knocked at 7:45pm. Jimmy went to answer it. As the door opened, stood on the other side was a giant shadow blocking out the whole world. Coming in at six feet ten inches and an easy 25 stone, his height extenuated by his frizzy hair, was Lee.

"Hi, I'm Lee."

The giant in front of him held out his spade shaped hand and shook Jimmy's.

"Welcome, Craig said you'd be in this evening."

Jimmy gave him a quick tour of the building and introduced him to the staff who were in. Everyone was taken aback by not just the sheer height of the young man but also the pure depth as well. He truly was enormous.

"This is my first door job; I've been a night watchman on building sites before but it can get a little lonely."

"I've a feeling you'll be just fine. Just follow the others and myself for instruction and don't get excited."

Jimmy stood looking at the man mountain before him as he signed in. The pen looked like a cocktail stick in his giant hand. Pete arrived not long after. He too was taken aback by the sheer size of Martin's replacement. Pete looked at Jimmy, who was well over six foot and not small at all, but even he looked like midget in comparison to his new colleague.

Over the next few weeks, the club got busier. Lee settled in and a few new problems arose. Mainly the need for extra door staff inside. This was, however, a pleasing problem to have. Craig sorted out some new guys, and as the first Christmas in the club came around, everything was settling into a steady pace.

Unbeknownst to Jimmy, this feeling of equilibrium was about to be shattered. Christmas is always an interesting time for pubs and clubs. You get the once-a-year drinkers who can't drink for toffee, the office workers who don't go out very often and cut loose on epic scales, the guys and girls who used to strawpedo Hooch back in the day and mistakenly believe they still can.

It was the Saturday before Christmas day and the evening had started well, and right up until 2am, everything was perfectly fine. Jimmy was in the DJ box playing singalong favourites to the crowd who were more than reciprocating as he led them in another chorus over the mic. Just after 2am, his attention was drawn to what looked a scuffle on the dance floor. He alerted the door staff but it was too late.

Approaching the aftermath, there was a man in his early 30s lying unconscious on the floor, a blonde girl crying hysterically, and unfortunately, no culprit had been detained.

Lee had already alerted the police and requested an ambulance as well. The gentleman on the floor was in a bad way. Basic first aid was given as they waited for the ambulance to attend.

At the end of the night, after statements had been given, a clear picture had emerged of the events that had unfolded. Jimmy watched the CCTV as Isabelle held court on the sofa entertaining staff with pictures of Jimmy playing with their son. It was a softer side of him not many who worked for him had ever seen.

The gentleman who'd been assaulted was dancing with the blonde lady when an older man, late 50s-early 60s, approached and randomly punched him once as hard as he could. It was a cowardly attack, a total sucker punch and came out of nowhere. Jimmy had spoken with the blonde lady and she had turned out to be the victim's sister.

Sunday morning came. Jimmy hadn't slept much. He had a feeling that this was an incident that was going to draw the attention of the higher echelons of the local constabulary. As he sat in his front room catching up on the news, at just after 9am, his phone rang. It was a withheld number which was never good news.

"Morning, Jimmy, this is Police Licensing Officer William Lewis…."

Jimmy soon found himself in the police station. It was just after 11am and the station was very busy. Jimmy thought they must have had a busy night with trouble in the city, not a real surprise at Christmas time. He waited in the reception area for quite a time before he was eventually shown through to an interview room. He sat in the interview room waiting on his own with just his thoughts for 15 minutes.

He'd dealt with these situations at Parker's but it felt very different with his own neck on the line. The door opened and in walked Mr Lewis and a colleague. He knew who Mr Lewis was but this was someone new, someone he didn't know.

"Morning, Mr Harris, I'm Chief Inspector Thomas. I believe you already know Mr Lewis, our licensing officer."

They sat down opposite him placing several files on the table. It was very well choreographed and a clear attempt to intimidate him; it was working well and he felt like he was the accused himself. The next two hours were spent arguing about whether the incident was preventable and whether the correct response was acted by the club.

By the time Jimmy left the police station, Jumping Jacks was having its licence reviewed by the local authorities. The review was very serious and could cripple the club if the licensing committee decided in favour of the police. Over the next few days, Jimmy found out all he could about the events and who was involved. However, it was not looking good.

Even though Jimmy had provided a great picture of the perpetrator of the attack, no one knew who he was. Yet, he was the key to defending the club from West Mercia's onslaught. If they had a culprit, there would at least be context to the events.

Jimmy had looked forward to the Christmas week but with everything going on, he just wasn't feeling it. Even the staff had started to notice the wind had gone from his sails. It had only taken five months to get into his first review and no amount of Christmas decorations and tinsel was cheering him up.

On Wednesday, Jimmy was having some new hand driers put in the toilets. He had had enough of clearing up the paper towels. Even though he provided a bin, they seemed to go everywhere but in the bin. He had bit the bullet and got some hand driers.

Harry Smith, a local electrician he knew, was fitting them for him. Jimmy liked him. He worked quickly, he turned up when he said he would, and he wasn't too heavy on the pen. Jimmy was in the office when the door knocked and he went and let him in.

"Morning, Harry, come on in. The kettle's on."

Harry was a short, stocky man who always had the look of a man who had got dressed in the dark. He shuffled past Jimmy carrying enough tools to restock B and Q. Harry went straight to toilets and set about the task in hand. Jimmy headed to the kitchen and made them both a coffee. Leaving his own coffee in the kitchen, he took Harry's cup to him.

"Here you go, I'll be in the office when you're done."

Jimmy placed the coffee down by the vanity mirror in the lady's toilet and Harry nodded. Jimmy was unsure if he had heard or even understood but figured Harry would come and find him when he was done.

Jimmy returned to the kitchen and collected his freshly brewed coffee. After rummaging in a cupboard looking for biscuits, only to discover they had all gone, he returned to his office. He'd got hold of the blonde girl's name from the fight on Saturday night and he set about going through her Facebook profile trying to find the assailant.

After about an hour and a half, his phone rang; it was Inspector Thomas. Jimmy answered.

"Good morning, Jimmy Harris here."

He attempted to sound as business like as possible with his heart attempting to restrict his ability to breathe.

"Jimmy, it's Inspector Thomas here. Mr Lewis and myself would like to come and see you this afternoon regarding your review."

"I'm in all day, Inspector. What time can expect you?"

"We'll be with you at 3pm sharp."

"I'll be here all day, Inspector. See you then."

The phone rang off. Jimmy looked at his computer screen and then stared intently at the camera picture from the CCTV of the attacker. He hadn't heard Harry come into the office.

"Why have you got a picture of Frank James on your desk?"

Jimmy jumped as Harry startled him from his thoughts. Harry lent over and picked the picture up for a closer inspection.

"You know him?"

"Yes. He's part of my old Masonic lodge, quite high up as well. One of the big dogs."

Harry explained how he used to be a member but hadn't been now for a few years due to politics.

"Have you got any photos of him with others to prove who he is?"

"Sure do. I've got to nip home and grab a few bits for these dryers. You know if you buy things from shops, they come with all the mounting brackets, Jim. I'll grab the photos whilst I'm there and bring them in if you pay me for the dryers today!"

"You get me a few pictures and I'll certainly pay you today."

Jimmy felt his heart beating faster as Harry left the office. Could this finally be the break he needed? A bit of luck that wasn't bad? He was having trouble reigning in his excitement but he knew he'd achieved nothing yet. Jimmy got up and let Harry out of the front doors. He watched as Harry scuttled away and Jimmy started to finally believe he might beat this thing.

Bang on 3pm, Inspector Thomas and Mr Lewis arrived at the club. Jimmy went and let them in. He bolted the front door and showed them in. Jimmy led them through the club and up into his office. Jimmy sat at his desk as they settled on the comfy leather chairs opposite him. Being fair they were part of a three-piece suite but Sammy, his dog, had eaten the arm off the sofa when she was a puppy and Isabelle had made Jimmy replace the whole suite.

"Inspector Thomas, Mr Lewis, what can I do for you?"

"Mr Harris, we are here to negotiate terms to stop the review becoming full blown and involving the committee."

Mr Lewis had hated Jimmy since his days at Parker's. They have had several run-ins and disagreements over the years. Mr Lewis had never quite been able to get anything to stick back then and so was trying extra hard with this turn of events. Jimmy could see he was itching to screw him, and his club, right up.

"We've put together several conditions we want to attach to your licence to stop this sort of incident from happening again. If you agree to these conditions, then the review will be dropped."

Considering the mass riots, brawling and shit that went on in the city, Jimmy knew this was personal. He also knew that they were aware he couldn't afford big time lawyers to keep the police at bay like the bigger chains did. Mr Lewis reached into his case and handed Jimmy an A4 piece of paper with the conditions that they wished to add to his licence listed on it.

"I don't see how we could've prevented the fight. It was a random attack with no build up and the attacker just punched and ran…."

"Don't you dare talk to us like that. We decide what you could've and should've done! You can't even get us his name from your CCTV! You and your staff couldn't even stop him disappearing into the night."

Jimmy felt cool and collected as he lent forward over his desk. He placed the conditions down on the side of his desk. He could almost hear his grandfathers' words in his ear: keep your powder dry until you are ready to deploy it. He reached into his top draw of his desk and from it produced a Dictaphone which he placed down on the desk and turned it on. He then from the same draw produced a picture of the assailant and placed it before them.

"I'm going to ask you one final time if you know this gentleman and I'm going to do it on record."

Jimmy leant back in his chair in an attempt to show he was relaxed about this situation. He sat there and he looked at them both.

"Of course we don't. This is your last chance to accept conditions or you'll be in review, and I'll make sure you never hold a licence in this city again."

Now the inspector was riled. The plot was thickening as to who was leading this review. Jimmy rubbed his chin, gently stroking the side of his face.

"I'm going to tell you what happened and then we'll see where we're at. The gentleman in question saw his son-in-law dancing with a very pretty blonde lady. They were clearly having a great time. He felt his blood boil that his little princess was being cheated on so publicly. He decided in a flash to deal with it. He ran over and punched the son-in-law as hard as could. Shattered his jaw so I've heard. He then ran for it."

"That's great but doesn't help us identify him, does it?"

"Now that's odd thing, Inspector."

"What is?"

"Neither of you batted an eyelid when I said son-in-law. How peculiar. Anyway, he was dancing with his sister who had just got back from South Africa where she works. But what is really odd is you two not recognising him."

Jimmy went back into the top draw of his desk and produced another piece of A4 paper.

"You see, gentlemen, I believe you do know him."

Jimmy placed the A4 sheet down in front of them. They both leant forward to get a better look at this second picture.

"You see, I believe you knew all I've just told you. I also believe as fellow Masons you are protecting him at my expense."

You could've heard a pin drop in that room. Just a very gentle hum of the computer and the CCTV units whirling in the background. Jimmy could see the panic rising in the pair of them. The inspector was gobsmacked that Jimmy had produced the picture. Mr Lewis was now as red as a beetroot and visibly shaking. *Got them*, Jimmy thought to himself, *now I've just stay cool.*

"This is…"

"This is a cover up, Mr Lewis. This is an abuse of power. I'll be honest though, it is a lovely picture of the three of you. Now what I'll do."

"You won't blackmail us."

The inspector was now properly rattled. Whatever their game plan had been, this was not part of that plan. The inspector was struggling to get his words out. Jimmy imagined their thoughts were now a blur. He knew this was his moment to strike, don't let them regroup at the police station or the Masonic lodge. This had to be finished now.

"What we'll do, gentlemen, is you will arrest the man you're stood by in the picture. If you've forgotten his name, I'll jog your memories for you. It is Frank James, and then this afternoon at some point, you'll phone me and let me know that the review has been concluded and Jumping Jacks and myself are free to carry on."

Jimmy sat back looking at them both. Mr Lewis had already started packing his leather file back together, not that Jimmy had really given him a chance to get it all out. He went to grab the picture of them with their fellow Mason and caught himself in the act.

"Take it, I've got the original. You can put that in your file."

They stood up and so did Jimmy.

"I'll see you out."

Jimmy motioned them out of the office. They walked through the club with great haste and Jimmy unbolted the front doors, letting in the harsh December wind that was currently thundering around the city.

As the inspector and licensing officer went through the door, Mr Lewis turned back and, in a very lowered tone, hissed at Jimmy.

"I'll see you real soon. Really soon."

"Have a good afternoon, gentleman."

Jimmy stood there on the front steps watching them disappear down the road. He was gripped by the feeling that he might have won that battle but had started a war. He shut the door and at least he knew he wouldn't have the review hanging over him for the whole of Christmas.

At just before 5pm, he had a short conversation with Inspector Thomas over the phone, advising him he could take down the review notice off the door as the matter was now concluded. Still the nagging thought of what would be next was living in his mind. He put it to one side and went home to get changed into his costume for the Christmas party that night.

Chapter 4
Jumping Jacks Keen

The early parts of any year are always a bit quiet in the night-time economy. Everyone is paying off Christmas, attempting to stick to New Year's resolutions or just avoiding the dark, cold nights that winter brings. Jimmy had pre-empted this and granted holidays for people throughout January and February. Killing two birds with one stone. He didn't want the staff stood around bored and also needed to get holidays shifted before April came round and the new tax year began.

His son was now over a year old and had become an even bigger driving force behind him, spurring him on. His relationship with Isabelle was now pretty strained and he buried himself in work. Probably the wrong course of action but at least he felt wanted at work. Isabelle would still come in most weekends and meet her friends so they did see one another, even if quite often it was only fleeting.

Jimmy did note how she revelled in the role of hostess, he was cordial and had learnt over the years most people only blow smoke up your ass as they want something. Still, perhaps, he thought he could still put this to good use as the club continued to get more and more popular.

As the months went by and the evenings grew warmer, he soon encountered new problems. Firstly, Jumping Jacks got hot, very hot. The antiquated air conditioning system simply couldn't handle the warmth and heat, especially when everyone started dancing. At the end of a night in early May, Jimmy could actually feel the condensation running down the walls. It was a problem that was rectified quite easily but it was not cheap. Still he had plenty of years on lease so it was an investment rather than a frivolous waste of money.

The second problem was not so much a problem but more an opportunity. Jimmy had noticed that a lot of people were coming after working in other venues as the dress code was more relaxed than that of his competitors. This meant when they finished at 3am, they were still practically full. He decided to challenge the city precedent that all licensed venues must finish business at 3am. He dutifully filled in the forms and applied for the club to have a 5am licence.

This was also the same city that stopped all hot food being served after 1:30am because people were congregating at fast-food outlets and there were occasional disturbances.

The licence went in, the fees paid, the advert put in the paper and the blue notices put up. Now he just had to wait the 28 days. The days ticked by slowly and Jimmy heard nothing from the council or the police. The wait felt like an eternity. After the consultation period was over, Jimmy was emailed by Edith Bowman from the council licensing division.

There had been some representations from the police and seven private representations from citizens of the city. She had emailed them all to Jimmy for him to read through. He now had a few days to negotiate with those making representations or off to committee they would go.

The police's representation was signed off by Inspector Thomas and basically stated the police didn't want a licensed venue open after 3am. This, whilst annoying, was going to be simple to deal with. Jimmy picked the phone up and rang Inspector Thomas. The inspector answered quickly.

"Mr Harris, I've been expecting your call."

"Good morning, Inspector. What conditions would the police like on the licence for you to support it."

"We never support applications, Mr Harris. Our position must remain impartial. Our only concerns are the licensing objectives and what is right for the night-time economy. As I'm sure you can see our position is based on the movement of people around the city. What would you suggest?"

The inspector sounded very confident in his position.

"Inspector, we don't want to cause ourselves any issues so we are willing to offer keeping last entry at 2:30am."

Jimmy was hoping that by not moving the last entry time, he would not only get people in but keep the police on side as best he could. He wouldn't be altering how people moved around the city, just getting more of them to come his way.

"I will put your offer to Mr Lewis and get back to you in due course."

The inspector put the phone down. Jimmy was quite pleased as it wasn't a straight out no and at least negotiations had begun. He hoped that by working with them, they could find a happy compromise and also start developing a better working relationship with them.

The other seven were puzzling him somewhat as he read them on the computer. Something wasn't right. He printed them out and reread them but he still couldn't put his finger on it. All seven purported to be local residents worried about the noise of a new club, worried about the mess and people coming to the area late at night.

"A new club?"

Jimmy was thinking out loud to himself in his office. This really wasn't making much sense. It was almost as if all seven had missed the fact that club had already been open nearly year. Six of the complaints came from flats about 300 yards down the road but one was from area over a mile away. He had their names and started Facebook stalking them to see what they were like and who they were.

It got even stranger. Over the course of the next week, he discovered that six of them were all college students under the age of 25. *Students like going out, don't they?* Jimmy thought to himself one afternoon as he strolled through their profiles on Facebook. Going out was something that students enjoyed, who goes to college to study? Something was not adding up.

The seventh was a man in his 50s, who apparently had nothing to do with the area, he lived several miles away. He didn't recognise him or anyone in his picture. What has he got against the club? Jimmy pondered long and hard over these people and their complaints.

The police had agreed to the conditions that Jimmy offered. Jimmy had to agree to extra door staff on certain nights but that was a minimal inconvenience as he already employed extra door staff. Jimmy was sure half the reason was Mr Lewis and Inspector Thomas were giving him enough rope to hang himself with. It just seemed too easy and he felt the inspector probably had an ulterior motive behind his support. It would be up to him to not give them the opportunity. He would remain vigilante and continue to keep them at bay…he hoped.

One Monday, Jimmy went with his son to see his mum and dad, just to talk over what was happening and have a little break from everything. He loved seeing his parents' reaction to their grandson. It just seemed to bring smiles all round.

Jimmy sat down and explained the whole saga to his dad, who having been a council official for many years, albeit many years ago, would hopefully give him some insight that he himself had missed. Jimmy sat in one of the armchairs in their front room as his parents sat on the sofa watching their grandson play with some Brio trains.

"I can't get my head round it, Dad. It's like they all have the same argument that they don't know we've already opened. They're acting like it's a new club opening. Not one that has been open for nearly a year."

"Have you got a copy I can read?"

Jimmy realised he'd left them on the kitchen side at home.

"I'll print you a copy out."

Jimmy got up from the chair and went over to their computer and logged into his email account. He printed one out for himself and one for his dad. So it wouldn't have to be being passed back and forth.

His dad studied the letters of consultation. As he finished reading, he peered over his glasses at Jimmy.

"Can you defend these representations?"

"Yes, but there's six so close that the committee will find in their favour on numbers alone. It's always a bit of a kangaroo court and the officials have to think about their voters. They don't get that people move to the city and then they're shocked at the noise. It's like people moving next to a farm and then moaning about the smell!"

"Leave them with me and I'll ring you tomorrow. Let's see what we can come up with."

He was proud of his son. He walked his own path and kept trying. The look of dejection on his face and slumped shoulders was not the Jimmy he was used to seeing. He'd spend the afternoon studying them without Jimmy peering over his shoulder asking questions every 2 minutes.

Back at home, Jimmy was in the kitchen making a coffee and half reading the letters. He stared at them intently as the coffee brewed. What was he missing? He picked up the letters and his fresh coffee and headed to the patio. Settling down at the picnic bench, he laid out his files. Isabelle was nowhere to be seen. His son was quite happy having a nap and finally he had some peace.

As he took the first sip of coffee, his phone rang and it was his dad. This was unusual at best. He rarely used the phone if he could help it.

"Hi, Dad."

"I can't hear you."

"You've got me on speaker phone, press the green button."

There was a clicking noise and Jimmy could hear some muttering.

"Hello, Jimmy, are you there?"

"Can you hear me now?"

"That's much better. Odd question but have you got a copy of these letters printed off a different printer?"

"Yes, I have, Dad, how come?"

"Put the same letter off our printer next to the same one off another printer."

He sounded quite excited. Jimmy laid them out side by side and stared at them. He still couldn't see anything. What was his dad excited about?

"Can you see the striation marks on all the letters?"

Jimmy looked again and there were five lines running the length of each letter, he picked up some other letters and every one of them had the same five very feint lines running their full length.

"Whoever wrote all the letters printed them all off using the same printer so that when they were scanned into the council system, they retained the striation marks, and there's more. The writer of the letter from miles away. His wife owns the building with all the flats in."

Jimmy couldn't believe it. All those years watching Columbo and Miss Marple had really paid off for his dad. This was amazing to hear. He wasn't even going to ask how he'd found out that final bit but he was grateful for the information all the same.

"Jimmy, are you still there?"

"Yes, I am. Just taking a moment to take all this in. Thank you so much."

"Not a problem, nice to be of some use every now and then."

Jimmy had gone over and over the letters and not seen a thing. The old adage was clearly true that sometimes what you need are a fresh set of eyes. He was so happy inside. He could finally challenge the representations. He had tried contacting all of them to negotiate but he had been stone walled in every attempt that he had made.

As he calmed down, he started to think a lot more clearly. The licensing committee was only a few days away, perhaps he could still put a stop to it and win without going in there. Jimmy hung up on his dad, went to his office, and phoned Mr Scott, the council licensing officer.

"Hello, Frank Scott, here."

He was quite a jovial old fella. Jimmy figured, at some point, he'd been a copper based on his mannerisms.

"Mr Scott, it's Jimmy Harris here. I wish to talk with you about the upcoming licensing hearing."

"Withdraw, Mr Harris, you are not going to win."

Jimmy had been hoping to find out what sort of mood Mr Scott was in before proceeding to far. The very abrupt reply had well and truly answered the question on his mood. Still Jimmy thought he should try. He didn't have anything to lose.

"Mr Scott, I have some relevant information which might make you want to withdraw."

"Pray tell, Mr Harris. This could be the highlight of my day."

"Mr Scott, I believe all the representations against the club are vexatious and I can prove it…"

"Mr Harris, I, as chief licensing officer, decide what is vexatious and what is not. I have, after very serious consideration, decided they are not. This is not a moot point for you to challenge. I have accepted all representations on their own merits."

"Mr Scott, if you look at the letters…"

"Mr Harris, I will repeat they are not. If you bring this up again, I will personally see to it you lose your personal licence. Am I clear?"

And with that, Mr Scott snapped down the phone ending the phone call.

Before Jimmy could even start, let alone finish, his sentence, the line went dead. Jimmy sat back in his chair at his desk. He half threw his mobile on the desk. This felt like a stitch up. Scratching his head, he started to formulate a plan. He knew this was the game changer. The bluster of Mr Scott did not faze him. Could he use it to his own advantage?

By the time Isabelle got home, he had a plan. It had taken all afternoon but he had worked out what he was going to do. She asked him how everything was going but he was busy plotting and didn't care much for the interruption to his train of thought. However, he knew for this plan to work he needed her. He was going on the attack.

Jimmy rationalised he had one shot at the late licence and at the moment, Mr Scott didn't realise the errors he had made.

"It's all coming together, tomorrow I'd like to buy you a suit."

Isabelle eyed him suspiciously. She knew he was up to something, but she also quite liked the idea of a nice suit.

"Ok, I'm free all day. I'd quite like a new suit."

"Wonderful, one new suit coming up."

Jimmy sat back in his chair and took a swig of coffee. He picked up his pen and made some notes on his desk pad. Isabelle left the office and disappeared into another room. Jimmy sat there contemplating how this would play out. He only had a few days to wait but it was the waiting and the anticipating that ate him up.

Hockington House was a massive Edwardian building where the committees were held. Jimmy had been up since before 6am preparing and rehearsing his role in the upcoming proceedings. He was determined to do everything without notes or prompts. The committee was scheduled for 10am. Jimmy drove into the car park and exited the vehicle.

He was wearing a full-on three-piece suit with full length black wool overcoat. Isabelle had been instructed to turn up separately. She arrived slightly after Jimmy and pulled into the car park. She was wearing a beautiful pin stripe trouser suit with full length wool overcoat. Her hair pulled back into a ponytail and looking as business like as possible.

She exited the car and retrieved three box files from the back seat; exactly as instructed. Jimmy waited outside the building and greeted her with a handshake. He knew full well somewhere in the recesses of that building the 'enemy' was watching. Theatrics were not a full part of his armoury but he was going to try today. They turned and headed towards the building making their way inside.

Committee Room Two was the destination. A beautiful oak panelled room. The large bench at the front, the chairs behind it, two tables set out on either side at the front directly in front of these. Jimmy and Isabelle were asked to sit on left. The chairs behind them were filling up. Some people were in attendance from the press and a few from the case that would precede theirs.

At exactly 10am, the clerk walked in. He announced the committee as they walked to their seats on the bench. Mr Scott walked in with a suited gentleman. They sat on the table on the right. Jimmy could feel the tension rippling through the room. The chair of the committee sat in the middle of the bench. Sir David Ramsey, an imposing looking man with white eyebrows that looked to be like an invading force on his head.

,Jimmy had been warned by TJ that Sir David took no prisoners and would not suffer fools at any costs, so no jokes. Sir David stood and banged his gable.

"I hope everyone present is familiar with the case before us."

He looked around the room eyeing up everyone who was present. When he was happy he decided to continue. He had made it very clear who was in charge.

"As such I would like to ask Mr Scott, head of council licensing, to outline his case."

Sir David sat back down and surveyed the room once more. He spotted Jimmy pouring himself a glass of water. Noting a slight tremor in his right hand that he doubted was caused by the weight of the jug. He knew that appearing here could be stressful.

Mr Scott stood up and looked directly at the bench.

"Firstly, Chair, Mr Harris has not provided the council with proof of his licensing application advert appearing in a local paper."

He reached down to his table and from a box file brandished a newspaper for all to see.

"This one is from June 2010."

"Objection, Mr Chair."

Sir David was a bit shocked to see Jimmy stood up. He quickly glanced over at the file on Mr Scott's table, saw it read Jumping Jacks licensing application 2010.

"Might I suggest Mr Scott has brought the file from last year, my original application to have a licence granted and not the file that is relevant to this current application."

Jimmy sat back down and Sir David stared hard at Mr Scott expecting answers. He was also impressed by the precise nature of Jimmy's objection. He had a fair point.

Mr Scott looked increasingly panicked as he looked at the bench and then in the box file he had brought with him.

"Uumm, Sir David, I believe…"

The gable hammered down on the desk in front of Sir David.

"Mr Scott, I expect everyone, especially you, to be prepared for my sessions."

"Might I have 5 minutes grace, David?"

"You have 3 minutes and it is Mr Chair or Sir David!"

Sir David banged his gable down again to bring the room to order. Mr Scott hurriedly made his way out of the back of the committee room. Sir David was also glad of the short recess, that last cup of coffee had gone straight through him.

"We will have a 3-minute recess whilst Mr Scott gets his house in order."

Sir David sat back down and whispered something to others on the bench not for the ears of everyone else present. He then excused himself.

Jimmy poured, and drank, his second glass of water. So far so good. He couldn't have predicted this turn of events but he would take it. He sat patiently in his seat. Time seemed to stop entirely before the heavy oak doors swung open and Mr Scott reappeared. Mr Scott hustled to the front, his ill-fitting suit seeming to slow him down with every step he took. He stood back at his table and stared at the bench.

"At the second time of asking. Are you now ready, Mr Scott."

"Yes, Mr Chair."

"And…"

"And what, sorry?"

"Very simply, Mr Scott, did Mr Harris submit the paper in time with his advert in it?"

"Yes, Sir David, he did. My assistant is bringing up the file now from the town hall."

Mr Scott looked incredibly flustered; this was not the ideal start to his day.

"Well, you will carry on without it until they arrive, Mr Scott."

Sir David's patience was clearly already at breaking point.

Mr Scott stood and took a deep breath, rolled his shoulders slightly, and for the second time, he began.

"The council has received seven representations against the application…"

"Objection, Mr Chair."

For the second time, Sir David saw Jimmy on his feet. Sir David's patience was not for trying. He stared at Jimmy for what felt like an eternity. *He's got tenacity*, he thought to himself.

"On what grounds are you objecting this time, Mr Harris?"

"Vexatious, Mr Chair."

"Outrageous."

"Mr Scott, you will await your turn when an objection is raised. Mr Harris will now explain his objection to the room and I'll remind you who is in charge of this committee and how members are to behave."

Mr Scott slid back down into his seat like a scolded child. The ill-fitting suit looking even worse when he sat down.

Jimmy stood up, fully aware everyone in the room was staring at him, especially those of the exasperated chairman. This had to be the pitch of a lifetime or it was all for nothing.

"Mr Chair, I have printed these letters off several printers, and it has become very apparent they were all created on the same computer and printed out using the same printer."

Jimmy was trying to act as coolly as he possibly could whilst his heart was beating faster than that of a cocaine addicts in the middle of a binge.

"Mr Harris, that is a very serious accusation. It is even more serious if true and the chief licensing officer has failed to notice it. Can you prove it further?"

Sir David was quite clearly still annoyed from the earlier disaster of protocol caused by the said licensing officer but was at least intrigued by what Jimmy had to say.

"Yes, Sir, I can. A Mrs Bolt, whose husband posted the 7th representation from a distance away, owns the six flats from which the other six representations came from. I believe she has printed them out and made her tenants sign them."

There was an audible gasp in the room at these remarks. Jimmy took stock and relaxed. The room was in chaos and he just needed to be the stability.

"I also know, Sir, that Mrs Bolt attended the same school as Mr Scott and that they are friends on Facebook."

The chatter in the committee room meant it took Sir David many blows with his gable to bring the room to order. Sir David was visibly furious, Mr Scott was visibly panicked, and Mr Lewis for the police was absolutely shocked. Jimmy, however, was just stood in the middle of it all looking unperturbed by the unfolding events.

Jordan O'Keef, the council's lawyer, was sat at the end of the bench. Upon hearing the accusations, he motioned the clerk over to him. He whispered something to him and the clerk preceded over to Jimmy's table.

"Mr Harris, the council lawyer is an expert in these matters and wishes to see the letters."

Jimmy handed him the three sets of letters and the clerk took them to Mr O'Keef.

"Mr Scott, how do you respond to these accusations?"

"Sir David, I did not believe them to be vexatious. I think it best we get Mrs Bolt here and she can explain."

Mr Scott was clearly grasping at straws. Isabelle kept scribbling on bits of note paper and handing them to Jimmy. He read them and put them in the file box in front of him.

"Very well. You have half an hour to get her to attend. Committee is excused until 11:15."

Before anyone could stand, Mr O'Keef, who had been examining the letters, stood up.

"Do you mind if I speak, Sir David?"

Sir David indicated that the floor was all his. This was supposed to be a very simple licensing application. How in 15 minutes had it descended to this?

"I can quite clearly see that these have all come off the same original printer, and thus, without good reason, they will be deemed inadmissible when we return. I, as the council lawyer, must advise everyone here present that they are to be treated as vexatious, and thus, inadmissible."

"Room dismissed."

Jimmy stood, watched the committee leave, and then scuttled out of the rear doors himself. He needed to regroup and get his thoughts together. He exited the committee room in a flash.

Isabelle found him sitting by a large planter outside sucking on a cigarette, looking a lot less happy than she thought he would.

"Ok, why do you look so down? It's going well, isn't it?"

"So far. Until Mr Scott gets her in here."

"Come on, Jimmy. You've just got to see it through, What's the plan?"

"He calls her. She lies through her teeth and we lose!"

Jimmy handed her a cigarette and lit it for her. He stood up, stubbed out the cigarette he was smoking and lit another.

"That won't help your cough."

"I have other things to worry about right now."

He stood there, taking a few more drags on his cigarette, looking very pensive. Isabelle had thought he would be ecstatic at the way things had gone so far.

"The moment she starts to speak, hand me a piece of paper with NO written on it. Ring it and pretend to scribble something, I've got this sorted. It's game over."

Isabelle took a drag, looked at Jimmy, and knew he was not messing around at all. His face was nothing but thunder and his eyes had developed a distinct darkness. She knew when it was best to leave him to his own thoughts brooding.

Jimmy spent the next 10 minutes pacing up and down; Lost in his own thoughts, chain smoking, playing out possible scenarios in his mind that might unfold within the committee room. The clerk appeared outside and announced that they were about to be back in session.

As the room reconvened, everyone sat down as they were. A table had been brought in for the aforementioned Mrs Bolt to sit at.

"Committee is back in session, Mr Scott, your witness."

Sir David began the proceeding for the third time.

"Committee, Sir David, I bring before you Mrs Bolt for her version of events."

Mr Scott sat back down and began waving arm at Mrs Bolt to stand up, implying to start her statement. She had obviously cobbled together a statement to read out, no doubt coaxed by Mr Scott on what to say. Isabelle did as she had told. Jimmy picked up the piece of paper and pretended to read it.

"Dear Committee…"

That was as far as Mrs Bolt managed to make her statement before Jimmy stood up.

"I object."

Sir David stood; he glowered at Jimmy and sighed. This was his third objection and he still hadn't heard a single representation.

"On what grounds, Mr Harris?"

"Very simple, Sir David. Only those who have made representations during the consultation period may speak at the committee."

Sir David stood, Jimmy raised his left arm in a stopping motion whilst looking at the end of the bench in the direction of the council lawyer, Jordan O'Keef.

"Mrs Bolt has two options. Number one, admit she wrote all the representations and forced her tenants to sign them making them vexatious, or deny it and not be allowed to speak."

Jimmy stared hard at Mr O'Keef. Mr O'Keef beckoned Sir David over to him and in the confer, he told Sir David much the same as Jimmy had told the room.

After 30 seconds, Sir David returned front and centre.

"Mrs Bolt, I ask you which is it? Did you write them or not?"

"I wrote them all and I will be heard. I will not have a nightclub open by…"

"No, Mrs Bolt, you won't. Mr Harris, Mr Scott, Mr O'Keef, to my chambers please at once."

Sir David banged his gable down incredibly hard that time. Jimmy was amazed it didn't break.

Jimmy had planned to divide and conquer but this was extraordinary. As he strode forward, he decided that keeping his own council would be very wise here. He hadn't got a scooby doo what was going on. The four of them went through the doors to the back left of the bench and into the Chair's chambers. Jimmy was last in. Sir David was fuming.

"What the fucking hell are you doing to my committee, Frank? You will withdraw immediately and the licence will be granted. Am I fucking clear? I have only brought you all here to save the council face in front of the press. Frank, you're a fucking shambles."

Jimmy stood at the back trying his hardest to not make eye contact with anyone. All of them stood around not talking, not saying a word. Jimmy thought time was standing still as they all just stood there. The only hint time was moving was the ticking of the ornate clock on the mantlepiece at the back of the room.

"Right, that's enough time, looks like negotiations took place and that we have resolved all issues. Let's go."

Everyone turned and left the Chair's office. Returning to the committee room and taking their seats, everyone in the room sat down as the session resumed.

"After a conference in my chambers, conditions are agreed. Mr Scott, are you happy?"

"Very happy, Mr Chair."

"Mr Harris, are you happy?"

"Yes, no problems from myself."

"In that case then, the licence is granted. Mr Harris, you may trade as you wished and the council will furnish you with the paperwork in due course. Committee is in recess until 1pm."

Sir David banged his gable one final time, stood up and left the chamber. The other members followed and stood up and tailed him out of the room.

Jimmy sat there in a bit of a daze. He had hoped to win but that was amazing. He looked at Isabelle who was sitting in shock.

"Did we win?"

Before Jimmy could answer, Mr Scott leant over their table.

"I don't believe I've met your lawyer, Mr Harris. We always have positions in licensing for sharp minds like yours!"

"Mr Scott, isn't it?"

"Yes, sweetheart."

"I'm Jimmy's partner. Pleased to meet you."

Isabelle held out her hand for him to shake. The ruse was up but it made no odds. Jimmy wasn't sat next to a legal super brain. He was sat by his girlfriend in a suit. Jimmy could see Mr Scott wanted the floor to swallow him whole. Jimmy couldn't resist a small smile as the chief licensing officer hurriedly made his exit.

As he watched Mr Scott leave the committee room and the door swing shut behind him, Jimmy scanned around to see what everyone was making of the proceedings that had unfolded before them. As he did so, he spotted his dad sitting in the front row of the viewing gallery. His dad smiled at him and gave him the thumbs up. Jimmy got his things together, gave Isabelle a hug, and they hurried over to see what his dad thought of their performance in his old stomping ground.

Chapter 5
5am, All That Jazz and a Pool Hall

There were a few things that needed to be altered before they could open until 5am. First thing Jimmy did was ring round all the staff and check they could actually work that late. Everyone was keen so that made life easier. Jimmy hadn't wanted to tempt fate and thus, hadn't ordered new posters with the new times on them before the licence was granted. He did order them though about 2 minutes after getting home from committee.

News travels fast in a small city and soon enough, Jimmy's phone was ringing nearly constantly. He ignored most of them as he sat writing the Twitter and Facebook posts to make the general populous aware of the decision. He posted the status updates and decided that was enough for one day. He still had to open the club that evening.

Standing on the front steps of the club as it opened that Friday, Jimmy felt a sense of accomplishment. They'd taken on the council and won. He'd stood there out of his comfort zone and managed to operate in that world of legality, now to reap the rewards of that hard fought victory. As he stood there savouring the moment, he noticed coming down the road the rather overweight figure of Tony Graham. He was the manager of the city's biggest nightclub, Klimax.

He walked with an odd gait, having injured himself falling off an inflatable banana being towed by a speed boat, so the story went. Jimmy could not stand him. He embodied everything that was wrong with industry. He approached the door of Jimmy's club and Jimmy himself.

"Jimmy, how are you?"

The over familiarity was odd as they had barely spoken five words to one another in the previous 5 years.

"I'm fine, thank you, Tony. What can I do for you?"

Jimmy was attempting to be cordial but he was no less wary of his competitor. It was blatantly obvious that this was not a social visit.

"Just wanted to see what all the fuss was about; I've never been in here before."

"Come on in, I'll show you round."

Jimmy pointed Tony through the doors. He was clearly on a scouting mission. He spent the whole tour fishing for information behind a facade of false friendship. Jimmy didn't trust him as far as he could throw him, and given his considerable girth, that wasn't far as all. This instinct was to be proven very correct over the next few months. He had been warned by quite a few people that he was a slimy cretin to be avoided at all costs.

With the 5am licence came a lot more customers, which was wonderful. Yet to begin with, it also bought quite a bit of hassle. Jimmy was very aware it put the club on the map in the city but it made them a target for others. Jimmy would often think how some people cannot create their own happiness so instead get joy out of attempting to ruin other people's.

Apart from a few teething issues, like getting customers to understand the last entry time was still 2:30am, the transition went well after the first few weeks. That was until the stink bombs started being dropped around the club. They absolutely stank. It was a very quick way to clear a club.

"Any idea who it was?"

Jimmy was pacing up and down as the staff enjoyed their post work drinks one evening. Another night of stink bombs had not put him in the best of moods.

"Not sure if he did it but I saw a lad off my course in here. He works at Klimax."

Maybe, just maybe, George had identified the culprit, or one of the culprits. It would make sense.

"Can we get his picture, Jimmy?"

Sebastian was clearly planning for next weekend and frisking the lad if he tried to gain entry again.

"Yes, I'll get that sorted. Can you text me his full name, George?"

This went on in a similar patten for about three weeks. Jimmy was losing his patience. He knew Tony Graham was behind it. The toilets were also getting routinely sabotaged. Toilets blocked and sinks flooded. It was becoming a very real problem that Jimmy knew he had to deal with, and quickly. It didn't take much to stop people coming.

One Friday, just after the latest stink bomb, Jimmy had had enough. He took a walk across the city to have words with Tony Graham. Arriving at Klimax's door, he asked to see Tony but was told he was too busy.

"Just tell him Jimmy Harris said enough is enough. One more stink bomb and it's not going to end pretty."

Jimmy was furious as he walked back through the city back to Jumping Jacks. This was just unacceptable. In big cities, he could understand it but this was just a big town. Sabotaging other venues was dirty and totally unnecessary. His phone rang, the caller ID told him it was Lee.

"Boss, there's been another stink bomb."

As he continued his walk through the city, a flyer girl quite innocently handed Jimmy a flyer. He instinctively took it so as not to be rude, he knew how hard their job was, and put it in his pocket as he continued his conversation with Lee.

"I'll be back in 5 minutes, crank up the air cons."

In the week, he'd bought a few toilet air fresheners with the jellies in them. Cut them open and sliced up the jellies. He had then strategically placed the slices in the air cons to create giant air fresheners.

By the time he arrived back, the smell had gone but so had half the customers. Jimmy went to the bar and got himself a drink. He sat at the table on his own, wracking his brain as to how to deal with this problem. He reached in his pocket and pulled out the flyer. It was for Klimax. It was their usual generic flyer. 'Free entry before midnight with this flyer', 'selected bottles just £2 each with this flyer'. As he stared at the flyer, suddenly Jimmy felt the flicker of an idea forming.

When the shift finished, Jimmy asked everyone if anyone had a friend who wanted to earn a few quid tomorrow night.

"My sister will."

Hannah instantly volunteered her younger sister for the job. She'd been angling for a job for her for a while but Jimmy had none going. This would get her foot in the door at least.

"Great; can you ask her to be here at 10pm tomorrow. If she can bring a friend even better."

Jimmy saw everyone out and made his way with the flyer to his office. Tonight was going to be long but it would be worth every second.

Saturday night soon came round. Isabelle was in with her friends drinking. It was one of their birthdays, but Isabelle never needed an excuse to celebrate and push the boat out. Jimmy went over and checked they were all having a good time. It was odd for him since he'd got a DJ in to cover every other Saturday so he could concentrate on other things. It did also, however, give him a break and a chance to relax. Hannah approached them all.

"Jimmy, my sister and her friend are here."

"That's great, can you show them up to my office, I'll be there in a few mins."

Jimmy turned to Isabelle and her friends.

"I've got to go. I have a few things to attend to."

"Don't be too long."

Isabelle knew he would be ages, he always was. There was always something he had to attend to or something that he needed to fix. Jimmy walked into his office and Hannah introduced everyone.

"Hannah, thank you. Thank you for agreeing to help this evening, it is very much appreciated. Right, very simply tonight, I want you to zoom around the city and hand these flyers out to anyone who is heading towards Klimax. Keep moving and don't stay in one place too long."

"Does it matter who?"

"No, it doesn't. However, don't tell anyone you work here. Don't come straight back here when you're done. Take a loop around the city to throw off anyone who might be following you."

He handed the girls two big wads of flyers and followed them down and out of the club. He stood on the doorstep and lit a cigarette as he watched them disappear into the city. The pure anticipation of the ensuing car crash was almost too much to bear.

He was getting a drink when the first stink bomb went off. It was so frequent now they could deal with them pretty quickly and he kept smiling. He was hoping tonight would be last night he, and they, would have to deal with them. Klimax did not know what was about to hit them.

Jimmy was sat with Isabelle and her friends just before 12:30 when his phone rang. It was Tony Graham. He ignored it as he imagined the panic running through the man's body at that moment in time. He was enjoying the mere thought of it all. He deserved everything he was about to receive. The first of his flyers had clearly arrived at its target. Jimmy smiled to himself.

"I know that smile. You're up to something."

Jimmy just smiled as his phone rang for a second time; again it was Tony Graham. He ignored that call as well. Barely a few minutes later, his internal radio went off.

"Jimmy, we've got a Tony Graham here to see you."

"I'll be out now, keep him there, do not let him go anywhere."

He excused himself from Isabelle's table and headed towards the front door. Stepping through the door, he could hear, before he could see, a very irate Tony Graham shouting the odds.

"Tony, good evening. What can I do for you?"

"You, you've done e-fucking-nough!"

Tony thrust a flyer into Jimmy's hand in a very aggressive manner. Jimmy looked at it as if it was the first time he'd ever clapped eyes on it. He read it and looked at Tony.

"I don't think I can compete with these offers, Tony."

"Fuck you. You did this, I know you are behind this."

Jimmy looked at him. Tony was nearly hyperventilating, he was so angry. Jimmy reached inside his jacket, took out a cigarette and lit it. As he exhaled, he held Tony's gaze.

"Tony, I've got a feeling that if I see no more toilets flooded and I don't get any more stink bombs, then you won't see any more flyers after tonight."

Tony stood looking at Jimmy flanked by huge two doormen.

"Fuck you, do you know how much this has cost us?"

"Do you think I care? Do you think after all the stink bombs you've had let off in here, I actually give a shit how much it's cost you? Now fuck off back to your club and leave us in peace."

Tony paced furiously in front of the club. He couldn't believe this little upstart had actually got the better of him.

"Think you're a big hard man with your doormen protecting you?"

"Tony, just so you know, they're not here for my safety, they're here for yours. Now fuck off."

Jimmy had now lost his temper; he couldn't believe the arrogance of the man. To be trying to ride a high horse after all he'd done to Jimmy's club. The doormen were both worried about what was going to happen next.

Tony stood still for a few seconds eyeballing Jimmy and his staff. He then headed away from the door cursing under his breathe. The door staff breathed a sigh of relief. They weren't quite sure what they were going to do if it had descended into a fight.

"What was that all about?"

Jimmy laughed heartedly and handed Lee the flyer that Tony had thrust in to his hand. Still laughing to himself, he walked back inside the club. Lee stood looking at the Klimax flyer that Jimmy had handed him. On one side it offered free entry all night and on the other side, it listed all bottle drinks just 10p each…buy one get one free.

The two towering door staff laughed as well, as they too were now imagining the chaos in Klimax that evening. They could also see why Tony Graham was livid with their boss.

And just like that, the stink bombs stopped and the toilets were no longer being sabotaged. Although, George did tell Jimmy one night that he'd heard of a friend who worked there that the odd flyer was still turning up at Klimax a few weeks later.

With the now much higher profile, came a few opportunities which were very welcome. Every August bank holiday, the Anchor hosted a giant beer and cider festival. Lots of real ales and traditional ciders from all over the nearby counties. To be able to sponsor something at it was great for the community as it raised a lot of money, and it was also great exposure.

As Jimmy sat having a pint with TJ one evening, TJ said his bosses had asked him if he wanted to sponsor the wristbands for the event, i.e. provide the wristbands for all the patrons.

"Yes, of course, I'll do it. How many do you need and what do you want on them?"

"I'll email you all the details but it's about 650 a day for each of the three days. Now Klimax are still one of the main sponsors but at least you've been asked."

"That's very true, thank you."

"You get five free tickets each night as well."

With the festival being only a few weeks away, Jimmy got to work quite quickly designing the wristbands. He wanted it to be right and not embarrass TJ in any way.

The Friday of the bank holiday, it all opened at 6pm. Jimmy had arrived early at the pub as the first people in were the sponsors. No one noticed very quickly what the wristbands said beyond 'Beer Festival' and the date for which the wristbands were valid.

Just after 6:30pm, Tony Graham and the Klimax contingent turned up. Jimmy made sure he could see them get their wristbands put on their wrists. Tony held his arm out and the wristband was placed on his arm. He inspected it and Jimmy was sure he could see his eyes flicker in disbelief. Although, they'd paid a lot of money to be the main sponsor, the wristbands read:

THE ANCHOR BEER FESTIVAL—Friday, 26 Aug 2011.

This Wristband gives free entry to Jumping Jacks b4 1am!

Sponsored by Jumping Jacks Nightclub; NO. 1 in the City!

Tony was so angry. His face flushed bright red; he was fuming and it was visible for all to see. He tore his wristband off and stormed out, leaving his entourage in his wake. Jimmy was in stitches. TJ wasn't pleased but there was nothing he could do about it, and they still had three days to go.

"If they pull their sponsorship next year, you'll be replacing them."

"It'll be worth every penny."

At the start of November, the floor above Jumping Jacks became available to lease. It had previously been a karate dojo but the owner had moved to an industrial unit slightly out of the city to save money. It was a large and cavernous space. Jimmy contacted the estate agents and went for mooch about to see if he could make use of it. It had a front area, toilets which would need replacing and a very large room.

Initially, Jimmy thought about connecting it to the club but soon dismissed the idea. Jimmy concluded it was a lot of work, would cause massive disruption, and ultimately wouldn't be worth the hassle.

As he sat in High Town having a coffee one morning with Isabelle, Jimmy suddenly had an idea.

"We could turn it into a pool and snooker club."

"Don't you think it'll be a lot of work? And you have plenty on already. Does anyone still play pool?"

"Well, if you did a few afternoon shifts there, it would be worthwhile, and I think pool is still popular. It just has less venues with tables as a lot of pubs are turning gastro and removing pub games."

Jimmy sat back enjoying his coffee as well as personally liking the idea of playing pool; he thought it might give Isabelle a sense of purpose. She might enjoy it. She was a clever girl who just needed a little push sometimes.

"I suppose I could."

For once, Isabelle was agreeing with Jimmy. She also liked the idea of freedom and a break from her normal life.

"Right, I'll phone the agents and set the ball in motion. I don't imagine it will take long."

With all the legal bits to sort and Christmas approaching, nothing got sorted until mid-January. Jimmy had negotiated the building rent free for the first six months as it needed quite a bit of work and the landlords were keen on a long-term tenant. It also helped he was the tenant downstairs. They seemed to very much seemed to like the idea of rent being paid.

It started taking shape quite quickly and soon, all the rooms were painted, and TVs installed all around for the sport. Jimmy had bought a transit van off eBay. Apart from 4th gear not working properly, it was pretty good and as he only paid £500 for it, he was pleased with his purchase. The van had a year's MOT which had very obviously been bought but Jimmy didn't care. It was functional and that was all that mattered to him.

He'd discovered the beauty of eBay whilst building the club. If you were prepared to travel a bit, it was a great way to save money. He was attempting to get four urinals for the gents but the prices of new ones in the city started at £150 each. The gent's toilets had been a changing room and so had plenty of space for extra urinals.

One evening, with a couple of beers on board after finishing work, he spotted a job lot of five urinals for £100. He cheekily sent an offer of £60 to the seller and the next morning when he woke up, this offer had been accepted. He paid for them and then messaged the seller asking when he could pick them up. It was only as he looked at the screen, he realised that his purchase was not in Newcastle under Lyme, a mere 90 miles away, but instead in Newcastle upon Tyne, some 265 miles away.

Oh bollocks, Jimmy thought. And he'd bloody paid for them already. The money he'd saved on the toilets he'd now waste on fuel and a twelve-hour round trip. Also the idea of taking his van on such a long trip was quite a daunting thought.

Lee had said he would come with Jimmy and keep him company on the journey. Jimmy figured it would also help keep him awake. They set off at 2:30am after the club shut to get there about 8:30am. Jimmy hopes of Lee keeping him awake all the way were soon dashed as Lee fell asleep within the first hour of the journey and did not wake until they arrived in Newcastle upon Tyne. Having collected the urinals, they got back in the van.

"Sorry I fell asleep on the way here."

"No worries, you were probably tired."

Jimmy was feeling the rigours of the journey as he stifled another yawn. They set off heading for home. Jimmy opened his window and turned the radio up to try and keep himself awake. This may have helped him but it was no help to Lee who was fast asleep again before they hit the motorway. He did wake up when Jimmy stopped at the services but that was only because he needed to go to the toilet, and as soon as they got back on the motorway, back to sleep he went.

Jimmy laughed to himself about how easily Lee found it to sleep anywhere. He'd found him a few times dozing off against a speaker stack in the club when he was supposed to be watching the dance floor so he wasn't completely surprised.

Having retrieved the toilets from the furthest place up north he had ever been, and bear in mind, he considered anything above Crewe to be Northern, he set about purchasing two snooker tables and six pool tables. He figured that by owning them himself, although he'd have to pay for the upkeep, he could retain all the money. He even thought he might get some rare 50ps which everyone seemed to be collecting these days.

Plus, he needed every penny he could get after Isabelle announced she was pregnant again. He wondered if his son would get a little brother or a little sister to play with. Either way, he found he was quite excited by the prospect. He loved being a dad.

It was the middle of March when he went to pick up the two snooker tables. Luckily, this time he wouldn't have to go far. He collected Lee and Sebastian and off they set in the super van.

"So how do you take a snooker table apart, Jimmy?"

"Well, I've been doing some research and according to YouTube…"

Lee and Sebastian looked at one another and knew they were in for a great day.

The first table was a snip at £180. They drove up the driveway of the large house that contained the table. The house was enormous. Getting out of the van, all three of them had a good stretch before approaching the front door. A man in his mid-forties answered.

"Good morning."

Jimmy instinctively held out his hand to shake the gentleman's.

"Morning, boys, come about the snooker table, have you?"

"Yes, we have."

"Great, if you'll just follow me, I'll show you where it is."

The gentleman shut the front door and headed around the side of the house. As the perfectly manicured garden appeared before them, they could see a rather lovely building situated behind the house.

"It's in here."

The gentleman opened the door and popped the lights on. It was a beautiful table; it could almost have been an antique, it was so beautifully carved.

"Been here since mother and father moved in during the 70s."

"So, it's not moved in 40 years?"

Sebastian was clearly already thinking this was not going to be easy to dismantle as he thought about the weight of the slates sitting there for 40 years.

"Not during my lifetime. I'll leave you to it, boys. If you need me, I'll be in the house."

With that, he exited the building and shut the door leaving Jimmy, Sebastian and Lee with the very settled antique snooker table.

"Right, Jimmy, did that YouTube video suggest what to do if a table has been sat for 40 years?"

"I've bought some WD 40 just in case."

It was a fair question though and after two hours of hammering and a whole can of WD 40 just to get the bolts undone, it would also be fair to say the lads were pretty pissed off with Jimmy. Still the table was nearly apart. The sides were off, the slates had been loaded into the van and the frame was nearly completely undone.

"Jimmy, that was a struggle for us three on flat ground."

"Yes, they were a bit heavy."

"How the hell are we gonna carry them up a flight of stairs? It's going to be *dangerous*."

Lee tried emphasising the dangerous bit, but he knew full well Jimmy was going to plough on regardless. He had a plan and he was sticking to it.

"We'll have more people at the club. But being fair, they were heavier than I thought they were going to be."

Jimmy concentrated on getting the final few bolts out of the frame whilst everything else was being loaded.

After they'd finished loading, Jimmy looked in the back of the van. It was already starting to get a bit low on the shock absorbers, but he figured that he only had ten miles to go to get the next table and then a swift 25 miles home.

Pulling up at the second house and removing the second table was much easier. It was a much newer table, nowhere near as pretty though and took less than an hour to dismantle. With the two being so different at least they wouldn't be mixing up the bits when they returned to the snooker hall. Once it was loaded, the van was now very, very low on its suspension but still 25 miles and this would all be sorted.

Jimmy noticed both Sebastian and Lee eyeing up how low the van was before they got in. Thank God, they didn't see how low it got after they had got in.

"It'll be fine, lads."

Jimmy tried to put them in a positive frame of mind but he was also trying to convince himself. He fired up the van and off they set on the homeward journey. The first hint there was an issue was going up the big hill eight miles out of the city as they got slower and slower, until they were being overtaken by everything else and crawling at below ten mph as they crawled up in the slow lane.

"Everything alright, Jimmy?"

"Yeah, just a bit heavy and it's only a two-litre engine. It'll be fine once we're at the top."

Jimmy realised they still had ½ a mile to crawl to the top before it plateaued out and he was already down to first gear. Looking back, the warning signs were there but hindsight is so effective in spotting the errors of your ways. Driving over the plateau was fine. It was as they began the descent, Jimmy twigged there might be bigger issues than even he had thought about as the van started gaining speed.

"Hold on to something."

Although, Jimmy's voice was very calm, the lads could sense something was afoot. His eyes were firmly focused on the road ahead and his knuckles were growing white as his hands gripped the steering wheel.

"Brake, bloody brake."

The van thundered down the hill gaining momentum with every metre it covered.

"I fucking am."

Jimmy was now stood on the brake pedal. The road swung left and then right. Just one bend to navigate and then they'd be on the flat, but the van had such momentum then that even the engine couldn't slow it down.

"JESUS CHRIST."

The van now going in excess of 85 mph as they took the last bend. Jimmy was hanging on to the steering wheel for fear of a grim death; Sebastian was screaming and Lee discovered that he was actually quite religious. On two wheels they somehow made it round and the road straightened out as it levelled.

A communal exhaling of air and nervous laughs filled the van. There were no more hills to the city and Jimmy thought they were home and dry just before he noticed the smoke coming from the front of the van.

"We're on fire."

"It's ok, the brakes have just got a little bit hot. I'll pull over at the next lay by and let them cool down."

As they all disembarked from the van feeling a pulpable sense of relief that they were exiting under their own steam, Jimmy couldn't help but feel he had put all their lives at risk.

"This is more dangerous than working the doors."

Jimmy lit a cigarette and started walking around the van. He knew how lucky they all were to be in one piece. He rang Isabelle and asked her to round everyone up at the pool hall as they would be back inside half an hour, and they were going to need as many hands as they could get. After a brief period letting everything cool down, the intrepid adventures carried on, heading for home.

Pulling up in the loading bay opposite the club and the pool hall, they felt like there should've been more fanfare for the returning heroes but there wasn't even as much as a coffee. So, in true British spirit, Jimmy went in and put the kettle on.

They loaded in all the wooden bits of the tables with relative ease and separated them in to two distinct piles to differentiate the tables. Once they were all in, everyone's focus turned to the slates. It didn't matter how hard they tried, you can only get four people on a slate going up the stairs. This was proper hard work. With each slate that was going in, there was always someone muttering about how many there were still to go.

After just over two hours and many pinched fingers, all ten slates were upstairs. Everyone was shattered except Lee, who as soon as they finished and it was clear he wasn't needed anymore, he got up and announced that he was off to the gym.

It took a week but everything was finally in place. The snooker tables had been reclothed, the pool tables installed, the games machines were ready and the toilets rebuilt. Rerack Snooker and Pool Hall could finally open for business in late summer. Now although, Jimmy had hoped Isabelle would be able to do some shifts, she was now 38 weeks pregnant, so she had a pretty good excuse to not do any bar shifts.

However, despite seemingly birthing a beachball and the fact she could not manoeuvre behind the bar, although she did try, she was upset at not taking up her role as bar manager. Jim reassured her that she could take up the role in a few months and that nothing had changed.

It had taken longer than anticipated to get it all ready and Jimmy had foreseen this problem with staffing and Isabelle's pregnancy. He hired a new guy to help him upstairs in the pool hall, John Bevan; although because of his superhero tattoos all over his arms and legs, everyone just called him Tatts. He was a big lad and very jovial. Jimmy had known him for quite a few years.

Tatts had first come to Jimmy's attention when he first started to attend gigs at Parker's. Jimmy enjoyed his company quite a lot and found his enthusiasm for everything quite contagious. He didn't really like employing friends but this seemed to make perfect sense. Tatts needed a job and Jimmy needed help from someone he could trust. It wasn't long before Tatts was not only working in Rerack but coming and helping in Jumping Jacks as well.

Rerack was a different kettle of fish to Jumping Jacks. It was open a lot more and for a lot longer hours—10am to 11:30pm, every day. Rerack was also more evolution than revolution. But even in the first few days, people were drifting in to have a look and play a few games of pool. Some of the guys and girls from the club were enjoying the overtime as Jimmy had them running around the city putting up posters and handing out flyers. Anything to let people know they were open.

His second son was born in the middle of the month so sleep was now at an absolute premium. Jimmy had grown up with a brother and Jimmy thought how wonderful it will be to see them grow up together. With sleep now an almost a nonentity in his life, Jimmy made use of the office space in Rerack. He had managed to get a sofa into it so he could actually grab a few minutes sleep every now and then.

By this point, some events were starting to repeat themselves. Mid-August, organise an A Level results party—attempt to stop the door staff keeping tally of how many students were thrown out or not even allowed in as they were celebrating a bit too hard; end of August sponsor the Anchor Beer Festival, after the wristband debacle, he was now the main sponsor, and then onto September and Threshers week, for the local art college and the knowledge that it wasn't long until he got to decorate the club for Halloween.

Every year, he'd order even more Halloween decorations so the celebration got bigger every year. It also took longer and longer every year to put the decorations up and take them down.

With the club becoming quite set in a pattern, Jimmy enjoyed having the challenge of Rerack. Starting something fresh.

"How many pool teams have we got signed up for the winter league?"

"Four pool teams and one darts team."

"Superb, regular customers every week. I've spoken with Bart at the chippy and they'll provide the food for the teams on league nights and deliver it."

"Good because I'm no cook."

Jimmy wasn't sure if Tatts was serious or not about being able to cook but at least he wouldn't have to find out the hard way.

It was in September when Darren, Isabelle's little brother, came to work for Jimmy. Jimmy had thought him odd for years. The first time they had ever met, Jimmy had asked him what his favourite music was and after a pause Darren had replied, "Elevator Music."

He'd just turned 18; he had no drive, he'd been kicked out of college, he had no friends and seemingly spent every day in his wanking chariot at his mother's house. Well, she had decided after he failed to get into college, that he was going to get a job and help pay the bills at home. Unfortunately for Jimmy, he hadn't managed to get one and so very kindly Isabelle had promised him one at the club.

"Right, Darren, I'm going to show you how to clean a pool table, after that you are going to clean the other five."

Jimmy produced a selection of brushes, sprays and a hoover. After he'd shown him how to do that, he handed the cleaning equipment over to Darren.

"Darren, have you got any questions?"

"Do you want me to do the big ones as well?"

Darren pointed at Jimmy's pride and joy, the snooker tables.

"No, Darren, leave the snooker tables for me and Tatts as they need ironing as well. When you're done with those five come and find me and I'll set you onto your next task."

Maybe this might work out well anyhow, thought Jimmy. He left Darren alone in the pool room and he wandered off to attend to some other pressing matters.

Chapter 6
Visitors from Foreign Shores and #fagboxwankers

Over the course of the summer, Jimmy had noticed, as had several others in the city, a general increase in numbers of patched up members of a bike gang that hung out in town. There had been a few kicking around for years and the numbers had always been fairly stable. In the city, there had often been quite a few gangs, nothing to worry about as they all tended to keep themselves to themselves.

However, this summer had been very different. A lot of new faces coming in, doing ride outs on the weekend, flexing their muscles and the numbers were getting a lot higher.

As Jimmy sat having a coffee with Isabelle and Tatts one Monday morning in early October, his phone buzzed and he received an email. It was from Mr Lewis and marked highly confidential. He sat there and opened it as he sipped his coffee noting it had been sent to every licensee in the city centre. He read it out to Isabelle and Tatts.

Subject: Bike gangs
Dear Sir/Madame,
Apologies for the group email but this is a very serious matter, and we don't have much time. I would politely ask everyone who can to please attend a meeting at the Carlton Hotel this Tuesday at 10am. It is a matter of much importance. This is in strictest confidence.
Please RSVP by this afternoon.
Mr Lewis
Police Licensing Officer.

Jimmy let them digest it but they had as much information as he did.

"Sounds interesting. Are we going?"

"Best had I suppose."

Jimmy knew he had already replied that he would be in attendance and if Tatts wanted to tag along, then that was all well and good.

"What do you think it's about then?"

Isabelle was just checking if Jimmy knew something and wasn't letting on. He always played his cards close to his chest, so sometimes it was worth asking.

"Not sure. They've probably heard something on the grapevine and shit themselves. It's a small city and this is probably the highlight of their year."

Tuesday came and Jimmy was at the club repairing the cigarette box outside the front as Tatts arrived.

"Morning, Jimmy. Broke another one, have they?"

"Morning, buddy. Yeah, this one is proper mangled. When we've done this meeting, I'm going to set a camera up to catch the little pricks in the act."

Tatts knew he was not joking. It was about the fifth or sixth cigarette box that had been destroyed. He also knew Jimmy had reported it to the police but nothing had been done about it. The other premises nearby, including the Ferrers, were also have the same problem and environmental health were biting his ass over the cigarette butts on the floor.

"We'd better get a move on or we'll be sat at the back trying to work out what they're saying."

Jimmy nodded in agreement. He alarmed and locked the club, and then off they went. They made their way to the Carlton Hotel near the railway station. There were a lot of police in attendance as they were shown through to the conference room which was already buzzing with other licensees.

As everyone finally found themselves a seat in the conference room, the table at the front was fully stacked. Mr Lewis, Inspector Thomas, his assistant that Jimmy didn't know, Mr Scott and Edith Bowman from Licensing. It was Mr Lewis who stood up to address everyone.

"Good morning, everyone, and thank you for coming at such short notice. What is discussed in this room must go no further and I want to make myself very clear on that matter. I will now hand you over to Inspector Thomas who will fill in on all the details."

With that, Mr Lewis sat down and Inspector Thomas stood up removing his police hat as he did so.

"Good morning, everyone. I will reiterate that what I'm about to tell you must go no further, everything is in the strictest confidence."

Inspector Thomas gazed out over the room trying to convey a sense of how serious he was about the message he was about to deliver. When he was satisfied that everyone was listening and he had their full attention, he decided to continue.

"We have some intelligence…"

"Bollocks…"

Someone in the audience yelled out causing rapturous laughter throughout.

"Alright, settle down."

Inspector Thomas put his arms up in front of himself to try to bring the room back under control. *It is like dealing with children*, he thought to himself.

"This weekend, The Tornados Bike club is holding its annual AGM. Unfortunately for us, they are holding it here in Hereford, with their Hereford Chapter as hosts. This means anywhere between 200 and 1000 bikers are coming into the city from all over England and Europe."

There was hushed mumbling going on throughout the room as everyone started chatting and putting their thoughts forward for their colleagues and friends.

"The Tornados in Hereford don't do much, but their other branches are heavily involved in drugs, prostitution and arms dealing. We want to make it clear to them from the outset that they are not welcome here. Thus, you will all be receiving an email letter later on. This email will remind you of your responsibilities as licensees namely crime and the prevention of. Anyone wearing bike gang colours or cuts is banned from entering licensed premises this weekend."

The grumbling in the room was growing, the discontent from the crowd was very apparent.

"Any questions?"

As most looked around taking stock, Mad Dave, who ran The Kings Head, stood up; half the room simultaneously thought, *oh shit here we go.*

"Inspector Thomas, the bikers frequent my pub every week, they don't cause any trouble. This'll just end up costing me a fortune. What do suggest I do? They'll need to go somewhere! Unless of course, your plan is to have them wandering the streets all night."

This was a good point and quite clearly caused a conference at the head table. After about a minute, Inspector Thomas stood up again.

"Dave, that is a good and valid point. We certainly don't want them marauding all over the city. After conferring with my colleagues, we want to put it to the room that the King's Head will be the pub we send all the bikers to. Much like controlling football fans. Any objections?"

No one spoke. Realistically, no licensee had ever had to deal with serious bikers in the city. Dave was welcome to have his pub smashed up by all the bikers, thought Jimmy. Most damage they could cause would be 50pence anyway.

As the room settled down, Mr Lewis stood up again.

"I will email you all this afternoon reminding you all of your licensing commitments and what has been agreed this morning. Thank you for coming and have a great day."

He looked very pleased with himself. It was very clear to see he loved exercising power over people. It was obvious to everyone who'd ever had to deal with him that he was on a power trip and got a kick out of it.

With that, everyone started disappearing out of the hotel and back to their normal lives.

As they walked back, Tatts looked at Jimmy who was seemingly mulling something over in his head.

"What's up, boss?"

"I've just worked out we're the closest late-night venue to The Kings Head. They shut at 11pm."

"Ahh, I see. And you think…"

"I think bikers have come to party not to go to bed early."

Now as they walked along, there were two of them walking along mulling things over.

Isabelle came to the club with the children that afternoon. She arrived as Jimmy was putting up the new camera at the front.

"Do you think that'll stop them smashing up the ciggie boxes?"

"I hope it might least act as a bit of a deterrent."

Jimmy screwed the sign to the wall warning them they were on CCTV. Failing that, he'd at least get a good picture of them to go on Twitter but he wasn't about to mention that part of his plan to Isabelle, she always told him to be more careful on social media.

"How did the meeting go this morning?"

"It was ok. It was about biker gangs and how they'll be lots in on the weekend. Can your mum babysit on Saturday? It'll be all hands-on deck and I'm going to have to weld myself to the front door to make sure everything is ok."

"She already is. Didn't I mention I was going out with the girls? It's Erica's birthday. I'm just off now to get my hair done. Can you watch the kids?"

Jimmy rolled his eyes; no, she hadn't mentioned it as if she had mentioned it he would have remembered it. Sometimes he really felt that Isabelle could've been a lot more inclusive in her life and what was going on rather than just dropping bombshells. However, he was very aware he was as guilty of this as she was. Sometimes it was better just to get on with it all rather than rock the boat.

"Yeah, that's no problem at all."

With that, Isabelle strolled off into town looking as if she didn't have a care in the world.

"Right, boys, let's go and have some fun. Who fancies going to the park?"

The boys were very on this idea. He shut the club and he too left all his problems there for the afternoon. This afternoon, there were more important things afoot, like who could scream loudest on the swings!

Friday rolled around and the police seemed to be right with the information they had gathered as motorbikes poured into the city from all directions. There were some really awesome bikes and Jimmy did take some time to stroll past where quite a lot had parked up to have a look at them. He quickly spotted they had two prospects watching the bikes making sure no one messed with them. He made his way to the club and up into Rerack.

"Good evening, how is everyone?"

"Evening, Jimmy."

Jimmy entered the bar and made his way through to the kitchen.

"Evening, Jimmy, all quiet on the Western Front so far?"

Jimmy laughed. Tatts was very much of the opinion that this was all a storm in a teacup and being blown totally out of proportion.

"Do you want a coffee?"

"I'm ok, thanks, Jim. Only just finished one. Darren's doing a good job. I got him to scrub the bins out earlier before he finished. He did a great job."

"That's good news; maybe he just needs a bit of confidence."

Jimmy checked his watch, 7:45pm. He finished making his coffee and headed down to the club with his coffee in hand.

The dark night came in quickly. Soon the streetlights were all coming on and it was just them and the club's lighting illuminating the street. Ever since the council had started replacing the old streetlights with new LED ones, the quality of street lighting had dropped massively. Lee and Sebastian were with Jimmy on the front door as the first biker approached.

"Good evening, I'm looking for Jimmy Harris."

The biker had a thick German accent with impeccable English.

"I'm Jimmy, how can I help you?"

The biker explained he had been informed they weren't allowed to come into the club that evening, and he would like an explanation. Jimmy explained to him fully the situation which the police had put all licensed premises in. The biker then thanked Jimmy for his time and headed back in the direction of the King's Head.

"That's not the last we'll be hearing of that this evening. That is just the beginning."

"What are we going to do?"

"What if it gets hairy?"

Sebastian nodded. Jimmy thought for a second or two. He'd already made his mind up about it

"You lock the doors, you go inside and have a beer and I will deal with it."

Jimmy, however, knew that that was a lot easier said than done.

As 10:30pm arrived, Inspector Thomas arrived at the front door with a clipboard under his arm.

"Good evening, gentlemen. Jimmy, can I have a word please."

The inspector pointed to a spot away from the door and out of ear shot of people eavesdropping. "*We* have a problem, Jimmy."

Jimmy did not like the use of the word 'we' in that statement but he let the inspector continue.

"The bikers want to come here after the King's Head closes."

"Well, they can't; you banned them from doing so."

He didn't trust this man much at all and this was starting to feel like a stitch up. There is nothing worse than feeling like you're being boxed in and he was aware he was being boxed in really properly.

"I've arranged to meet a few of them so *we* can come to solution."

Jimmy felt annoyed yet again, there was the use of that word 'we'.

Jimmy lit a cigarette and even though he knew this was not his wisest idea, he could see he had no other option open to him. He smiled at the door staff. They knew that without his say so that the bikers were not to come in.

"Come on then, let's go."

The inspector led the way and together they walked down the road and around the back of the club. As Jimmy stood in the entrance to an unlit car park, he could see at least four maybe five silhouettes moving. He walked beside the inspector and as they got closer, Jimmy could see at least seven bikers. *You fucking idiot*, he hissed quietly under his breathe at the inspector. He reached into his jacket and put his gum shield in. This could go south in a heartbeat.

He was now standing directly in front of the bikers. His only protection was a moron inspector with a clipboard, his gumshield and his wits. *I'm screwed*, Jimmy thought to himself.

"The inspector tells us that it is up to you if you let us in?"

It was the biker that Jimmy had met earlier on the front steps of the club.

"I'm afraid that is not the case, the inspector has misled you."

"Jimmy, it *is* up to you."

Jimmy felt fury burning inside him. He was being stitched up. Jimmy reached into his jacket and produced a white piece of paper and he unfolded it.

"The inspector has obviously conveniently forgotten the email that he had sent to all the pubs and clubs this week in the city. He is now very, very *conveniently* passing the buck to myself."

He handed the piece of paper to the biker. The biker got his phone out and turned the torch on his phone on so he could read the email properly. After two seconds, he put his hand into his leather cuts pocket and produced his little reading glasses out of a little leather pouch.

Having thoroughly read the document, he looked at the inspector.

"You have not been truthful, Inspector. It clearly states here we can't go into any pub or club wearing our cuts or club colours."

The biker removed his glasses, put them back in their little case, and put them safely away. The whole time he did so, he didn't take his eyes off the inspector.

"Well, I...someone in my office may have jumped the gun or...umm misunderstood what I was intending."

"To me, Inspector, and back in Germany I am a lawyer, this is discrimination and I'm sure I needn't tell you that discrimination is frowned upon by courts in all European nations."

Jimmy was going to let the inspector stew for a bit but decided better of it; he might end up tarred with the same brush if they decided to kick the crap out of him.

"I do have a solution if you'll bear with me. I'm not a lawyer, but I believe the wording of that email does give us some leeway."

Jimmy looked up making sure he had everyone's attention. The inspector was being particularly attentive.

"I fully understand how important your cuts are to you and how club colours are not to trusted to non-members. However, if you would be prepared to put a prospect in the cloakroom, there is nothing to stop you coming in if you leave those items with the prospect in our cloakroom. That, gentlemen, is the best option I can offer."

"One moment please."

The bikers formed a huddle and spoke in German to one another, totally ignoring the inspector and Jimmy. Jimmy didn't understand a word of German but it was very clear some of the party were not happy; others were shrugging and Jimmy felt this could still go either way.

"Ok, Jimmy, whilst we are against the idea of leaving our cuts unattended, if one of our men can look after them, then we accept your proposal. This does not mean that this is last you will be hearing of this matter, Inspector."

The biker finished and held his hand out to shake Jimmy's hand to seal the deal.

"Can I keep this email?"

"Of course, I'll go and let my team know what's happening."

Jimmy turned and walked away from the car park, back into the light. His heart was beating thunderously in his chest. He took his gum shield out and lit a cigarette. He smiled to himself; he had achieved part one of his plan and outsmarted the inspector. Part two was to now earn a lot of money from the bikers. All he needed was a little bit of luck, good luck for once.

Friday night passed without a single incident and there was almost a collective sigh of relief as the last customer left and the doors were bolted.

"I think we got a bit lucky there."

Stuart was one of the older doormen and he had been around the block a few times. Looking at everyone who was sitting down, he clearly spoke for all of them. The room had a general consensus for which Stuart was speaking for.

"I couldn't agree more, but at one point, I thought I was going to die in a car park."

"Now that would've been quite funny. All the crap we get in here and you get flattened with a copper in a car park."

"Well, we do it all again tomorrow, and let's hope we are just as fortuitous tomorrow night as we were tonight."

Jimmy picked up his drink and headed to the smoking area. Tatts followed him out.

"What's up? I thought that went well all things considered. We survived and we've made a few quid and we've still got all our teeth!"

"They didn't really drink much tonight. They want to go out riding tomorrow in the day so they wanted to keep clear heads. Saturday night is party night as they have Sunday to sleep it off before they head home."

Jimmy took a drag on his cigarette contemplating what was going to happen tomorrow tonight. Stuart was right, they had got lucky. Proper lucky so far.

"Tomorrow, they will go hard at it. Tomorrow is the night they will cut loose and we will have to bring our A game from the moment we open until the moment we finish."

"Ah, I see. So what's the plan?"

"Not a clue, maybe some praying!"

Jimmy stubbed his cigarette out, finished his drink, and they headed back inside.

As Saturday evening began, Jimmy wondered how a group of bikers would take to the Dirty Disco. As it turned out he needn't have worried. Jimmy stood by the dancefloor. Partly because he could see the front door, the dancefloor, and the bar just by moving slightly but also to make sure the DJ was ok. As *Stayin' Alive* came on, Jimmy watched as 50 bikers all did their own impersonations of John Travolta. There was a slight surreal feel to the whole evening, and he was just starting to relax when Stuart sidled up to him.

"Jimmy, can you come sort Kimbo Slice out please?"

"Ehh? Who?"

"You'll soon understand."

Stuart pointed Jimmy towards the smoking area. As Jimmy entered the smoking area, he knew exactly who Stuart was talking about and why. Stood on the far side of the smoking area, chatting with some fellow bikers, was a man who stood over seven feet tall, easy 25 stone, and it was all muscle. Jimmy had spotted him earlier on the dance floor. Unfortunately, he was wearing a Tornado bikers vest.

Jimmy swallowed and walked over to the man mountain. He would rather lose face than not stand up to the man mountain, he had to cover up or remove the top. Gingerly, he tapped him on the shoulder, the man spun round. He looked down on Jimmy from his imperious height.

"Good evening, I'm Jimmy, the owner. Can I have a quick word please?"

As confident as Jimmy sounded, and was trying to look, he still felt like a little boy popping over to a neighbour to ask for his football back.

"Of course, you can. What have I done?"

"I'm afraid you can't wear biker colours or clothes in here, that's the rules."

The biker immediately looked mortified. He took his t-shirt off and put his jumper back on.

"I'm very sorry. My mistake. Please don't kick me out. I got hot dancing and I totally forgot."

"Not a problem. Are you having a good evening?"

"Yes, it's very good. Needs more ABBA though."

Jimmy shook the man's hand and left him to continue his conversation without further interruptions. Quite how the biker thought Jimmy was going to throw him out made Jimmy laugh inside. Jimmy took himself back to the dancefloor and continued enjoying the rest of the very bizarre evening.

Jimmy felt very smug with himself as he mopped the club that Sunday morning. He'd out foxed the police; he made a shed load of cash off the bikers, and the whole weekend had passed without a single incident. He'd tried phoning Isabelle several times that morning, but her phone was off. He hoped she was ok, but this was becoming a regular occurrence now. He knew she'd surface before mid-afternoon, but he did feel a simple text wasn't too much to ask.

As he emptied the mop bucket in the street, Jimmy noticed the cigarette box was demolished for the umpteenth time. *I'll have the little bastards this time,* he thought, hoping that the cameras had caught a good image and that the vandals hadn't bothered to cover their faces. He finished cleaning and then started reviewing the CCTV. Soon enough, he had the little shits. A really good picture of them busting it open and pouring the contents into their coat pockets.

He took a picture on his phone and with a few hashtags like #fagboxwanker #vandal, etc., he posted the tweet. He'd given up letting the police know. They didn't care and they didn't have the manpower. It was more about creating a paper trail so that environmental health, who kept moaning about the fags on the floor, could see he was doing something to try and rectify the problem.

Isabelle had not emerged from whatever pit she was in so Jimmy had to ask her mum if she could possibly stay Sunday night whilst he ran Rerack; very graciously she agreed she would. He was getting a bit annoyed as he was having to ask so many favours of the boys' grandparents. He was very grateful for their help though. He wished Isabelle could act like an adult but as time went on, it was getting harder and harder. Her attitudes and priorities lay elsewhere.

He didn't blame her though, she'd put up with him not being home a lot. She had tolerated a lot and Jimmy did understand that she felt neglected. He did feel the flip side was she enjoyed a lifestyle that was the envy of many. He could see both sides of the argument.

At 6am the next morning, the doorbell went, and it was promptly followed by a lot of shouting and arguing. Jimmy lay in bed for a few seconds and then realised that the commotion was coming from within his own home. He hauled himself out of bed, grabbed his dressing gown, and ran down the two floors to the ground floor where he found Isabelle's mother arguing with a bailiff.

"Get out of my house!"

Jimmy yelled as he jumped the final few steps. The bailiff had his foot wedged in the door which Isabelle's mother was trying to shut. Without even thinking, Jimmy throw himself at the bailiff and soon they were rolling round on the path outside. The struggle continued for quite some time but Jimmy managed to get the upper hand and soon the bailiff said enough. Jimmy was very aware of the lights coming on in the street and the curtains twitching.

"Here."

The bailiff was gasping for breath as he handed Jimmy a letter. Jimmy quickly scan read it.

"This isn't me, that's not my name."

Jimmy released his hold on the bailiff. They both sat there on the path. The bailiff looked a lot better than Jimmy did as he readjusted his boxers and tied up his dressing gown. As Jimmy digested the letters contents, it transpired that the owner of the house had gone bankrupt and completely forgot to tell anyone that he rented the house out.

The poor bailiff was there to repossess the house and was under the assumption that the owner was living there. Jimmy couldn't believe the owner hadn't told anyone he'd been renting it out for the past few years.

The bailiff made a phone call to his head office and advised Jimmy that his bosses had said he had a week to vacate and then he would be back and would have to take possession of the house. Jimmy felt he'd done that mainly as a courtesy as there were two young children living at the property. He was grateful either way.

By 9am, Jimmy was standing at the letting agent's door. He was still absolutely fuming at what had happened that morning. The letting agents were absolutely aghast at what had happened. They showed Jimmy all the available properties they currently had which could be moved into immediately and within the hour. After multiple apologies, he was viewing a house on Walnut Avenue. And by teatime, the let was agreed.

That evening, as Jimmy sat at his kitchen bar, the front door went. Isabelle had finally reappeared.

"Good evening, I gave up on sending search parties out for you. Care to explain where you have been?"

"Don't start. I'm not in the mood. I'm going for a shower."

Isabelle looked like hell and smelt like a brewery. A shower was probably a good thing all round as she was still wearing the same clothes she had gone out in on Saturday night.

Jimmy sat there for over 45 minutes awaiting her return. Eventually, she graced him with her presence.

"Have a seat."

He poured her a cup of coffee. She sat stirring it for what seemed an eternity. Maybe she was trying to work out if she could keep it down if she drank it. Eventually, Jimmy could stay silent no more. "This isn't much fun anymore."

A deafening silence descended as Isabelle continued to stir her coffee. Jimmy just sat there impassively looking at her. Searching for a response of any kind, even just an acknowledgement he existed.

"We have an opportunity to start again. It's up to you. Either way, we have to move out of here."

Still Isabelle didn't say a word, although she had now taken a sip of coffee. Jimmy got up and poured himself a vodka and red bull. He took the time to look at her and try and ascertain what was going on.

"Why do we have to move?"

"Our landlord's gone bust. This house has been reprocessed. I have mega apologies to make over this morning to both your mother and a bailiff."

"You? Are you ok?"

"I'm fine. I'm always ok. Gave as good as I got, just bloody embarrassed about it all. We, however, are not fine. You know it, I know it, Christ even our parents know it!"

Finally, one of them had said it. Isabelle took another sip of her coffee. Jimmy finished his drink and fixed himself another one. Jimmy stood with both hands on the kitchen side staring out of the window. The rain coming down somehow made everything seem even bleaker than it really was.

"I know it's not been easy. I know I've been working a lot and I've not been home as much as I wanted, or what you needed me to be. It's getting better though. You've got to work with me."

"Everything that's going on though."

"Let's draw a line under it. We have two children to think of. I've found us a new home. No ghosts of the past. We can move on as a unit."

"I don't know. That's a lot of water under the bridge now and I haven't even seen this new house!"

"I tried calling you repeatedly and I had to sort something immediately or we'd all be homeless. It's not like I had a choice."

"I'll sleep on it and let you know tomorrow."

Jimmy smiled to himself as Isabelle left the kitchen. He couldn't help but feel he'd be better off just walking away before the toxicity got too much. He had to try though for the boys. A new home, new surroundings, no neighbours that had seen his bare ass brawling with a bailiff. Jimmy noticed Isabelle had left three quarters of her coffee. It was probably for the best she went and slept it off.

Morning came. Jimmy made himself a coffee after feeding the boys breakfast. He sat on the patio and enjoyed a cigarette as the boys watched *In The Night Garden*. Jimmy couldn't help but think whoever wrote that was off their head on mushrooms. It made no sense to him but the boys adored it. The storm that night had cleared the morning air and it had a beautiful freshness to it.

Jimmy sat on the patio enjoying the freshness of it all. Isabelle emerged and came out to join him.

"Good morning. Did you sleep ok?"

"I slept a bit. I spent a lot of last night thinking about what you said. Do you really mean a fresh start after everything?"

"Yes, I do."

"Draw a line under everything and start again? No bringing up the past and throwing it in one another's faces at the first opportunity."

"Yes, we can move on if we want to."

"Ok, let's give it one last go. Let's do it."

Isabelle came round the patio table and they hugged for a long time. Just holding one another. The only sound was that of the boys playing in the background. The thing that united them above all else. Still Jimmy couldn't shake the feeling that they were papering over the cracks. However, what were the other options? Giving up simply wasn't in his nature.

Plus, Walnut Lane was very spacious and was four-bedroomed so they each could have their own room. It provided options beyond those their current accommodation did.

Chapter 7
Trick or Tweet

Everything was thrown in boxes and hastily labelled. Jimmy was amazed how much they had accumulated since they had started living there. He remembered back to when they moved in and all they had was a sofa, a bed, a microwave, a kettle and a few odd tit bits. The clothes had all lived on the floor for months until they sorted out dressers and a few wardrobes. They had even been taking their washing to their parents for the first few months until a reasonably priced washing machine had been found.

Moving house is never fun but luckily, Jimmy had a whole retinue of staff to call upon for help. They were only moving just over a mile away but each journey seemed to take forever. Load the van as carefully as possible and then drive off only to hear stuff clattering around in the back.

Their new home was a mish mash of boxes stacked all over the ground floor. Jimmy did, however, take a toilet roll on the first trip. he had forgotten one when they'd moved into Moat Street and he wasn't going to make that mistake ever again.

It took over a month to finally get settled in and work out where everything was going to live. Even then, Jimmy still spent quite a while every morning trying to find clothes to wear.

Jimmy and Isabelle were trying hard to work through their difficulties. They set aside time every morning to talk. To find out how each of them was and what they had planned that day. Isabelle was even attending a therapist for Post Natal depression. Jimmy hoped against hope this was going to work out well.

It did feel like this was their final chance to make it work or they would simply end up making each other miserable forever. As it turned out, Isabelle only attended one session before never returning.

Their new home was set slightly out of the city on a hill overlooking a flood plain. It had extra space, a double garage, and a much larger garden for the children to play in. Jimmy immediately set about trying to find a giant climbing frame on eBay for the children to play on. This time, he also made sure of where it was before he purchased it.

His attention had also turned to the garden and how to maintain it. He was looking forward to buying his first lawn mower, it somehow seemed like a very adult thing to do. Isabelle had already vetoed several ride on mowers that he had seen on eBay. The garden was quite big but not that big.

As December began, the club nights were going well with the people coming in spending plenty per head. The weeks weren't too bad either with lots of Christmas parties popping in for one more drink before calling it a night and the pool hall was ticking over nicely.

Jimmy and Isabelle were at least communicating and Jimmy felt things were improving greatly. His mood had lightened and he had a genuine optimism about how life was going and where it was heading.

Jimmy stood taking stock on the front door looking forward to another Friday night. Fridays were never quite as busy as Saturdays, so the pressure wasn't nearly as great. Jimmy was able to enjoy Fridays. However, West Mercia police had other ideas to interrupt his new found sense of peace.

He stood watching up the street as two PCSOs made their way towards his front door. It wasn't unusual to see the police as they often went around the pubs and clubs to check numbers and get a sense of how the night was unfolding. Do walk throughs and check everything was in order. The only issue they ever encountered was a drunk Andy occasionally playing The clash I Fought The Law if he clocked them early enough.

This time though, Jimmy could sense something was wrong. He could tell by the way that they walked, they were uncomfortable. They visibly slowed down as they approached the door.

"Jimmy Harris?"

"For all my sins, yes I am."

"We need to talk to you about abusive online communication."

"Pray tell, I'm all ears."

"We have a letter here from a young man you have abused online, he's dreadfully upset. If you don't delete or remove your tweet, we'll be forced to arrest you for malicious communication."

"Are you actually being serious?"

Jimmy was absolutely stunned by this turn of events. After the amount of grief he had received from Environmental Health and the number of times he had reported the vandalism to the police, he couldn't quite believe what he was hearing.

"Yes, this is going to be treated as a Hate Crime."

"Interesting. Very interesting. You're on my doorstep defending a vandal who has been causing mayhem to myself and other businesses. So you're now in the business of defending criminals?"

"Mr Harris, it is you who have abused him."

"That letter you have. Does it have his name and address on it?"

"Yes, Mr Harris, it does."

"And I assume you have the crime reference numbers for when I reported the criminal damage to you multiple times?"

"Not to hand but I'm sure they're on the system somewhere."

"So just to clarify, you have in your hand a confession to an outstanding crime and yet you choose to stand there and threaten to arrest me?"

"Mr Harris, I don't think that you are grasping the situation very well. This man has had his picture printed out from your tweet and put all around his local village. You've made his life hell."

The PCSO was trying as hard as he could to get his point across and he had not expected this response or level of resistance. They had been warned back at the station before they set out that Jimmy was not afraid to take on the authorities and he was pretty sharp, but this was way more than they had anticipated. It should've been a simple apology and a deleting of the tweet.

"Good, I hope everyone he knows can see him for scabby little vandal he is. Tell him I'll do him a deal. He pays for the new fag box then I will take the tweet down."

"Mr Harris, we're not here to do deals with you. We're here to tell you to take the tweet down or there will be repercussions."

By now several people in the queue were heckling the PCSOs. This simple assignment was fast becoming a nightmare for the PCSOs.

"I told you my offer and you know as well as I do PCSOs cannot arrest anybody. You have the same rights of arrest as every citizen in this country does. Now if there's nothing else, I have work to do and I assume you'll be off to try and bully other people for standing up for themselves when you haven't done your jobs properly."

Jimmy turned and started walking away from them back inside the club.

"I haven't finished talking to you."

Jimmy walked inside. The two PCSOs stood there for over ten seconds after he had left. A few people in the queue laughed at their predicament. Inside Jimmy sat himself down and thought that he probably hadn't heard the last of it. He thought to himself that perhaps he shouldn't have walked away but it was too late to change it now. Why could he always think of so many better responses after the event?

Jimmy was in his office the following Monday morning. He was pleasantly surprised he hadn't heard any more about the tweet. He was damn sure he wasn't going to take it down and if they pushed it he was going to the press. As he lounged back reading a paper and enjoying his coffee, there was a knock at the door.

"Come in."

Darren popped his head round the door looking sheepish even for him.

"Err, Jimmy, how much is the green stuff?"

"What green stuff, Darren?"

Jimmy folded his newspaper up and sat upright.

"The big green stuff."

"*What* green stuff? Oh sod it, just show me."

Jimmy stood up and threw the paper on the sofa. Darren could drive him to distraction most days but Jimmy was not in the mood that morning for silly games. Darren led him through Rerack and into the large pool room at the back.

Jimmy didn't have the words. In the corner of his lovely snooker table, burnt into the once green baize, was the perfect shape of an iron.

"How the hell did you manage that?"

"I thought I'd help you by ironing the table. I needed the toilet and put the iron down and…well…it umm as you can see…it's sort of burnt a hole."

Darren could see just how angry Jimmy was and he guessed it wasn't cheap or easily repairable.

"Go away."

Jimmy stood staring at his ruined snooker cloth. Darren continued to loiter a few yards away also looking at the ridiculous hole in the table. Jimmy looked straight at Darren.

"Just go away."

Darren didn't need telling twice. He slunk off very quickly and far away from the visibly enraged Jimmy. As Darren walked down the stairs, he passed Tatts. Tatts did a double take as he had never seen Darren move so fast.

"Everything ok, Darren?"

Darren kept going and just shook his head. Tatts made his way through the pool hall and found Jimmy holding an iron and just staring at the snooker table. Tatts looked at the table and couldn't help himself. He just started laughing. He didn't mean to but he couldn't stop himself, it looked ridiculous.

"Don't."

"Did Darren do that?"

Tatts was still trying very hard to laugh. He looked at Jimmy.

"Oh come on, it does look funny."

He got absolutely no response from Jimmy who was staring at the table with a mixture of pure puzzlement and fury. Tatts decided to leave it be before Jimmy launched the iron in his direction, so he left Jimmy to his own devices by the table. He figured he would come round soon enough.

It was over 15 minutes later that Jimmy appeared in the kitchen. He had an absolute look of defeat on his face by now. He placed the iron on the side. By the look of it, the cloth was burnt to the heavy iron, that would also be expensive to replace.

"Sorry I snapped. I just couldn't believe what he'd done. I will admit that it does look slightly funny."

"No worries. Sorry I laughed."

"I best give Gavin a ring at the Snooker Lab and organise getting it reclothed. It was only Saturday the moron was glass collecting in the club and somehow he lost the brush for the dust pan and brush. He lives on a different planet to the rest of us."

"I don't think anyone will notice."

Jimmy face was now just fury, he looked like he was chewing on a wasp. Tatts was finding it harder by the minute not to laugh out loud. He knew it wasn't good but it just looked so stupid.

"Too soon?"

"Too soon."

Jimmy disappeared into his office. *Probably for the best*, thought Tatts, *let him regroup and come out firing on all cylinders. Hopefully, he would see the funny side in time.*

It turned out that this was just the start of one of those weeks that it was best to forget. On Wednesday morning, as Jimmy descended the stairs at his new home, when he got to the bottom step, he noticed a slight purple colour encroaching into the cream-coloured carpet by the kitchen door. Hesitantly, Jimmy had pushed opened the kitchen door to see his eldest son stood on the kitchen windowsill, which was also a seat, clutching an empty two litre bottle of Ribena.

"Floor is lava, Dadda."

"For crying out loud."

Jimmy rubbed his face to check he wasn't having a bad dream. It was not a dream, it was very real and very sticky. It might have only taken him an hour to clean up initially, but Jimmy was sure several months later that parts of the kitchen floor were still slightly sticky!

Christmas always brings out the odd crazy person and this Christmas was to prove to be no exception. Just after they finished on the Saturday night before Christmas, the door hammered. As was the protocol, two doormen went to see what all the commotion was about. Sebastian opened the door and in front them was a man in a suit.

He was pretty intoxicated and unsteady on his feet. Neither he nor Lee recognised him as being a customer at the club that evening.

"Can I help you, Sir?"

"Yes, I want my coat please."

The man was slurring his words badly. He fumbled around in his trouser pockets looking for his ticket. Both door staff were worried he was about to faceplant the floor as his balance was all over the shop. Eventually, after some rummaging in all his pockets, he handed Lee a cloakroom ticket.

Lee examined the ticket and handed it back to the man.

"We don't have your coat here, Sir. Are you sure you were in here this evening?"

"Of course, I was here. Are you an idiot?"

What the man was lacking in sobriety, he more than made up for in profane language.

As the situation escalated, Jimmy made his way to the door. He could see Sebastian pushing a man back out of the door who was clearly trying to gain entry.

"What's up, guys?"

Jimmy approached the door to see if he could help resolve the situation and assist his colleagues.

"This guy wasn't in tonight and yet somehow he believes we have his coat."

By now, Sebastian especially was finding the situation quite amusing for the farce that it had now descended into. The man, however, was not. His temper was rising and his mannerisms were becoming much more unpredictable. He was swearing at everyone indiscriminately and Jimmy decided he'd seen enough.

"Shut the doors, guys, we can't help everyone. Don't forget to wish him a Merry Christmas!"

Jimmy walked away having made his instructions clear. The door staff did as they were told and bolted the man outside in the cold. For a couple of minutes, the door was knocked a few times and then it stopped. Everyone just thought the man had given up and gone home. Drunks like that normally run out of gas and get themselves home.

20 minutes later, the door was hammered again. This time with much more force. Jimmy was the only one left apart from Isabelle who was tidying the bar up. Jimmy approached the door and upon opening it, he was surprisingly greeted by several police officers.

"Evening, Jimmy."

"That's him, that's the wanker that's stolen my coat."

The drunk from earlier was pointing at Jimmy whilst knocking into the officer he was standing next to.

"Get him then. He's stolen my coat."

"Is he still banging on?"

"Jimmy, we haven't got time for this. It's proper silly season in town. If you give him his coat, we can carry on and you can go home."

"We haven't got his coat; we've never had it. I've explained that to him"

With that, the man lunged at Jimmy before he was restrained by several officers and wrestled onto the floor.

"Jimmy, he says he has a ticket. Have you lost his coat?"

"Ask him for the ticket."

"What?"

"Just ask him for the ticket."

The officer turned to his colleagues and asked for the ticket. The officers were all frazzled from the night's entertainment in the city and they had way better things to be doing than deal with this. They stood the drunk up and he produced the ticket. The officer returned to Jimmy clutching it like it was a prized trophy.

"Ticket number 67, Jim."

"Look at the ticket. It's for Diamonds not us."

The officer examined the ticket.

"Oh, for crying out loud, I fucking hate Christmas."

"The door staff tried telling him and I have tried telling him for over 20 minutes. He's just an idiot who won't listen. He's got tunnel vision, got his drunk blinkers on."

The officer returned to the drunk and told him the same thing. Even taking the time to point out his ticket had Diamonds written on it and that he was now stood at Jumping Jacks as proven by the eight by four name above the front doors.

"Pigs! You're all in it together, get me my fucking coat!"

The drunk started yelling more profanities as he started pushing officers away from himself. It took possibly ten seconds from that point for him to get himself arrested. Jimmy stood by the front door enjoying a cigarette watching the drunk trying to fight the four officers. He was soon handcuffed and thrown in the back of van. The doors slammed shut and the officer made his way to the driver's seat.

"Goodnight, Jimmy. Merry Christmas."

"Merry Christmas all."

Jimmy put his cigarette out, watched the police van disappear into the night, and he walked back into the club.

As the New Year began in earnest, Jimmy turned his attention to keeping customer numbers up during the doldrum months. After spending too much time googling ideas and watching too many cats do the funniest thing videos, he eventually found an idea he liked and that was workable. He certainly had never seen anything like it before.

When the team arrived on Friday evening, they were quite taken aback to find the dancefloor had about 200 balloons attached to ribbon, all attached to glow wristbands. The balloons were emblazoned with the usual 'Free Entry to Jumping Jacks with this balloon'.

"What do you reckon, guys?"

Jimmy was obviously excited to see how everyone reacted to his creations. Hannah came and took one off him, pulling the string down to get a closer look at the writing on the balloon.

"Everyone loves balloons."

Jimmy could not see a downside to this plan. The advertising from people carrying these balloons around the city would be epic. Jimmy followed the flyer team out into the city. He smiled as he watched them walk off down the road with a canopy of balloons above their heads. He headed to the Anchor for a pint. It was a lovely crisp January evening, cold but dry. It was perfect for his balloons.

Once he had arrived at the Anchor and sorted himself and TJ out a pint, he kept quiet to his friend about his latest advertising idea. He found a good table outside from where he could watch all the goings on. He was hoping to be able to gauge people's reactions to the balloons and also see what TJ thought. He was pleasantly surprised he didn't have to wait too long for the reaction as the first couple of people wandered in off the street with the balloons attached to them that they'd got from the flyer team in the city.

TJ looked at the balloons and then back at Jimmy.

"Bloody hell, Jimmy."

TJ raced down the yard and into the pub after the first few balloon carriers. However, it was too late. TJ trudged back to where Jimmy was sitting, his face was not a jovial one.

"Your balloons are now well and truly wrapped around our ceiling fans."

Jimmy just burst out laughing imagining in his mind the customer still attached to the balloons swinging around in the pub.

"I hadn't even thought about that."

"How many of those monstrosities have you sent out tonight?"

"Just over 200."

He took a swig of his drink and started to think about the damage they could do around the city. It was too late to stop it. Within the hour, he'd turned his phone off to stop the texts and the phone calls from enraged landlords about the city. This was starting to become a headache. He still thought it was quite funny.

On Monday morning, he was sitting in his office with Mr Scott and Mr Gough, the head of Environmental Health. They read him the riot act over the chaos the balloons had caused. Jimmy listened intently and apologised profusely. Inside though, he still thought it was quite funny but realised it probably wasn't his best idea.

The conclusion of the meeting was that Jimmy could never again go out flyering using helium balloons as the bait. Jimmy agreed and now he just had to work out what to do with the other 800 balloons he had left.

Mr Gough had let him know his balloons managed to snarl up fans in at least four pubs other than the Anchor and somehow one had popped and ended up melting to the counter in a fish and chip restaurant. Jimmy didn't tell them he'd seen social media videos of Tony Graham attempting to burst several in the queue to Klimax which seemed to result in a brawl breaking out in the street. Still the profile of the club was raised even further which wasn't a bad thing.

As he walked Mr Scott and Mr Gough out of his office and to the front doors, they crossed over the dance floor. Jimmy saw Mr Gough smiled as he looked up and saw Jimmy's ceiling had over 50 balloons bobbing about above their heads.

"Yes, Mr Gough, even I didn't escape the fun my balloons caused."

Jimmy saw them out and went to get his long ladder to fix his own balloon problem.

Chapter 8
I Could've Been a Contender

Through certain lines of business, Jimmy had come into contact with a lot of different people from many varying sources. Come the Autumn of 2013, Jimmy found himself in procession of ten tickets to go and see George Groves vs Carl Froch at the Manchester Arena. Jimmy had only ever attended hometown bouts and charity events. He'd never been to a major boxing match. He was quite excited to see this spectacle first hand. Rounding up a few friends and some staff on that mild November day off, they all headed off to Manchester.

They arrived at their hotel mid-afternoon and discovered that up north, the temperature was decidedly a lot colder and included wind that seem to come from all directions at once. It was bloody freezing.

Jimmy booked everyone into the hotel and handed out the room cards. He was amazed as he looked at some of the luggage his entourage had with them. Some, like himself, had an overnight bag, others seemed to have enough luggage with them for a week on the Costa del Sol.

"Right, everyone, we'll meet in the hotel bar in 30 minutes."

Jimmy informed his entourage making sure they understood that stragglers would be left behind to fend for themselves. Everyone trouped off to their rooms to get ready. The traffic had been pretty heavy and six of them in Jimmy's Land rover had been a bit of a squeeze, but at least they'd made it in one piece and the old girl hadn't exploded on the motorway, although at 75 mph, it did feel a bit like a lunar landing.

Jimmy freshened up and got changed. He had brought with him his quite expensive three-piece suit and woollen overcoat. He was very pleased he'd brought the overcoat with him having felt the Manchester cold. It seemed to chill him straight to bone earlier and he'd only gone across the car park. He knew

Isabelle would take a little longer than he did to get ready so left her to give her some space and get out of her hair.

"I'll meet you in the bar."

Isabelle was in the en suite bathroom. He heard a muffled reply and made the assumption that she had understood, or at least hoped she would figure it out. He certainly wasn't waiting around for her to blow dry her hair and apply her make up. This was his night off. His first Saturday off in years and he was going to enjoy every moment of it.

Making his way into the bar, he saw TJ was already sat there waiting. He too was suited and booted and at least together they looked the part, even if they didn't have much of a clue about boxing on the whole.

"Evening, you've scrubbed up alright."

TJ pointed at a beer he'd already got for Jimmy sat waiting for him on the table. Over the next 20 minutes, everyone came down to join them. It looked like a right rabble to be honest. Some in jeans and jumpers, some looked very smart in their suits and dresses. Lee had obviously missed the memo and was wearing what could only be described as a knock off white John Travolta suit from Saturday Night Fever, complete with red frilly shirt.

They had a few hours to kill before the bouts actually started and so took leave from the hotel and headed to a few bars on their way to the arena. The Manchester night life was buzzing. Fans attending the bout, some taking up residence in bars showing the Pay Per View event if they didn't have tickets, Hen dos, stag dos and ticket touts buying and selling tickets. Jimmy was finding the sheer vastness of Manchester both exhilarating and hard to comprehend. He couldn't help but see ideas and opportunities everywhere that he looked.

"You're not working tonight."

TJ had spotted Jimmy making some notes on his phone. He just wanted his friend to relax and enjoy a night off for once in his life. *He's got to have an off switch surely*, TJ thought to himself. However, after knowing him for 15 years, he hadn't found it yet. He wasn't even sure Jimmy knew how to switch off.

"I'm always working, you are too."

"I'm not. I'm enjoying a beer and having a night off."

Jimmy put his phone down on the table in front of them and looked straight at TJ over his glasses.

"So you're telling me, in all honesty, that you haven't already made a mental note of all the exits from this building and where the door staff are positioned."

TJ smiled at Jimmy.

"Well, maybe just a little bit. Come on, enjoy your beer. Have a night off for once in your life."

Jimmy now smiled, it had sounded more like an order than a request. He took a sip of his beer and joined in the conversation with everyone else. It was a little rude to be working he guessed.

By 8:30pm, they had arrived at the arena via four or five very hospitable pubs. Everyone was in a great mood as they waited in line to get inside. Thousands of people all queuing up to go through security. It was like a military operation. As they filtered forward, Jimmy got himself positioned at the back of the group to make sure no one got left behind. They started filing through and as Jimmy approached the desk he had been pointed to, Lee was in the adjacent queue.

"Search him properly."

Jimmy nodded at the security guard patting Lee down.

"Behave, boss."

This caused both the security guards patting Lee and Jimmy down to stop and confer with one another briefly at the back of the search station they had been assigned to.

"Why did you call him boss?"

The one patting Lee down had stopped the pat down and was now standing straight in front of him looking him up and down, all six feet ten of Lee looming large.

"He is my boss."

"And what do you do?"

"I'm his security, he runs a nightclub."

Lee innocently, and honestly, had answered the security guards interrogation questions which was quite possibly the worst thing he could have done.

"So, you've brought security to boxing event?"

The guard in front of Jimmy was now eyeing him up for both size and distance. Jimmy initially shot Lee a scowl but then he sighed. He had been on enough security courses himself to know the protocol and he knew this was only going to end one way. True to form, within 2 minutes both Jimmy and Lee were being strip searched as the eager guards looked for weapons and drugs.

It was a cold night to be stood in just your boxer shorts as hundreds of people filed past, heckling and wolf whistling. With the search complete, and nothing unsavoury found, they were permitted entry without so much as an apology.

They made their way up the long flight of stairs to the entrance of the arena, rearranging their clothing as they went. Jimmy couldn't help but see the funny side as they walked, especially as Lee was struggling to redo his buttons on his frilly shirt. At the top, they quickly spotted the rest of the group and made their way to join them.

"It was good they've waited for us."

"They've waited Lee as I have the tickets."

They strode towards the rest of their entourage.

"Where were you?"

"Isabelle, thanks to that idiot we were being strip searched."

Jimmy pointed at Lee as he adjusted his waistcoat so it was comfortable once more.

"How come?"

"Because numb nuts over there doesn't know when to bite his tongue."

Lee, who was still trying to do his frilly shirt up, just smiled. They headed through the giant entrance and TJ held the door open for him and Isabelle.

"What kept you?"

"I'll explain later."

They filed through the turnstiles and Jimmy handed over the tickets. Finally they were in. The foyer was a complete hubbub with people trying to get drinks or food or find the correct entrance to get to their seats. TJ and Jimmy queued for beer whilst everyone else went to secure their seats. Years of bar work definitely helped as they navigated their way through the melee carrying five pints each.

They all sat there taking in the atmosphere. The sheer size of the arena was breath-taking. Over 20,000 people sat around all just waiting to see two men fight. The lights swirled and flickered around and the volume of noise was deafening. The cheers as the new boxers made their way to ring caused a complete cacophony and Jimmy could barely hear himself think.

Sat in the first tier, the view they had was amazing. They could perfectly see the ring and all the celebrities sat in the ring side seats. They could even see the TV companies conducting their ring side interviews. Jimmy watched his group pointing stars and celebrities out to one another. It was nice to get away from the club, but Jimmy couldn't help but wonder how the club was doing. It was his first Saturday not being in the club in over 3 years. It was an odd feeling.

He was also receiving several text messages from the guys working which were not designed to put his mind at rest.

'Club is on fire.'

'Jimmy, I'm writing an incident report, is 20 people fighting a melee or a riot?'

'The lager is coming out at 85 degrees, should we put ice in it?'

Jimmy decided to avoid looking at his phone again until tomorrow morning.

"You look lost in thought."

Jimmy heard TJ but could see no point in attempting a conversation where the only way to be heard was shouting. He feigned it was too loud to hear but truthfully, he was trying to work out if he wanted to continue running clubs. He liked the money but the idea of Friday and Saturday nights off to do his own things had entered his mind a little while ago. He passed it off as the grass always being greener but still it nagged away at him. It was getting a little louder every week.

The main event was exciting with Carl Froch winning by knockout having been put on the canvas in the first round. As soon as it ended, 20,000 people made their way out of the arena and into the Manchester nightlife. The time to exit the building was seconds compared to the 20 minutes it took to get in.

After initially finding every venue they went to full, they found a dive nightclub that was still letting customers in. It was down a flight of stairs and dingy. It was both horrendous and brilliant all at the same point. The place itself might have been grubby and dark but what it had was atmosphere. The vibe was contagious.

"You're not supposed to be working."

Isabelle sat down by Jimmy on a sofa which he had taken up residence on and handed him a drink. However, the ideas Jimmy was busy setting to memory were all coming back to his club.

"Just doing a little bit of market research."

Jimmy gave Isabelle a look with the wry smile of a little boy who had been caught with his hand in the cookie jar. Isabelle knew he was taking in every nuance of the building and that this was making his mind really tick over. It had many similarities to the club but it just had an extra dimension that even she could see and feel. Jimmy sat there furiously making notes on his phone. Taking pictures of the surrounding and generally absorbing it all at the detriment of ignoring everyone else. They all knew what he was like though so it wasn't unexpected.

As the night went on, everyone was soon to be found on the dancefloor. It had been a long time since Jimmy and Isabelle had danced together. Neither of them could dance but what they lacked in ability they made up for with effort. Jimmy almost didn't want the night to end as they all clambered into a taxi to head back to the hotel.

The next week in Jumping Jacks, he set about bringing those ideas home with him. He set up TVs around the bar area so he could play funny videos interspersed with the odd advert for the club. He fished some old spirit bottles out of the waste, washed them, and put fairy lights in them. He ordered a new sign for the front of the building.

An eight feet by four feet sheet of checker plate with Jumping Jacks cut out of it and back lit. It had been over 3 years since the club had opened and it felt right to refitting the club for the next three.

Jimmy took a great deal of pride in the fact that many in the city thought they wouldn't last more than six months. Yet here he was, over 3 years down the line, refurbing the club for the next three. Not only that but they'd added a pool hall and that too was thriving. He just hoped this Christmas would be a little less stressful than the previous one. Soon he was day dreaming of a whole Christmas that was fight free and everyone drinking sensibly.

Jimmy was looking forward to the weekend. He'd shut the club all week whilst he refurbed it and he couldn't wait to see everyone's reaction to it. He was sat in his kitchen having a coffee and reading a book before work as he was just trying to pass the time. He been dressed and ready for several hours. It was the first Friday in December so the first proper day of silly season. As he sat there, his phone rang and it was Emma, Tatts' girlfriend.

"Jimmy!"

Emma screamed down the phone. She was hysterical.

"Jimmy!"

"Emma, just calm down and breathe, breathe through your nose. What's going on?"

There was a lot of sobbing and wailing and eventually, Jimmy could hear her start to regain her composure of sorts. *What the hell was going on*, he thought to himself.

"It's…it's Tatts. He's been in an accident; he was cycling along and….and…he's gone."

"Emma, what do you mean he's gone?"

"Tatts is dead, Jimmy. My beautiful John is dead."

Jimmy felt sick, he couldn't speak, the phone call was now just silence. He waited in vain hope that there was a punchline coming but nothing came. He knew it would never come. A wave crashed over him in that moment. He could feel the pressure in his eyes build and soon the tears were flowing freely down his cheeks.

"Jimmy? Are you still there?"

"Yes, yes, I'm still here, Emma. Are you ok? Where did it happen?"

"I'm alright, Jim, could you let the guys know? I can't face calling anyone."

"Of course, Emma. You need anything you call me. I'll call you later."

Emma hung up and the phone went dead. Jimmy just sat in his kitchen. His mind swirling, going 100 mph. He leant back on his stool and stared off into space. He held his head in his hands. No matter how he was he couldn't get comfortable.

"You ok?"

Isabelle entered the kitchen and could see Jimmy was in a state of great distress. He wasn't one for crying but he clearly had been. His face was all puffy and red. Her question snapped Jimmy out of his trance that he was in. It might've been for ten seconds, or it could've been an hour he didn't know.

"*Jim?*"

"It's Tatts, Isabelle. He's gone."

He turned and looked at her. He'd never needed a hug so much in his life as he did in that moment.

"Where? Who's poached him?"

"No, no. You don't understand. He's dead."

The tears started streaming down his face again as he sat there sobbing. Silence descended and all Jimmy could hear was the sound of himself breathing and the gentle hum of dishwasher nearing the end of its cycle. Isabelle put her arms round him and held him tight.

"How?"

"He's been knocked off his bike and, well that's all I know. Emma just phoned me."

Jimmy adjusted himself so he could wipe his eyes and cheeks on his sleeve, he pulled himself free of her embrace.

"I've got to go and get ready for work."

Jimmy got up and left the kitchen. He just wanted to be on his own.

That evening was one of the most uncomfortable nights Jimmy had ever faced at work. He was trying to keep everyone together and get their jobs done whilst he also tried to hold himself together and get his jobs done. By midnight, he worked out he had the attention span of your average nat.

"There you are."

TJ tapped him on the shoulder and sat down at Jimmy's table.

"Thought you might want some company this evening."

"Cheers, mate, although I don't think I'm much company at the moment to be honest."

"That's ok. We can sit and be grumpy bastards together."

"Everyone's heard then?"

"Yes, mate, it's all the staff in the pub were talking about earlier. Fate is a cruel mistress, my friend."

He could see the distress etched on Jimmy's face. He knew how close they were and how much this was likely to affect Jimmy.

TJ was 10 years older than Jimmy and had looked after Jimmy like a little brother since they'd first worked together. Jimmy had been wild when TJ first employed him at Parker's. He was just 18 and to say he was a live wire, would be an understatement. TJ had liked him at first sight. Full of ideas and plans on what he was going to do, and to the shock of pretty much everyone, he did what he said he was going to do and more.

He also knew that Jimmy saw Tatts as a newer version of himself, a protégé to be encouraged and helped. His major weakness was occasionally, he wore his heart on his sleeve too much. He was emotional at times.

"What was the name of that band you put on in Parker's which brought out the mounted police to control the queue going round the city?"

TJ decided he was going to take Jimmy back to happier memories. Stop him being so morose and dwelling on the subject.

"Ironically, they were called Violent Delight."

Jimmy laughed as he recalled in his mind the sight of police on horseback trying to control the queue across High Town. It must have had 800 people in it and the venue only held 400.

After that, the rest of the evening was spent recalling funny stories from their combined past and drinking a serious amount of whiskey.

The next morning, Jimmy woke up on the sofa in his office at home. He couldn't really remember getting home. He made his way into the front room where his two boys were playing around on the floor.

"Good morning, boys."

He gave them both a big kiss and lay down on the sofa in there just watching them play. He had never suffered from hangovers; he was immune to them. It was an odd trait but in his profession, a very useful trait. The boys both looked most content without a care in the world. The way it should be.

Jimmy decided that lying prostrate on the sofa was not going to make him feel any better about Tatts. He got up and started playing with the boys. He was quite sure they were being extra loud that morning but it could also have had something to do with how sensitive he was feeling. After a few minutes messing around with his boys, he made his way upstairs to get ready for the day. There was a lot to do to get both venues ready for the day and only one of him to do it now Tatts wasn't about to help. Saturday was going to be very long.

Come Saturday night, the news had filtered through to everyone who knew Tatts. He was very popular and Jimmy was already fending off questions about when the funeral was and what the arrangements were. To be honest, he didn't know himself, he had only been dead for a day. Jimmy stood on the front door that night noting how the mood, although still sombre, was a large improvement on the previous night.

For Christmas time, there had been only a few niggles and nothing to really worry about. Stuart and Pete came through to the front door holding a gentleman in his early 30s. They put him out in the street and told him to be on his way. The man readjusted his clothing including light up Santa jumper and hat.

"What did he do?"

"Just being a pain in the ass to girls on the dancefloor, being a pest really."

Stuart was not taking any prisoners that night. Jimmy looked at the man in the street and noticed he was quite drunk considering it was only just past midnight. Jimmy and Lee both noted he hadn't left the area and he kept lingering on the opposite side of the road. As 12:30am rolled around, two police officers turned up to do the usual licensing checks.

"Is everything ok?"

"All good, apart from laddo over there lingering around. He was thrown out for being a pest and just won't go home."

"Do you want us to have a quick word?"

"Might help."

Lee was pleased with the two officers for taking a proactive view to policing. He watched as the two officers strolled over the road and had a chat with the man. They promptly returned to the front door.

"He says he's waiting for his wife to pick him up."

"No problem."

Jimmy hadn't spotted him on the phone but maybe it was a prearranged pick up. Perhaps she knew he didn't handle his drink very well. The officers did a quick walk through of the venue and once they were satisfied everything was in order, they wandered off into the city to continue their tour of duty.

Lee and Jimmy were sharing funny stories of Tatts to pass the time. Jimmy was regaling Lee with the time Tatts tried to clean the glass washer with washing up liquid and the first thing he knew that there was a problem was when the soap suds poured into his office. Lee was in stitches and neither of them noticed the man approach from the other side of the road.

"You're laughing at me."

The man on the opposite side of the road was slurring his words, joining in a conversation that wasn't his to do so and also standing lopsided.

Here we go, thought Jimmy to himself. He'd seen this scenario quite a few times. A misinterpretation of a conversation being assumed as an insult or a slight.

"Not at all, Sir, merely reminiscing about a friend of ours."

Jimmy thought Lee's attempt at defusing the situation was pretty good. He wasn't going to bother himself, he was looking for any excuse for a dust up.

"Liars."

The man was getting louder and also coming a lot closer to them. Eventually, he stood right in front of them.

Jimmy had taken up a stance half a yard back and to the left of Lee as the events unfolded in front of him. He radioed the city CCTV.

"Echo Alpha, can you get the cameras on our front doors please."

"Everything ok down there?"

"All fine, just a precaution at the moment."

Almost before he had finished his radio call, the man charged closer and swung a giant hay maker at Lee. Catching him clean in the ribs, Lee didn't flinch but Jimmy heard the cracking noises. Immediately, the drunk hit the deck, rolling around screaming clutching his arm. Jimmy looked at Lee. Lee hadn't touched him in retaliation.

"Echo Alpha, can I get the police and an ambulance."

Jimmy didn't fully understand what had happened. Lee hadn't even pushed him back. He watched as Lee offered the man first aid. It was to no avail. Jimmy saw the man's arm, it was quite clearly shattered as it flopped around. It was quite a sickening sight. It looked like it was fluid rather than an arm.

The two police officers from earlier came sprinting down the road almost at the same time as the ambulance came round the corner. Jimmy was dumbstruck. He knew Lee was a big lad but how the hell had that happened. They had to just deal was it as it was. They'd offered first aid and called for medical assistance, it was as much as they could do.

"We've got it all on camera."

"We have too."

Lee explained to the officers what had happened and that he didn't wish to press charges. The man was walked into the back of the ambulance and taken away.

"How the hell did you break his arm?"

The two officers were as intrigued as Jimmy.

"Sorry, boss, I've joined a re-enactment group."

Jimmy and the officers looked at him slightly puzzled. Lee decided it would be easier to show them rather than continue trying to explain. He unzipped his door jacket and rolled up his shirt to reveal a full chain mail shirt underneath.

"I was breaking in my chain mail for tomorrow's re-enactment."

Jimmy and the officers fell about laughing. The moronic drunk had punched Lee with all his might and connected with a full set of chain mail. No wonder his arm had bust. If Lee hadn't been wearing it, he probably would've had some broken ribs.

Tatts' funeral was held a week before Christmas. It was a beautifully crisp winters day; the frost was quite hard and as Jimmy waited with the other pall bearers at the church, he noted how crunchy the grass was. The church was filling up very quickly and everyone was hurrying to get inside as it was so cold. Soon inside the church it was standing room only. Jimmy could almost hear Tatts in his mind telling him to give everyone a flyer for the club!

Jimmy waited with the others outside stamping his feet to keep them warm. He knew three of the other bearers and they'd already been told the order in which they were to walk. Jimmy had never been a pall bearer before and even though he didn't really want to be one he felt he owed it to Tatts.

The hearse drew up outside the church with the family cars following in due course. Jimmy felt his heart break all over again as he looked at Tatts' mum and dad. Their eyes were red and raw but looking incredibly dignified. They both made their way over to the pall bearers who were now all stood at the back of the hearse as it opened.

"Don't drop him, lads, as funny as he would've found it."

Tatts' dad was trying to break the ice and put everyone at ease. It was a lovely gesture.

As they lifted the coffin off the trolley, Jimmy couldn't help but notice the weight even though there were six of them. They managed to get him in safely and soundly to the plinth in front of the altar. Getting him there safely meant a lot to all concerned and they returned and took their seats as the service began.

Jimmy drifted off as he listened to the reverend. It always amazed him that the coffin actually had the person in. It didn't seem any time ago that he and Tatts were joking how funny it would be if after their funerals, someone could take their phone and text everyone 'Thanks for coming'. It seemed like a lifetime ago.

Chapter 9
Landlords from Hell

As the new year wound its way on, life had returned to a sense of normality. Jimmy found himself attempting to call or text Tatts a lot less as the days rolled by. Time has a way of remorselessly grinding away until all we have left are memories of those who have gone. It had been February before Jimmy had stopped putting Tatts on the rota. Every time he had done so, he had cursed himself.

March had bought a new, unexpected challenge. The owners of the building had sold up without telling any of the tenants, including Jimmy, what was going on. They had sold up to a new group from Sheffield. The new owners were very different to the old ones. Firstly, they had come down and decided the whole building needed smartening up; secondly, they had decided that some of the little shops and hairdressers nearby needed much tighter leases, none of these six months rolling contracts a lot of them were on.

It had become apparent very quickly that the cost of the renovations was to be paid for by increased rents. Jimmy still had over 4 years left on both his leases, so he was largely unaffected by the initial changes.

The renovations were nothing more than a slap of paint and some plastic flowers in hanging baskets, but the rent increases were extortionate and more in keeping with major cities. A lot of the independents started moving out and by the time summer came, the lovely independent quarter Jimmy had watched grow over the last 4½ years had been decimated.

Jimmy felt like the patriarch of this area. He had watched them come in and grow, watched them develop into flourishing businesses. To see them abandon their shops and hairdressing salons upset him greatly. He was not going to take it lying down. The new landlords finally got around to wanting to talk to him and arranged a meeting.

"So please tell me what the next part of your plan is?"

Jimmy was sat in the office in Rerack with Zoya Chandry, the representative from AJL Properties, the new landlords.

"Mr Harris, what do you mean?"

"Well, Mrs Chandry, so far you've slapped a bit of paint on the building, hung up some pretty God awful plastic flowers and managed to convince half the tenants in the area to vacate. I, of course, wondered what the next part of this great plan was?"

"Those tenants, they're better off gone. We'll get better ones. Next we will be fixing the guttering and renaming the quarter. Anyway, Mr Harris, we have a much more pressing matter for your consideration. Pressing enough that I would call it urgent. Your leases are both up in January."

"Think they run until January 2018."

"In January, we as your landlords, have the option of a break clause, this gives us the opportunity to reassess all rents and tenancy agreements. I will be back next week. These are your new terms if you wish to agree to them."

Zoya was very clearly not messing around. She stood up and handed Jimmy a brown A4 envelope. With that, she was gone and the meeting was adjourned until the following week. Jimmy escorted her out of the building and hurriedly shut the doors.

After Jimmy quickly checked the cameras to make sure she had completely left, he disappeared into his office, shut the door, and opened the envelope that she had handed him. Highlighted in yellow was the new rent charge they were going to be asking for. It was nearly double what he was currently paying. He was livid. He went out for a cigarette to calm himself down. Once he returned, he reread the whole article and discovered that he would also have to pay for his car parking space. "Bastards!" Jimmy yelled out loud.

Jimmy couldn't see how they could justify these increases. The cost of the refurb they were saying was adding value had at most cost £2000, and the idiots doing it were cowboys. Jimmy felt as if they had some ulterior motive. Perhaps they did want all the tenants to leave? Perhaps they wanted to redevelop the whole area and they needed to get everyone out. He spent most of the evening crunching numbers to see what he could make work.

"It's your night off and you spend it hidden in your office!"

Isabelle brought him a cup of coffee and making it clear she was not impressed with how Jimmy was spending his Monday night off. He explained to her what was going on and how he was trying to work out what they could afford. Isabelle felt a bit guilty for snapping at him but also that he could've said what was wrong before it had got to that point. He had literally come in the house and disappeared into the office without a word to anyone.

The next morning when he arrived at work, there was a Cherry Picker and three lads in harnesses setting up at the front corner of the building.

"Morning."

Jimmy made his way over to introduce himself to the contractors.

"Good morning."

"You guys sorting the gutters out?"

Jimmy already knew the answer but wanted to just double check.

"Yes, only be here a few days. Won't get in your way hopefully."

"Just wondering if I gave you a few quid would you clean the windows of my pool hall whilst you're up there."

Jimmy pointed at the windows on the upper tier. The oldest of the group, who had been the one engaging with Jimmy, tilted his head upwards and counted how many there were.

"£50 and we'll do them all."

"£30."

"£40."

"Deal, I'll be in the pool hall when you've done them and want paying."

With that, they shook hands and Jimmy disappeared into the club. He always hated going up the ladder to clean them and so he thought he might as well turn the situation to his advantage. He also hoped that they would come in and spend the said £40 on beer in the pool hall.

That evening, Jimmy was in the pool hall at around 8pm when he heard a slight commotion outside. The noises got louder until he could no longer ignore whatever it was and so made his way down the stairs and into the street. Outside, there was a group of young teenagers. They were on the opposite side of the road all milling around the Cherry Picker which the workers had been using earlier on in the day and had been put it to bed for the night when they had finished. Jimmy watched in astonishment as the Cherry Picker started to move.

He grabbed his club radio off his belt.

"Hannah, can you come out the front of the club and bring the city radio with you please."

"Coming, is everything ok?"

Very quickly Hannah appeared at the front doors of Jumping Jacks and started heading towards Jimmy who stood outside the pool hall. She too could see the Cherry Picker. It was now well and truly on the move down the street.

Hannah looked at Jimmy.

"I know."

Jimmy was having trouble stifling the giggles. Jimmy took possession of the city radio.

"Echo Alpha, this is Jumping Jacks."

"Go ahead, Jumping Jacks."

"If you spin the cameras on our street so they're facing us. You'll see a Cherry Picker."

"What's it doing?"

The CCTV operator sounded quite confused as Jimmy heard the archaic cameras at the end of the street start to turn in his direction.

"About seven miles per hour."

Jimmy had to cut his transmission short as he and Hannah were both now laughing out loud.

"And what's the problem, Jumping Jacks?"

"Mainly, it's being driven by a lad who looks about fifteen and more importantly, there are about ten teenagers with him in the cradle, which is about 15 foot in the air."

Jimmy watched as it trundled quite sedately to the end of the road and turned right into the city and out of Jimmy's line of vision.

It took less than 5 minutes for three police cars to go zooming past Jimmy with their lights on and sirens blasting. Jimmy and Hannah just stood outside waiting for the next chapter in this saga to unfold. Luckily, it wasn't far away. 10 minutes passed before they heard the trundling of the Cherry Picker come back into to ear shot. Four police officers were walking beside it. The teenagers were still in the cradle.

The Cherry Picker retuned to its original position opposite the pool hall. The police at the bottom were imploring the teenagers to lower the cradle with them in it and the teenagers, for their part, were negotiating for their pardons for returning the Cherry Picker.

Jimmy couldn't take anymore as he laughing so much he thought he was going to be sick.

"I'll see you in a couple of hours, you'll have to let me know how this ends."

He handed Hannah the city radio and left her watching the goings on as he ascended the stairs back into the pool hall still laughing away to himself about what he had just witnessed.

Zoya returned the following week as she had promised and was sitting with Jimmy in his office. The atmosphere was frosty to say the least. Zoya was obviously a very well-educated lady in her early 50s. She dressed well and wore a very expensive watch loosely on her left wrist. She had clearly been doing her job a long time and had no issue in destroying other people's businesses to further her own interests. That was business though and Jimmy knew that.

Jimmy placed a cup of strong black coffee down for her and that signalled for battle to commence as soon as he too was seated.

"Have you had a chance to read the amended terms?"

Zoya knew full well that he would have and was just attempting to start the conversation.

"Yes, I have."

"And what are your thoughts?"

Zoya led with a very leading question attempting to extract as much information as possible without giving anything away herself.

"To be frank with you, these are horrendous. The prices you want to charge are big cities prices and to take away the car park spaces is a very underhand move."

"I haven't taken away your space, I just want you to pay a fair price for it."

Zoya knew they had taken it away and now wanted Jimmy to pay for it, every penny she could generate was important. It was her job to make money. Jimmy knew this too and was angry that Zoya thought £1200 a year for a car park space was throw away money.

"I can't accept the terms as they are. The slap of paint does not befit nearly doubling the rent, furthermore the car park space was included in the previous terms. It should still be. You wouldn't rent out a house and charge extra for using the driveway, would you?"

Jimmy took a sip of his coffee and awaited a reply. Jimmy hoped the frosty atmosphere and lack of idle chit chat would put Zoya on edge and unnerve her. Jimmy attempted to appear as cool and calm as he possibly could. Trying his best not to fidget or give away any little tell that would give Zoya an edge. He had already seen she was good at these sort of things, he was still trying to learn.

"Mr Harris, my company has to make money, mortgages to pay, maintenance to pay, insurances to pay. You've been paying a very low rent for a long time and that needs to be addressed. This area is thriving."

Zoya was trying to sell her deal as best she could. She knew that the increases were steep but hoped Jimmy would at least try and meet her somewhere and not just dismiss her out of hand.

"It was thriving."

"Sorry, what was that, Mr Harris?"

"I said it was thriving, but since you've taken over and over half the tenants have left."

"I will admit that we've lost a few tenants but we'll get them back, those units won't be empty for long."

Jimmy had already decided he was going to stay but he had also decided he would try and get the best deal he could. He also wanted that car park space; being totally honest, he needed it and she probably knew that. He couldn't really lug creates of beer several streets from the nearest council car park.

"I am willing to pay seventy-five percent of what you are asking. Not a penny more and I want the car park space included at no extra cost. However, I don't want 10 years, I just want two."

Jimmy had laid his cards out fully on the table, he'd made his mind up to play hard ball. It was a high-risk strategy but he could see no other way to really deal with this company and their aggressive tactics. He also only wanted 2 years because if they carried on losing tenants then he could end up stuck in a totally derelict building paying very high rent. He had to have some wiggle room.

"I have better things to do with my time than bat this back and forth with you all morning. I feel that what I have offered to pay is fair. I don't think you'll get another tenant very easily for these two units and bear in mind, I pay the bills."

With his little speech over, Jimmy sat back and watched. Jimmy was hoping that she would see the logic in his argument. In a curious way, she also needed him, as she had said she has bills to pay.

Zoya smiled a little bit, a slight tell giving away the fact that she had roughly got what she set out to achieve.

"Jimmy, I will take your offer back to my office and see if it's acceptable to my partners."

Zoya made a few little notes on her pad, finished her coffee, and stood up. Leaning over Jimmy's desk, she held her hand out to shake his. Jimmy stood up and shook her hand.

"I'll see you out."

Jimmy walked around his desk and opened the door for her. He might have been playing hard ball but he certainly hadn't forgotten his manners.

A few days passed by and he had heard nothing. Jimmy thought about contacting Zoya but eventually talked himself out of it. *Patience is a virtue*, he told himself repeatedly. He kept himself busy organising Isabelle's upcoming surprise birthday party. Inviting everyone she knew and swearing them to silence on the matter. He even managed to get his mum to baby sit both boys so Isabelle's mum could attend.

He knew that Isabelle's parents had been divorced for many years and that the animosity between them was very deep and very real. Still he had made the choice that as they were both adults, they should both attend and he had reached out to both of them with the same message. They had both agreed to come. Jimmy had explained to both of them that he wasn't asking them to sit together, just come for their daughter.

The party was shaping up to be an awesome night. He'd spared no expense on making sure that it would be memorable and Isabelle would enjoy it. He'd arranged a magician to go round all evening entertaining people, a fire breather, and some burlesque dancers. This Saturday would be spectacular to say the least.

Saturday evening came round incredibly quickly. That evening to start, Jimmy took Isabelle out for a meal. Things hadn't been great but he had decided to keep on trying. It was difficult as Jimmy felt they were on such different trajectories these days. Mid-way through the meal, a bottle of champagne arrived as he had requested it would.

"Happy birthday, Isabelle."

Jimmy poured them both a glass and raised his glass in the air.

"Thank you, Jimmy. I'd like to talk to you to be honest."

"I'm all ears, sounds serious."

"it's nothing to worry about. I'd just like to work more; I'd like to be involved more."

"That would be good. I'd like you to be more active in the businesses."

Outwardly, Jimmy was taking this information fully in his stride. Inside he was amazed. He couldn't believe that after over 6 years together, she was contemplating actually doing some work.

"Thank you, I wasn't sure how you'd take that."

"I'll see when the next licensees' course is being held nearby and book you on it."

They finished their meal and headed to the club. For the first time in a long time, it was almost as if they were on the same hymn page. They arrived at the club and walked in. Isabelle's face lit up at seeing all her friends and family there to greet her. She ran around hugging everyone and making sure she did greet everyone.

"Thank you, Jimmy."

She gave him a kiss on the cheek as she breezed by him to dance with her family and friends.

Jimmy spent the next three or four hours busying himself with running the club and ignoring the fact she was drinking copiously and had ignored him for several hours.

As Jimmy returned from the stockroom and started to replenish the fridges, Hannah knelt down beside him out of earshot of everyone else.

"Are you ok?"

"Just trying to keep myself busy."

All the staff could visibly see Jimmy's pain when Isabelle behaved like this. But, they all knew, like Jimmy, there was not a single thing they could do. Jimmy had watched it over the years; it was like she could just hit self-destruct and then everything else was collateral damage.

As the lights came up and people dispersed from the club, Jimmy surveyed the aftermath. The magician had left playing cards everywhere, there were remnants of balloons all over and Isabelle was absolutely paralytic on a sofa. Jimmy went over and made sure she was decent. He asked George to grab him a few blankets from the office. He knew Isabelle wasn't for moving that night.

Jimmy cashed up, checked the toilets, and then he set the alarm and locked the club. He figured he'd either get in before she arose or when she arose, she'd set the alarms off triggering his phone.

"Do you want a lift home?"

Jimmy was a bit shocked Hannah was waiting outside. It was a kind offer but the walk home would help clear his mind.

"I'm cool, thank you. I'll walk."

He was still hanging onto the threads of hope that Isabelle would awaken from her drunken slumber at any moment so he could get her home too.

"Alright, Mr Harris, can you at least walk a young lady to her car?"

"Of course I can."

It wasn't far to her car and as they stood there, Hannah turned and looked at Jimmy. She saw him as he was behind all the charades and the smoke and mirrors.

"She won't change…ever. You know it. You're hanging on to something that now only exists in your memory."

Jimmy looked at Hannah. He knew in his heart she was right.

"Drive safely, I'll see you Tuesday night."

Jimmy watched her drive away and returned to the club. He walked over to Isabelle and made sure the blankets covered her. He finished his drink that he had left on the bar, turned off the lights, set the alarm once more and let himself out. He walked the back streets home taking in the sights.

In the morning, Jimmy's phone alarm went off at about 9am. He got up and showered and got ready to face the day. He went into the kitchen and started brewing some coffee. Within a minute, Isabelle was phoning him.

"Jimmy, can you turn the alarm off in the club please."

"Of course, I'll be down in 20 minutes to let you out."

"Thank you."

Isabelle hung up the phone and Jimmy turned off the alarm. He resisted the temptation to look at the cameras on his phone to see exactly how she was. He would see her soon enough.

They didn't discuss her birthday or the fact her father had somehow run up a bar tab of over £100 trying to impress people, which would never get paid. Jimmy could see no point. It would just lead to more arguments; it was easier if he dealt with it all, let it go and moved on.

Jimmy set about getting Isabelle on a course to get her personal licence. He was very keen on having the odd day off. The flip side also meant Isabelle also taking on some responsibilities. Jimmy hoped that with these new responsibilities would come a change in attitude. Maybe it would help her grow up. He could but hope.

In the following week, Jimmy got two emails and both, for different reasons would change the whole direction of his life. Firstly, Isabelle had got on to a course to get her licensee qualification and secondly, he had been accepted as a mentor to help young people in the city.

Isabelle was really pleased as Jimmy handed her the textbook from which she was to revise for her course. Jimmy was just as pleased to be attending his first mentoring session. A real chance to give something back to society. Jimmy had spent most of his adult life trying to help people after the dam had burst. This was a real opportunity to help people before they were carrying all the baggage.

In the middle of November, Jimmy got a letter from Zoya and all conditions had been agreed. He felt relief that he had not only managed to secure his future for the next 2 years but also that of his staff. It gave him elbow room to manoeuvre. 2 years would take him to nearly 20 years in the industry.

Isabelle had manged to pass her licensee course at the first time of asking, she did appear to be taking it seriously and Jimmy had caught her a few times revising. Jimmy laughed to himself a bit that unlike him many years ago, she didn't have to stand before a magistrate and explain why she should have one. Times change he figured. When he'd done that, there had been no social media; the world was different, it was throw away almost.

Chapter 10
You Run the Show

The world changes very quickly if you stand still. You can end up left behind or just grasping at straws. Jimmy honoured his deal with Isabelle and soon she was running two nights a week in the pool hall. He didn't want to throw her in at the deep end by giving her shifts at the club. He was also very acutely aware how the other staff saw her and this variance of nepotism would not sit well within the club.

It would also give her a fair chance to learn about the job. It was after all her first job. It was a solution that over time would hopefully appease everyone.

Jimmy, for his part, was loving being at home playing with his boys and then managing to get to bed before 9:30pm. He thought back to his childhood sometimes and how he riled against his parents to stay up later and realising as an adult, the epitome of it all is being tucked up in bed by 10pm. He couldn't help but chuckle to himself.

"Isabelle, the bar takings are down, any reason?"

Jimmy was cashing up after pool league night and normally, the takings were pretty similar every week, give or take £100.

"It seemed busy."

"It was busy. We had four home teams but the takings aren't where they should be, or where they normally are. Looking at the stock levels, we should be well above the average takings."

"I did treat a few people to a few pints and some shots."

"Right, I will explain this once, and once only, you do not give away free beers at my bar without my say so. Are we clear?"

"It's not just your bar, it's my bar too and I'll do as I please when I'm in charge. I'm not one of your staff, Jimmy."

"It's not. It's my bar. When you are here, you are working for me, unless of course, you don't want any wages."

"Well, I'm not doing it for free."

"So you agree that you are working for me."

Isabelle was not happy with herself for walking into that one. Jimmy could tell she was angry as she screwed up her eyes to glower at him.

"Fundamentally, I think you are too immature to run this bar. You can't tell who your mates are and whose taking you for a ride."

"When I'm in charge, I'll make the decisions, and without my friends coming in, it would be just a load of muppets playing pool."

"It's a fucking pool hall and those people you call friends, they are not your friends, they're not your mates. They're leeches. I don't think I've ever seen you with them except in the club or in here."

"So it's not my call."

"No, it's mine, and you act in my name. Do you realise every drink you give away is rent, bills and wages? It's toys for the kids for fuck sake!"

Jimmy knew this was a battle of will power and, if he was to have any time off, he had to win. Knowing Isabelle, he also knew he had to make her feel like she had not lost. She was not one for saying sorry or admitting to any errors.

Isabelle sat in silence looking at Jimmy and he swore he could hear the cogs going round in her mind.

"How am I supposed to play the role of host if I can't give away the odd drink?"

"You're here to sell drinks not to give them away. Isabelle, you only appear to be playing hostess to your friends. They don't spend any money. They only come in to drink free, drinks from you. The host makes the customers who spend money feel special, kind of like giving out patronage. If you get the pool team a round of Jager bombs for winning or a round of consolation shots for losing, it's very different to plying your friends with gin or wine all night."

"Ok, I see. So this is about me hanging out with my friends? You don't want me to hang out with my friends?"

"Not at all, but you are here to do a job. A job for which you are paid. What is the name of any of our pool team captains?"

"I haven't met them."

"They were all in last night. They would've been pretty hard to miss. You should've introduced yourself. We'll try it again next week. You must make more of an effort with the teams. They're the bread and butter of the pool hall. Come on, let's go get a coffee. I need a change of scene and subject."

Although, Isabelle was pretty disgruntled with Jimmy, she was also pretty hungover and a coffee seemed like a good idea at that point so she didn't argue.

Things soon settled in the pool hall after a few weeks. Jimmy had to admit, Isabelle was making a reasonable stab at running the show. She had even helped the pool team out a few times when they were short of players. Jimmy was taking the time at home to improve the advertising and keep on top of the social media accounts.

There always seemed to be something that needed fixing or some paperwork that needed sorting out. Even though he'd managed to get a few nights off, the endless grind seemed to just continue regardless. Jimmy would often wonder how he found the time before. It'll all be worth it in the end, he would tell himself as he ploughed through another mountain of paperwork and incident sheets.

As July approached, he was planning a big party at home to celebrate 5 years of the club being open. He had hired a bouncy castle for the garden, magicians to entertain everyone; he'd got caterers organised to come and sort the food and he had as much booze at home as he had within the club. All he needed now was a good dose of sunshine.

The day finally arrived and Jimmy was up early making sure everything was perfect. The weather forecast promised sunshine all day. Jimmy felt pleased as punch as the giant bouncy castle was erected. It was a huge affair with an inflatable obstacle course on it as well.

As soon as the boys saw it being inflated, they wanted to get on it. Jimmy had a task on his hands just trying to stop them getting on it before it was fully inflated. He also wanted a go himself so he knew how they were feeling. Eventually, it was ready and the three of them bounced around without a care in the world. The sun was shining and everything was great in the world.

He had invited all the staff and their partners and children, all his friends and most of the children from the boys' nursery. 1pm could not come fast enough.

As 1pm finally came round, all the guests started to arrive and the party started to get into full swing. He had also invited a few of the regulars who had supported them from the start, though whether they turned up was another matter. Jimmy walked into his kitchen to find TJ assisting the caterers.

"You found the food then?"

"Of course, just a little quality control."

TJ was laughing at the fact he had been caught in the act of trying to nab some food early. He had already had quite a bit before Jimmy popped his head round the door. They walked outside together and sat at one of the picnic tables on the edge of the garden. The air was full of the sound of music, children laughing and giggling, and the gentle hum of the generator powering the bouncy castle.

"5 years isn't bad. You should be very proud of yourself. If I'm honest, I wasn't sure you'd make the first Christmas."

"I was figuring Halloween was a stretch at one point."

Jimmy took a sip of his drink as he watched Isabelle show a few people through to the garden. Seems Isabelle had invited some of the pool teams as well which pleased him greatly. As they day wore on, everyone seemed to be having a wonderful time. As the afternoon ticked over, some of the children and their parents left but new people were turning up.

Some who had been working or just couldn't make it earlier, and some who just didn't fancy the party with children running everywhere. It was continually busy and Jimmy felt like he was entertaining people almost non-stop.

He couldn't believe how much food and drink everyone had consumed. Luckily, Jimmy had ordered plenty so they still weren't running low just yet.

Just after 8pm, the last of the children left. Jimmy could hear the odd child cry as they weren't allowed another last go on the bouncy castle. Jimmy put his two to bed with Isabelle. They were exhausted. They had also been promised if they went to bed that daddy would turn the bouncy castle back on tomorrow morning before the hire company collected it. They had spent all day running around and making everyone smile with their exuberance for life. Now they were shattered and they fell asleep very quickly.

"What time do you think everyone will stay until?"

"Who knows."

Now all the kids were gone, he fully intended to let his hair down. They made their way downstairs and back to the party. Turns out, adults love bouncy castles as much as children. Jimmy stood there sipping his drink watching his door team playing their own version of British Bulldogs. *Hope it's made of strong stuff*, Jimmy thought to himself as he wondered if he could kiss goodbye to his deposit on the bouncy castle. He turned and made his way back to his picnic bench to continue observing the shenanigans that were now taking place.

About 15 minutes passed before Gary, a friend of TJ's who had tagged along, approached their picnic bench.

"You guys might want to come and see this."

Jimmy and TJ got up and followed him across the garden and beyond the conservatory, Jimmy noted Isabelle was in the conservatory with a few of her friends and a couple of lads from one of the pool team as he passed by. As they rounded the conservatory, they could see the giant garden swing set that Jimmy had bought the boys. Jimmy had specifically moved it out of the way so he didn't have to spend all afternoon babysitting children on it. Somehow, wedged in the one swing seat was Lee. Judging by the efforts of everyone surrounding him, he was well and truly wedged.

"Seriously?"

"Sorry, Jimmy."

Jimmy stared hard at him with his arms folded attempting to look as furious as possible before eventually getting phone out.

"Right, everyone, get together, this has the makings of the club's Christmas card all over it."

He burst out laughing as everyone surrounded the stranded Lee and posed for the picture. Jimmy took plenty of photos.

"Right, best get you out I suppose. I'll be back in a few minutes, don't go anywhere."

He disappeared into the house to grab a sharp knife to cut the cords holding the swing. Going through the conservatory, as he made his way to the kitchen, he saw Isabelle and one of the pool lads.

"Sorry, didn't mean to interrupt you."

Jimmy spoke just to make them aware he was there. He just stood and looked at them. No one said a word. Everyone was completely still, as if time had stopped. Jimmy motioned he needed to get past them to get into the kitchen and the lad saw this as his opportunity to scurry away as quickly as he possibly could.

"Turns out chivalry isn't dead. I have to get a knife to cut Lee out of the swing."

"Jimmy, look..."

Before Isabelle could even start trying to explain, Jimmy had gone.

Jimmy retrieved the knife and walked back outside. The lad from the conservatory clocked him holding the knife, shit a brick and ran for it. Jimmy laughed to himself as he watched the lad run for his life as he bolted out the bottom gate to supposed safety. Jimmy made his way to get Lee out of his current predicament.

It took four of them to pull him out once the swing had been cut from the frame. Lee was dreadfully embarrassed by it all and probably a little sore.

"I'm really sorry, Jimmy, I'll pay for the damage."

"What did you think was going to happen?"

Jimmy gave Lee a hug as he showed him the pictures that he'd taken on his phone. It was certainly a talking point.

"No harm done; I've got some rope somewhere to fix it."

For what seemed like forever, everyone sat around the picnic benches telling stories of past events from the club's first 5 years. Jimmy sat and listened knowing how most of the stories would roughly end even with the embellishments that had been added over time. Isabelle had excused herself and gone to bed. *Probably for the best*, Jimmy thought to himself determined not to put a downer on the night.

"What's up?"

TJ had noticed Jimmy was for once listening to the stories rather than telling them.

"Nothing really, Isabelle's just being a dick."

"I did notice. I think a few others did as well."

"Great."

"So what was the boss like working for you? Bet you could tell a few stories!"

Just what Jimmy needed, a drunken George.

"There's plenty of stories, most of which should remain unspoken."

"Just one."

Drunk George was a persistent human being and was not going to let this go.

"Alright, alright. Just one though. We had a band play once. Quite a big band. Jim had booked them way in advance but by the time they arrived, they'd gained a lot of traction in the press and by the time the chart came out on the Sunday before they were to play at Parker's, they were at number two."

"I'm going to nip to the toilet."

Jimmy excused himself from the table.

"Don't you want to hear the story?"

As Jimmy steadied himself as he stood up, noticing both his legs had gone to sleep as he'd been sat down for so long, he looked at George and winked.

"I'll be honest, I'm pretty sure I know how this one ends!"

"So they arrived and…"

TJ continued the story as Jimmy walked back into the house. He just wanted 5 minutes peace to clear his head. He ducked in the kitchen after going to the toilet and downed a pint of water. Hoping that would sober him up a bit. It had been a long day and a lot had happened. This was going to take a while for him to process. He then made his way back to the picnic benches.

"…so I arrive at about 10am the next morning to find Jimmy in the car park with the environmental health officer, and Jimmy is trying to explain why half of the local park forest is in the club's car park and not where it should've been in the park."

TJ had just finished his story. Everyone was roaring with laughter and Jimmy was pleased with the timing of his return.

"Oh how everyone laughed except when the bill for the damage came through. We had to do another gig just to raise the money for the fine!"

Jimmy sat down by Hannah who was wiping tears out of eyes.

"You were a nightmare back in the day by the sounds of it!"

"I wasn't that bad, just a bit high spirited at times. Are you having a good time?"

"It's been great fun, Jim, I've got to make a move in a bit. I've got to pick my sister up on the way home."

"Well, thank you for coming."

The party gradually wound down and everyone left except TJ, who had made himself comfy on a sofa in the front room. Jimmy knew he wasn't going to be moving before morning so left him be and went to bed.

The club itself was having its birthday party the following Saturday. A heroes and villains theme. It was already a sold-out event before the Saturday had even arrived. Jimmy got a taxi to work that night, he didn't really feel like walking through the city dressed as Banana Man. He had chosen Banana Man as by the time he'd gone to the costume shop in the week, all the other costumes that would fit him had gone.

He was quite excited to see what the staff were dressed as. He'd promised at the party on the weekend that the best staff costume would win £100. *I must've been hammered to agree to that*, he thought to himself as he arrived as the club. He noticed he was not the first to arrive and quickly knocked the door not wanting to be stood on the doorstep dressed as he was.

When everyone had arrived, Jimmy took a group photo. Everyone had tried really hard to impress and had definitely succeeded. He had everything from Zorro to He Man, an array of marvel characters and also a Chesney Hawkes, a real hero for getting so far, for so long on one song! It was a bit odd Isabelle not being there but with everything that was going on, it did make sense. She had politely said she couldn't get a babysitter to make it easier on them both, even though they both knew she could have very easily if she had really wanted to.

The whole night went off amazingly well. The magicians entertained all, the exploding balloons had all gone off with perfect timing; Jimmy was not looking forward to clearing up that mess but at that moment in time, he didn't care. Loads of people had dressed up and there was only one scuffle all night. That scuffle was going to cause problems though as it had involved the mayor's son and his friends.

The mayor held considerable sway in the city and the fact his son was viewed by all and sundry as an absolute idiot was neither here nor there.

It was 4:30am and Jimmy, still dressed as Banana Man, was accompanied by two police officers in his office as they all surveyed the CCTV from that evening.

"So, Mr Harris, if I am reading my notes correctly and if I am to believe your version of events things unfolded as follows. Victim one grabbed Captain America's arm and felt his muscles."

"Yes, that was the start of it."

Jimmy sat there regretting wearing the Banana Man costume as he could feel himself sweating through every pore of his body. It was insanely hot; it had also been a complete nightmare to go to the toilet wearing it as he had discovered earlier on in the evening.

"Then he made some derogatory remark and Captain America pushed him away, then Captain America turned to walk away. The alleged victim then grabbed Captain America's shoulder, turned him back round and punched him in the face?"

"That's bang on so far."

Jimmy strolled the CCTV through which was corroborating his story perfectly so far.

"Then the second victim took matters into his own hands and joins in as well by throwing a punch at Captain America. The two alleged victims then set about Captain America. Next, the Incredible Hulk charges in and tries to defend

Captain America. The Hulk then exchanges punches with both alleged victims as Iron Man joins the fray."

"I told you what happened. I'm just glad I have CCTV to back it up!"

"Then, as the melee unfolds and everyone is trying to restrain alleged victims one and two, Hugh Hefner enters the fray with his bevvy of beauties and attempts to calm the two victims down. *Hugh Hefner?*"

"I asked the same thing earlier, apparently Hugh Hefner is a real superhero we can all actually aspire to be."

"Then Banana Man, which is you, and a giant man dressed as the Punisher, Lee, one of your doorman, enter into the fray. You split everyone up and it's all calmed down."

The officer seemed pleased to have got through reading all that without giggling once.

"Mr Harris, I have seen some things in my time but this, this is first. The mayor is not going to be happy. Can you burn me a copy of that footage please? The sarge is going to want to see this the moment I file the paperwork."

The three of them all stood around the monitor and watched it one more time. This time both officers and Jimmy did laugh. Seeing it at full speed somehow made it even funnier.

By the time the police left, everyone else had gone and Jimmy was very aware he was on his own, in a nightclub, dressed a Banana Man at 5:30am in the morning. He decided to walk home as it would be pretty impossible to get a taxi at that hour. It also wouldn't take long and he would be able to have a good think about his current situation with Isabelle. It couldn't go on as they were. They were like ships in the night, tip-toeing around one another and eventually, this would have a detrimental effect on the children as well as themselves.

He managed to grab a few hours' sleep but soon enough, Jimmy was sitting at the breakfast counter in the kitchen. He was nursing a coffee and running through his mind everything he wanted, and needed, to say. Isabelle came downstairs a little after 10am.

"There's coffee if you want some."

Jimmy pointed at the cafetiere.

"Thank you. I didn't expect you to be up so early. How did last night go?"

Isabelle poured herself a cup.

"Really well except the fight."

Jimmy then explained what had occurred. Isabelle couldn't quite believe what she was hearing from the description Jimmy gave. She was going to have to see this for herself when she was next in. She knew Jimmy always kept copies of every incident in case it was ever needed at a later date. Some unscrupulous people had worked out that most CCTV is only kept for 28 days and thus if you made a complaint after that period of time, then most clubs only had written accounts of incidents.

"Sounds like a very entertaining evening."

"It was certainly very different. Look, Isabelle, we need to talk."

"I know we do."

Isabelle looked at Jimmy. She was acutely aware how bad things were between them. It was hard not to be aware of it.

"We can't continue like this. It's making us both unhappy. The boys will notice soon enough, our parents already have."

Jimmy sighed and took another swig of coffee.

"What are we going to do?"

They just sat there for quite a time. A relief that everything was out on the table, finally there would be no more facade but neither of them having any real answers.

"Let's stop pretending for starters, that isn't helping at all. We haven't been a real couple for months. Look, the house is big enough for both of us to live in and we've still got over a year on the lease."

"So live together but not be together?"

Isabelle was fidgeting on her seat which Jimmy was finding a bit distracting but he tried to ignore it.

"Yes. We can work out who is looking after the boys and what days but let's give ourselves a few days to adjust; let's just take it all one day at a time."

Jimmy poured himself the remaining coffee and added a splash of milk.

"Ok, Jim, I'm sorry you know."

She looked down at the breakfast bar and couldn't bring herself to look at him. Jimmy reached over and took her hand. He gave it kiss and smiled at her. Both of them had tears in their eyes and Jimmy had to remove his glasses to wipe his face with his sleeve.

"It's ok, Isabelle, we tried, we really did. Somethings don't work and it's no ones' fault, it's just life."

"What do we tell people?"

"The truth. Let's be honest and open. That way at least we won't end up with everyone tiptoeing around us. Anyway, I've got a club to clean, there's thousands of bits of balloons everywhere, so I'd better get a wriggle on."

He stood up, and so did Isabelle. Jimmy finished his coffee. They stood there in just the two of them and just hugged. Neither wanting to be the first to break the embrace.

Monday over lunch, they worked out a few of the details. Jimmy wanted to make sure that Isabelle was able to make a living on her own so he resolved to sign her over the pool hall. Although, they weren't married, Jimmy was determined she would receive a fair share of their businesses. He did make it clear that he was keeping the club, that was his baby.

"How will I find the time to run the pool hall?"

"I'm not going anywhere. I'll still help and do bits for you."

"I'm not sure, Jimmy. I think if you're out and it's mine, it will blur the lines with everyone if you're still involved."

Jimmy sat and thought for a minute. She had a fair point and the reasoning behind it was sound. She would have to put her own stamp on it and he didn't want to be getting in the way.

"Ok, that's fair enough. I guess you'll need a few extra staff then. I should be able to transfer it all inside a few weeks. That'll give you time to get some people on board."

"I'll work it out. I've got a bit of time and I'm sure some of the girls would be willing to do some shifts."

"You can keep Darren though!"

"That's not fair, I had to put up with him growing up!"

"Unfortunately, Isabelle, these are the sort of problems you'll have to deal with now that you run the show."

Chapter 11
Locked in and Loaded

Alice, the cloakroom girl, was off to university after putting it off for a gap year that had lasted 3 years. Jimmy had to get someone new in. He liked having a settled team, everyone knowing their roles and capable of looking out for one another. He hated altering the balance but sometimes needs a must. His search eventually led to a very sweet young lady called Catherine.

She'd just started at the art college and only wanted to work Friday and Saturday nights, which was absolutely perfect for what Jimmy needed. She was friendly, always turned up looking immaculate, and never lost a coat. She was perfect for the role.

Jimmy had got used to not being involved in the pool hall. He found it hard at first and did get a slight kick when Isabelle would ask for his help but this occurred less and less as she learnt all there was about running the place. He was proud of her but it did leave him feeling a bit deflated. He had even stopped popping in before work sometimes for a game of pool and a catch up with some of the regulars as he felt like he was intruding. Isabelle had told him that was nonsense but the feeling was very real and he thought she was just being polite.

Everything had settled down into a very pleasant normality. Jimmy enjoyed his nights off and not being beholden to two places. Hannah had stepped into the manager role with great aplomb. She'd taken control of many aspects of life in club. Phones behind the bar were banned, drinking on the job was banned and, even though it was different for Jimmy, it was working well. Finally, he was beginning to reap the rewards of all his hard work.

Jimmy was taking his role as a youth counsellor very seriously. Meeting the group he was mentoring once a week. He was getting a great deal of satisfaction out of talking to these older teens. Their issues and problems were the same as many people and he almost felt that with most of them the issue was they had

had to grow up to soon. They were worried about money, their mum or dad's rents, helping put food on the table.

Some of them suffered from a great deal of frustration and that was why many had fallen foul of the law. Sheer desperation. There were a few just general idiots but the most had made life choices based on family situations. Jimmy knew he couldn't fix them all but he could at least offer them a friendly ear and some solid advice.

Jimmy was enjoying a late breakfast one morning with the boys when his phone went off.

"Morning, Jimmy. I'm a bit short of vodka and Jack Daniels and I haven't got the time to go to the wholesalers. Can I nip into the club and borrow a couple until tomorrow?"

"Course you can, just make sure you put the alarm on when you leave."

He was already regretting giving her Tatts' old keys with the club keys still on them. This was something he should've foreseen, but it was too late now. If he asked for those keys back, she'd only kick off.

"Thank you, Jimmy."

Jimmy knew he'd never see those bottles returned but anything to keep the peace was fine with him. The lack of arguments had been wonderful, the tranquillity it had bought to many aspects of Jimmy's life were much appreciated.

That evening in the club, he was met by Hannah who was in a furious mood. It didn't take long for Jimmy to find out why.

"You've got to tell her to fuck off."

Hannah was taking no prisoners as they discussed why there was no Jack Daniel's in the club that evening.

"I know there were three litres here last night. She hasn't taken one bottle, she has taken two bottles. How can I run this bar if she keeps running off with the stock? It's embarrassing when we run out."

"I'll get some tomorrow. I know it's annoying but it helps me keep the peace. A few more months and I won't have to share the same roof as her and things will get better."

Jimmy chalked his cue and lined up his next shot meticulously, he promptly missed horrendously.

"Getting to you, is it?"

Hannah knew Jimmy wouldn't normally miss such a shot. She could see the tension in his shoulders. Jimmy ignored the comment as Hannah cleared up the rest of the balls.

"You've got to learn to say no her. We can't support her and us. If she's selling out, she must have some money to buy her own stock."

Hannah was right but Jimmy didn't want to hear it. All he wanted in his world was peace and quiet. He did know that she had made a very valid point about the money, she must have some. He would have to tackle the problem before it got completely out of hand.

For now though Jimmy's mind was elsewhere though. He had been given notice that week that on the weekend it was his club's turn for environmental health sound initiative. They were going to be setting up shop outside the club and monitoring all noise emanating from the building from midnight until they closed. Jimmy had mentioned this to the door staff but he felt confident that their sound proofing was more than adequate.

He just wanted to be sure the guys were on top of making sure that doors were closed quickly as people entered or left the building. Still he knew any mistakes and Mr Scott would go straight for his jugular.

As Friday came round, Mr Gough and Mr Scott arrived outside the club at just after 11pm. Out of the back of the council van, they started setting up their sound monitoring equipment. Jimmy stood on the opposite side of the road to the club and offered them full assistance in setting up their gear.

"Do you want me to tell Andy to turn the sound levels down?"

Jimmy's radio had been almost non-stop with the door staff trying to help get through this situation.

"No, Seb, it's fine."

The door staff shrugged at one another and carried on with their duties. Jimmy was super confident and they couldn't for the life of them work out why. It was also perplexing Mr Scott and Mr Gough who were much more used to levels of hostility. It got to 11:55pm and the volume was fully pumping.

Outside was a gentle hum and you could make out a few bits as doors opened and closed to let people in and out. Overall Jimmy was pleased the door staff were doing their jobs with meticulous attention to detail.

"Boss, I can get him to turn it down if you want."

"No, Lee, it's cool, they've told me they're turning it on bang on midnight. So just hold tight, everything is going to be fine. They must see us as we really are and, guys, just trust me, we've got this!"

Mr Scott and Mr Gough stood opposite the club looking pleased as punch with their work. Finally, they'd get him. They did a few last-minute checks and they were set.

"Tell Andy to turn it up."

The door staff ignored this request and assumed Jimmy was joking. They all wondered what the hell he was playing at. This was their livelihoods, why was he acting with such brazen behaviour? Surely they could just turn everything down a bit for one night.

As the churches nearby struck midnight and the bells tolled, Mr Scott turned to Jimmy and looked him square in the eyes.

"Here we go, Mr Harris."

Jimmy just smiled at him and looked at his watch. Mr Scott could barely contain himself. Finally, he was going to nail Jimmy Harris, that son of a bitch who had embarrassed him so much and made him look like an idiot in the committee chambers.

As soon as Mr Scott turned the machines on, BANG and WHOOP, the first fireworks started exploding overhead. Almost unknown to anyone except Jimmy, the local cathedral was having an arts celebration culminating in fireworks display at midnight. The whole sky above their heads was lit up as if it was almost daylight and no one could hear a thing over the fireworks exploding.

"Mr Scott, I will be a witness. Let's go round and confront the bishop!"

Jimmy was having to shout to be heard. Mr Scott was incandescent with rage. He stared hard at Jimmy. If looks could kill Jimmy would have been a dead man. He then looked at the sound monitoring equipment. All it was picking up was the fireworks. The fumes were palpably coming out of his ears now. He was red with rage. How had he done this again?

There was a moment's hesitation as Mr Scott opened the back of the council van and with no finesse at all, he threw the very expensive, and highly delicate, sound monitoring equipment inside.

Jimmy was roaring with laughter as fireworks continued exploding overhead. Mr Scott adjusted his council issue high visibility vest and approached Jimmy.

"I'll get you. One day, Mr Harris, I will nail your balls to a fucking cross."

"Not tonight, Mr Scott, not tonight!"

Mr Scott walked around of the side of the van and got in. He drove off as fast he could away from the club. As he approached the bend at the end of the road, everyone could hear the tyres screeching.

"Well played, boss man."

The door staff could not believe what they had just witnessed. He must've known all along.

Jimmy stood there opposite the club and looked at Mr Gough, who Mr Scott in blind fury, had left behind. Mr Gough looked completely dazed by the events of the evening and he felt very embarrassed that his colleague had left him stranded.

"Would you like drink, Mr Gough, as your date has bailed on you?"

Mr Gough managed a small smile, pleased that Jimmy had acknowledged his plight amongst Mr Scott's rage.

"Yes, Mr Harris, that would be most cordial of you. Don't suppose you could call me a taxi?"

"Of course, Mr Gough, I'll get one of the lads to sort that out for you now."

The two of them walked over the road and into the club. As Jimmy walked through the entrance, he saw Catherine wanted a quick word with him as she beckoned him over to her.

"Boss, I'm running out of coat hangers."

Jimmy couldn't quite believe that as he has bought loads just a few months ago but at that precise moment, he had someone important to entertain. So it was a problem to be dealt with at a later time.

The next morning as he was doing all his checks, he concluded that Catherine was right. They were down to less than 100 coat hangers. He immediately took himself off to Dunelm and bought 200 more and spent the afternoon laminating new cloakroom tickets. *It was odd though*, he thought. He had several hundred hangers and then less than 100. It didn't make much sense.

Isabelle phoned again and borrowed a few bits. Jimmy reminded her what she owed. She promised to replace it all in the next few days. Jimmy actually thought to himself he hadn't seen her in several weeks and her mum had taken up what seemed to be permanent residence in his house. This would be the last thing he lent her until she had brought back all she owed. Enough was enough and he did not want to encounter Hannah's anger again.

That evening as everyone set about their tasks, Jimmy didn't take himself off immediately for his pint in the Anchor. He sat at a table on his own with a coffee waiting for Catherine to turn up, he had a few questions for her.

As Jimmy sat there with a coffee, Hannah approached.

"Good evening, Mr Harris, can I get you anything?"

"I'm all good, thank you."

Jimmy smiled at her as she rewiped the tables he'd rubbed down himself just a few hours before. He didn't know why but he was drawn to her, he was determined to remain professional though. He knew he was fighting it with every sinew in his body but he had to maintain that level of professionalism. There was no other option at the moment.

Plus inter staff relationships caused tension and never ended very well for everyone concerned. He had learnt that the hard way back in Parker's and as his nan would've said, 'once bitten, twice shy'.

Charlotte came in and ducked into the cloakroom to set up for work. Jimmy let her get completely settled in and then he approached her.

"I have replaced the hangers and there are now over 300. So tell me what constitutes a broken coat hanger?"

"Well, when they come back and there's no corresponding ticket, or the tickets are all frayed and knackered. I bin it."

"Eh? Can you explain that again please?"

"You know, boss, two tickets, etc."

"Are you telling me when the hanger doesn't have two tickets or the tickets are damaged you bin the whole hanger?"

"Yes, boss."

Jimmy stood there trying to digest that Charlotte was throwing away good hangers because the tickets were a bit screwed as Hannah walked out into the foyer. She placed one hand either side of Jimmy's waist and then reached into the cloakroom for the incident sheets from Friday night.

"Just going to write these up in the incident books, Jim."

"Thank you, that's much appreciated."

He was bit taken aback by how her touch on his waist had made his whole body feel and he had briefly totally lost his train of thought talking to Charlotte. As Hannah left, he managed to return to his conversation with Charlotte.

"From now on, don't throw the hangers away. Just place them on the floor in the corner and I'll replace the tickets."

"Ok, boss."

Jimmy was fully convinced she lived on another planet but the customers liked her and the other members of staff thought she was great fun. A few hangers lost were a very small consideration to pay when someone is as welcoming to customers as Charlotte was.

Come Monday morning and Jimmy arrived early at the club. He had listened to those around him, especially Hannah and he'd arranged for Michael, a local lock smith he knew, to change the bolts and locks on the front doors of the club. He could not go on funding the project upstairs. He wasn't sure if they all realised how embarrassing he thought it was that they came down and took his beer and his change. It was costing him a fortune.

Jimmy wanted to do his best by everyone but Isabelle was now in the category of taking the mickey. Jimmy knew it, and as much as he didn't want to enter into the silly games, he was now at a point where he felt he had to make a choice, and thus he had. The locks were duly changed. He handed out the new keys to the club keyholders and sat back waiting for the response. He had wanted to tell Isabelle in person but he had not seen her to do so.

The following Saturday morning, he didn't have to wait any longer. Jimmy was sat in High Town at the coffee cart enjoying a coffee with TJ in the late September sun. No sooner had they sat down at a table than Jimmy's phone started ringing.

"Does that thing ever stop?"

TJ looked at Jimmy as he took his phone out of his pocket. He looked at screen and it was Isabelle.

"I'd better get this."

Jimmy was not looking forward to this conversation but he knew he had to answer the call regardless. On the other end of the call, Isabelle went absolutely ballistic that she could not restock the pool hall from Jimmy's club. The phone call that accompanied it sealed the whole deal between them.

"What are you playing at? You've locked me out of the club!"

"You owe 10 1.5 litre bottles of Jack Daniel, 6 1.5 litre bottles of vodka, several bottles of tequila, God knows much Sambuca and at least 15 crates of beer. And on top of that, there is £850 worth of change owed, enough is enough. And that doesn't include what you owe at our home."

Jimmy knew he getting very angry and that was not going to help the situation, but he couldn't help himself. After putting up with so much for so long, it wasn't really surprising his temper was a little frayed. It was, in all honesty, a surprise something had not given before. Their relationship had always been quite lopsided but now it was just pure one-way traffic.

"Jimmy, be reasonable. I need it. I can't open without anything to sell. You know you'll get it back as soon as I can."

"Isabelle, you're using a lot of stock, you're not returning any of it and you're not contributing to the bills at home. Where's the money going?"

"Stuff, things you know."

Jimmy could hear Isabelle grasping at straws as she tried to figure out a response. Isabelle, on the other hand, was well aware that Jimmy did have a point whether she liked it or not.

"This isn't cutting it. I can't keep restocking your bar and paying every bill at home. I want to buy stuff and spend money on things but I can't because I'm funding your lifestyle."

"Fuck you, Jimmy."

With that, the call was ended. Jimmy let out a big sigh and put the phone down on the table.

"Sorry you had to listen to that."

"Don't worry about it. Trouble in paradise, is there?"

"Like you wouldn't believe. It's like my own personal nightmare."

Jimmy explained the whole sorry saga to TJ who sat and listened impassively. When Jimmy finished his tale of woe, he looked at TJ for even the slightest flicker of emotion.

"Not to say I told you so but I did warn you where this was going to go. It sounds like she's being pretty unreasonable but you did let her get away with it to begin with. I told you that you should've made strict ground rules for anything like this."

TJ had always been very level-headed and straight to the point on any issues like these. Jimmy figured it was his Northern upbringing, a spade is a spade and all that.

"You're right, you were right to begin with and of course you're still right. Now I've got to find a way of fixing it and quick before it gets silly."

"Sit her down and talk with her. She's probably angry with herself as well as at you. All these negative emotions and feelings are no good at all. You've got to nip them in the bud, and quick."

Jimmy nodded in agreement; he was well aware of the errors he had made. By trying to be kind he had made the whole situation worse. This was his own fault in many ways, he had helped create the situation.

After leaving TJ at the coffee cart, Jimmy went to meet his mum who had taken both the boys to a small breeds farm for the morning. He saw them before they saw him as his mum pushed them through the city in the double buggy. He approached them and greeted them both with a big hug.

"How was it, boys?"

He couldn't make full sense of their answer as they both excitedly tried to tell the story of their morning. The general gist he got was they loved it and they both now wanted a pet goat, which was not happening. Having a dog was quite enough.

"I've had Isabelle on the phone, she is not happy. I don't want to get involved, love, or take sides but couldn't you just give her the spirits?"

"It's not quite that simple. I'll sort it, so don't worry."

Having already retold the whole sorry saga to TJ, he wasn't in the mood to regale his mother with the same story as well. It didn't seem to get any better with each recollection.

"You better had, Jimmy. I don't want her stopping you, me or your dad from seeing the boys."

His mum looked at Jimmy with that worried look all mothers give their sons regardless of their age. Jimmy decided to change the subject to something more pleasing on a Saturday morning.

"Thanks for taking the boys today, Mum, they appear to have loved it."

"No worries, love. You alright with them from here? I've got a bit of shopping to do."

"Of course, say goodbye to nanny, boys."

The ensuing cuddles, hugs and giggles made Jimmy's heart melt. There's nothing quite like a connection between boys and their nanny.

He decided to take a stroll around the city with the boys to pass a few hours. It was a lovely day and quite frankly, he didn't fancy being couped up in the house all afternoon. An afternoon in the park with all that fresh air would do them all the world of good. Eventually, he wound up near the club and the pool hall. He pushed the push chair to the bottom of the stairs of the pool hall and rang Isabelle.

She didn't answer. So he text her instead. 'There's two little boys here to see you'.

About a minute later, Isabelle appeared on the stairs and both boys' faces lit up when they saw her. She to then had to try and make head or tail of the recounting of the small breed's farm but on top, she was hearing how daddy almost made the swing go over the top!

"I'd better get them home to your mum so I can get ready for work."

"Ok, thank you for bringing them to see me."

Jimmy had hoped it would break the ice between them and also thought they'd all like to see one another. Their working life did not need to encroach on their parenting roles.

"We should sit down tomorrow morning and have a good chat about everything."

"I think we should leave it a few days. Let everything calm down. Things said in anger cannot be taken back. You've told me that enough times, Jim."

Isabelle kissed the boys goodbye and made her way back up into the pool hall. Jimmy didn't like leaving things to fester but could clearly see Isabelle was in no mood to talk. On the walk home, he decided to leave the ball in her court.

The talks never materialised. The atmosphere at home was frosty and every time Jimmy even tried to start a conversation about anything, it was the wrong time, or Isabelle had something much more pressing she needed to be doing. In the end, Jimmy stopped asking. She had resolved to make this as uncomfortable and difficult for him as possible.

The following Friday after work, all the staff sat down for the usual post work beverage. The main topic of conversation was the upcoming Halloween and what the plan was this year. Everyone loved it, the costumes, the decorations, and all were throwing their ideas in about this year's theme. Gradually, as was always the case, everyone started drifting home and soon it was just Jimmy, Lee and Hannah.

Hannah was just checking the stock; Lee was investigating another pint—Jimmy swore he must have hollow legs—and Jimmy had just finished locking the safe up. Finally, Jimmy got to sit down with a drink, he felt like he'd been on his feet for hours.

"What about a Halloween pub crawl?"

"How do you mean?"

"Well, we pick a pub to start at, all dressed up and then we take everyone through several pubs before we end up here for the rest of the night. Each pub could have a special drink or cocktail you've got to drink but we end up with all the customers."

As soon as Lee stopped talking, he immediately finished another pint off and went to replenish his glass.

"I like it, we go round flyering anyway except this time, we'll take all the customers with us."

Hannah was very enthused by the idea and could clearly see the potential benefits even if it meant a bit of extra leg work.

"I think it's a brilliant idea, I'll get on it Monday. Great idea, buddy."

Jimmy too could see the benefits and was already working out how to pitch the idea to the other pubs.

After locking everyone out, Jimmy wandered home through the city and up the hill to go home. It was a pleasant morning to be strolling along. One day, he would take Hannah up on the offer a lift home, probably when it was raining, he thought to himself. As he approached his front door, the security lights came on and he could see exactly what he was doing. He produced his door key from his pocket but it did not fit in the lock. It was a new lock. *What the hell was going on?*

He phoned Isabelle who eventually answered after about five calls.

"Sorry to wake you but my keys don't work."

Jimmy suddenly realised just how much he needed to pee. Must have been habitual, walk home, go in and pee. Unfortunately, Jimmy's body had not realised he was still stood on the doorstep as it attempted to go into auto pilot mode!

"You don't live here anymore."

Before Jimmy could even reply, she had put the phone down on him. Absolutely dumbstruck, he stood on the doorstep just amazed. His only solace being that it least it wasn't raining that would've properly compounded his misery. *Guess hell does have no fury like a woman scorned*, he thought to himself.

He tried Isabelle's phone again but it went straight to voicemail, she had obviously turned it off. Jimmy then rang the doorbell, and then he rang it again, and again and eventually, Isabelle appeared at the door. She opened it but kept the chain on.

"What the hell's going on?"

"I said earlier *you* don't live here anymore, please stop ringing the doorbell."

Isabelle went to push the door shut not noticing Jimmy had placed his boot in between the door and the frame.

"Isabelle, I pay all the bills, the lease is in my name, it's 5am and I'm dying for the toilet. Just let me in, we can argue about this tomorrow."

Isabelle paused and thought for a moment. It was late and she didn't want to wake the children, or the neighbours up.

"Ok, you can stay tonight but after that you leave. Take your boot out so I can unchain the door." Jimmy did so. He half expected the door to just be pushed shut and locked but she did open it and let him into his home.

"We are most definitely talking about this in the morning, you are bang out of order."

Jimmy headed straight past her and made for the toilet at breakneck speed. He was determined he wasn't going to fully humiliate himself by pissing himself in front of her.

In the morning, Isabelle found Jimmy in the kitchen when she eventually got up. She could see he was angry but he'd locked her out of the club and so fair was fair in her book.

"Have you packed already?"

"No, and I have no intention of doing so. This is my home. I pay all the bills, I buy all the food, I pay the rent."

"I'll sort that out. I don't want to live under the same roof as you anymore."

"That we can sort. I'll help you find somewhere else to live."

"Jimmy, I'm staying, you are leaving. I don't want to see you every day. I don't want you in my life anymore. It's too much."

Isabelle started to cry. Then the crying became full on body sobbing. This out pouring of emotion had clearly been building for quite a time. Jimmy was not in the mood for her histrionics.

"SIT DOWN."

Jimmy shouted. This shocked Isabelle into doing so as he was not one for shouting and her crying stopped immediately.

"Right. Fuck it. You want me out of here, no problem but it will take a while. Do you think I am enjoying this experience? You're making my life a living hell."

Jimmy stared out of the kitchen window and down onto the flood plain. The downcast dreary weather seem to be fully taking its cue from his mood.

"You will also have to go see the letting agents and take over the lease and all the utilities. If that's what you want, then fine I give up."

"How long will it take?"

"A few weeks normally."

"Ok, two weeks and you no longer live here; I don't want you in my life anymore in any way."

"No problem. Do you think I want to live like this? Live with you being like this? I've also had enough. We'll go see the letting agents on Monday morning. Now give me a key, I have things to do. And I want all the stock replaced in the club this week."

Isabelle reached over to the kitchen side and handed Jimmy a key. Jimmy stood up and walked out of the kitchen. He was incandescent with rage but could take no more of her puerile behaviour. It was also no good to be walking round in his own home feeling like he was walking on eggshells. There was no way he was ever going to get that stock back but he did enjoy firing that over the bows.

Jimmy had decided to get a flat. Nice and simple and all he needed. He wanted a two-bedroom flat so he could put bunk beds in one bedroom so the boys could stay over. The lease on the house had been signed over to Isabelle but her mum had to be the guarantor for the rent. She'd asked Jimmy but he had flat out refused. Jimmy had no idea how she was going to afford it but that was her problem to deal with not his.

Having seen three flats and been given a tour of each, he had chosen his new home. It was quite a spacious two-bedroom flat with off street parking and had everything he needed. He had decided Isabelle could keep everything in the house, quite frankly he didn't want another argument. He just took his clothes and from there he would start again. A fresh start.

It was just a royal pain that he was flat out at work as well. There quite simply wasn't enough time in the day to fit everything in. He hastily moved his clothes to his new home and pressed on with his work commitments.

Having gone around to 6 or 7 pubs, Jimmy had the Halloween pub crawl sorted out. The sheets for everyone joining in had been printed, they could fill them in as they went along. The pub crawl was to begin in the Anchor and that is where he waited for everyone to turn up dressed as Dracula. He had arranged for a few members of staff to meet him there to help run the event as smoothly as possible.

Initially, he had hoped for 20 or 30 people to be involved but he was amazed to find that come the start time there were over 80 people all dressed up and raring to go. He'd got Charlotte on hand with a camera and was making sure that plenty of photos would be going on all the social medias.

"This is going great."

TJ he approached Jimmy and at first, he didn't recognise him as he was fully kitted out as Freddie Krueger and looked awesome.

"It's going a lot better than I expected. Do you mind if I stand on a bench to get this rabble moving?"

"Be my guest, Dracula."

Jimmy stood up on a bench in the beer garden and welcomed everybody. He looked quite impressive stood there as Dracula with his cape blowing in the breeze. He handed out the sheets that everyone participating was to use to get stamps in every pub. He then handed out a few charity collection buckets so they could raise some money for the local hospice as they meandered through the city. With that, the fun began.

Jimmy spent much of the next three hours corralling zombies, ghosts and various other creatures of the night through the city pubs and eventually, he made it back to the sanctuary of the club. He collected the collection boxes from everybody and secured them in the office; the club was still collecting at the door and the bar and would do so all night. It was for a good cause after all.

Andy was playing the usual Halloween specials and Jimmy was going to chalk this one up as an especially good Halloween. As the last of the revellers left, Jimmy felt a distinct sense of accomplishment. He collected all the donations and after Hannah had finished cashing up, they sat down and counted it all. The people in the city had been very generous and they had in total raised over £1500.

"You should contact the papers and let them know. You always get bad press so it's about time you got some good."

"That's a good idea. Charlotte got some amazing pictures tonight, perhaps we could send them some of those as well."

"Can't do any harm. I think I raised a few quid just by shaving my head."

George had really thrown himself into the event and even shaved his head to be Uncle Fester. The remaining staff all sat around and drank the remaining few pints of the Ghoul Juice that Jimmy had made. It was surprisingly palatable considering it was 75% Barnstormer cider!

Monday morning that is exactly what Jimmy did. After explaining the whole story, the Journal was only too happy to run the story. Their usual headlines were pretty boring non-events anyway and they knew it. 'Pothole in road', 'Cow escapes farm', 'Pam clocks up 50 years working in the same bakery'.

Come Thursday, it was emblazoned on the front page of the newspaper. 'Halloween Pub Crawl Raises £1562', accompanied by pictures from all the pubs and many of the people who participated. Jimmy bought two copies, one to read and one to keep as a memento. For once, it was a good piece of press about the club.

Jimmy often thought that pubs and clubs never got the recognition they do for fund raising in the community. Whether it be hosting charity nights, by having collection tins on the bars or by donating things to charity events. It was never quite sensationalist enough or headline grabbing. That was something he would raise at the next pub watch meeting. It was about time they all started getting better press coverage.

Chapter 12
Snow Day

That November started out very mild and then turned incredibly bitter very quickly. The wind chill was awful and Jimmy spent a lot of time worrying about keeping the club warm so people wouldn't freeze to death. On the flip side, on a Friday and Saturday night as soon as enough bodies came in, the temperature soared and he had to try and cool it down. It was a constant balancing act.

As December 2015 began, so did the snow. To start with little flurries with nothing really settling or sticking. It all just turned into that horrible brown slush. Then came Thursday, 3 December 2015. A day that would forever be etched in everyone memories who worked that day as Snow Day.

As Jimmy walked down into the city to go to work just before 5pm, the snow began. By the time Jimmy had arrived at the club, there was nearly half a foot of snow on the ground. This time, it was sticking and the city had ground to a standstill as roads became blocked up and drivers lost their heads from waiting in the queues. Hannah was already there setting up when he entered the club.

"Is there any point in us opening tonight?"

"We're here so we meres well."

Jimmy also didn't really fancy walking back home at that moment. He was completely frozen and had intentions to sit by a radiator and thaw out for an hour at least. By 8pm though, they hadn't had a single sole come in and the streets were deserted. Jimmy stood just outside the front doors having a cigarette. The snow always seems to mute all the noise so that everything is perfectly quiet.

Jimmy's phone buzzed and he took it out. It was TJ; they were shutting early at the Anchor and he was wondering if the club was open. Jimmy replied it was and would be staying so.

That pattern repeated itself several times over the next few hours until almost everywhere else had shut and Jumping Jacks was full of staff from other venues.

It was a most peculiar sight to see so many work shirts and no one else, no normal customers at all.

Jimmy knew that a few of these places had some quite heated rivalries but none more so than Diamonds door staff and Klimax's door staff. They worked for rival door companies and they hated one another. A few of the lads were already in bad moods having lost out on a shift with Christmas coming and presents to buy.

It had just gone 12:30am when TJ handed Jimmy a pint. He'd been busy playing pool with Gary and a few others from the Anchor.

"You keeping an eye on those door guys?"

TJ was sure Jimmy was but he also wanted to reassure him that he was as well. A friendly reminder that he wasn't on his own if this went completely Pete Tong.

"Yes, mate, think I might call last orders at…"

Jimmy never got to finish the sentence as the brawl erupted right before his eyes.

"Christ!"

Jimmy walked over to the mass of bodies brawling and started pulling people apart. It was utter chaos. It took over 5 minutes to throw out everyone who had been involved. Jimmy rested for a minute in the foyer, his hands on his knees, gasping for breath. He was certainly glad Gary and TJ had got stuck in with him otherwise he'd still have been fighting.

"You ok, Jim?"

Hannah entered the foyer and could see Jimmy was completely out of breath but other than that he looked in one piece.

"I'm all good. You?"

"I'm fine, I've brought you the radio. I did radio it through so the CCTV guys know what's happening."

From within the foyer, they could hear noises growing louder outside. Jimmy opened the front door. He could see the door staff were throwing snowballs at one another and that was enough to see them start to fight again in the snow. In his peripheral vision, he could see the blue lights of the police four by fours turning up as their blue lights bounced off the buildings near by announcing their arrival before he could actually see them. Jimmy and TJ headed over to brawl and attempted to separate people.

Gary stayed watching the front door with Hannah. The police vehicles slid to a stop and officers started running to join in as well. Absolute mayhem ensued. Hannah watched on as Jimmy got wiped out by one of the fighters falling over and going straight through the back of his legs. There was well over a foot of snow on the floor and it was still falling.

It took 15 minutes to split the brawling parties apart and by this point, Hannah had called time in the club and the remaining revellers had left. Everyone was told to go their separate ways and very forcefully told that licensing would be round to see them that weekend. Jimmy was helped back to club by TJ. He'd taken a big fall and it had not gone well for him.

Jimmy sat down at the bar in the club and TJ poured everyone a drink. They had well and truly earned it.

"That was fun."

Jimmy was trying work out quite what he'd done to his back. *Can you bruise an ass?* He thought to himself. Hannah reappeared from the office and handed Jimmy a cushion to sit on. Everyone laughed and Gary patted Jimmy on the shoulder. There was suddenly a lot of banging at the front door. Jimmy eased himself up and hobbled over to see who it was.

As Jimmy opened the door, he saw the reflective coat of a police officer.

"Evening again, Jimmy. We've got a little problem."

"What's up?"

Jimmy was praying it wasn't another fight as he wasn't in a fit state to help stop another one. He was just beginning to notice how cold his feet and his fingers were as the temperature returned to his extremities as they thawed out.

"I've lost the keys to the car."

"The police car?"

"Yes."

Jimmy laughed as the officer pointed at the stranded four by four in the middle of the street.

"Sorry, it's not funny but it is. GUYS, GIVE ME HAND A MINUTE."

Jimmy called back into the building. Everyone begrudgingly trouped back outside into the cold. Between the two officers and Jimmy's group, they strategically went along searching in the snow until eventually Gary found the keys.

"Thank God for that."

The one officer gladly took possession of the keys.

"Would've been quite funny at the police station if you'd turned up without a car."

Gary commented to amusing chuckles all round. The two embarrassed officers got into their car and slid off down the road, sprayed snow every time they accelerated.

Everyone was absolutely freezing and hurried back inside as quickly as possible once the police had left, stomping shoes outside to remove any snow clinging to them.

"What a bloody night."

TJ wandered back into the club. All of them huddling around a radiator just to get warm. If anyone had walked in, it would've made them laugh to see radiators around the club covered in random clothes and a rather strange group sat drinking next to another radiator. With a few drinks and the boiler cranked up, it took about 20 minutes for everyone to start warming up.

"How's your back?"

"It's alright, it's more my ass to be honest."

This caused a little ripple of laughter amongst those present. Jimmy was not expecting any sympathy and he certainly wasn't getting any.

"How am I gonna get home?"

Hannah lived quite a few miles outside of the city and there was no way she could drive it not with the amount of snow on the roads. It would have been far dangerous and simply not worth the risk.

"You can stay at mine if want. I'll sleep in the boys' bunk beds."

"Thank you, Jimmy, are you sure?"

"Yes, no problem at all."

Jimmy poured everyone another drink noticing he could now fully feel his fingers once more.

As they walked home together, Jimmy was very conscious of the situation he had put himself in. It took longer than usual as Jimmy and Hannah tried their hardest not to fall flat on their faces in the snow. Eventually, they made it to Jimmy's flat. He unlocked the front door and ushered Hannah in out of the cold. He took her coat and hung it up. He then showed her through to the front room.

It was quite a large room but the most noticeable thing about Jimmy's front room were the boxes. Although, he'd lived there for nearly two months, he had still not really sorted the furniture. He had a sofa and a television but everything else remained in the boxes which they had arrived in.

"You live like this?"

Hannah was struggling to take in what she was seeing. It resembled a warehouse.

"I haven't really had much time to build it all."

Jimmy appeared with a set of pyjamas for Hannah and a towel.

"Here you go. Not perfect but at least dry and clean."

"Thank you, where's the bathroom?"

"Down the hall second on the right. Would you like a cup of tea?"

"Yes, that would be nice, I'm impressed you have cups."

Hannah exited the room and made her way to the bathroom.

Jimmy made the cups of tea and went and got changed. Hannah returned to the front room to find Jimmy sat on the sofa in his batman pyjamas and a dressing gown.

"Did you find everything that you needed?"

"Yes, thank you. Can I hang my clothes on the radiators?"

"Pass them here, I'll put them in the tumble dryer for you, they'll be perfectly dry by morning."

Jimmy stood up and took her clothes to the kitchen and the aforementioned tumble dryer. As he re-entered the front room, he smiled at Hannah who still looked dumbfounded anyone could live amongst boxes like this. She did like the fact he had a load of books stacked on top of a box that apparently contained a bookcase. He had everything to make it a home, that's the beauty of on-line shopping, he just hadn't found the time to build half of it. He'd promised himself repeatedly he'd do it after work but most days when he got in, he just wanted to sit down and relax.

"Jim, this is a bit awkward, isn't it?"

Hannah placed her cup of tea on one of the boxes that seemed to be doubling up as a coffee table.

"I was going to put on some Barry White and light some candles but I don't really think I'm in the best shape for dancing."

Jimmy sat down on the sofa next to her. Not too close, he didn't want to be invading her personal space, but he also wasn't sitting on the arm of the sofa insinuating that she had some sort of contagious disease.

"That would've been very cheesy. What are we doing, Jim? You like me, I like you. Neither of us is attached. What's the issue?"

"It's not that simple, is it? We work together, or moreover, you work for me. I've always had a really strict rule about this sort of thing."

Jimmy took a sip of his cup of tea and turned to face her on the sofa. They just sat there looking at one another. Nothing else seemed to matter in the world. Jimmy was finding it very odd to have such a connection with another person. It was uncomfortable but it was also a feeling he quite liked.

He'd realised that much when she held his waist to duck into the cloakroom. He was adamant she could almost read his mind. If she leant over and kissed him, he would have reciprocated.

"Fine, I quit. If that's the only issue you have, I'll just find another job."

"That doesn't help, does it. You love working at the club and you're amazing at your job. Plus, I'd have to find someone to replace you and so I'd just end up working all the time and wouldn't get to see you. And what if we don't work? Where does that leave us?"

Jimmy sighed heavily and put his cup on the makeshift coffee table. Hannah got up from the sofa and finished her cup of tea. She leant over and kissed Jimmy on the cheek.

"Goodnight, Jimmy. Which bedroom should I take?"

"First on the right. Goodnight, Hannah."

Jimmy watched her walk away and down the hallway. He heard the bedroom door shut and the light switch click as she put the light on. Jimmy sat on the sofa finishing his cup of tea. This was definitely not going to help the sexual tension building between them. He thought of a hundred different things he should've said or done. There was a part of him very proud of his resolve and another part of him that just wanted to punch himself in the face.

As Jimmy was about to get up, he heard the bedroom door open and Hannah appeared in the doorway to the front room. At first she said nothing as they just looked at one another.

"Jimmy, I'm not sure what the etiquette is but I'm damn sure if you don't join me in this bedroom in the next minute, I'm going to throttle you on the sofa."

Maybe that was the punch in the face he had been waiting for. He didn't need asking twice that was for sure.

As Jimmy sat at home the following Monday evening, the doorbell went. He rarely got visitors, primarily as he hadn't told many people where he lived. The only people who ever came round were his parents and the boys. He opened the door to find Hannah with Lee, George, Catherine, and Sebastian all stood there.

"Good evening. What can I do for you all?"

"Well, Mr Harris, it has been brought to our attention that you have a lot of furniture that is currently in boxes."

"That's very kind of you, guys, but there really is no need. I'll get round to it."

Jimmy felt slightly embarrassed about being the subject of his furniture being common knowledge with everyone and also being the recipient of such attention.

"Well, we're here now so we meres well put a few bits together for you."

Lee walked straight into the flat followed by everyone else. Jimmy noticed Lee was carrying a bag full of cider so he was in for the long haul.

As Hannah passed Jimmy last of all, she leant over and whispered in his ear.

"If you think I'm spending comfy evenings here watching movies surrounded by boxes, you've got another thing coming."

She carried on past him with everyone else and Jimmy shut the front door. As Jimmy walked down the hallway, he could hear Lee tell everyone.

"I didn't know he lived so close to me; I can pop round more often now."

Great, thought Jimmy to himself and shook his head. For all his reservations about the situation that was thrust upon him, Jimmy had to admit he actually enjoyed spending an evening with them all. He had always kept himself at arm's length to everyone who worked for him but perhaps that was something that needed to change. He was also incredibly pleased to have furniture and that his home now resembled a home more than a warehouse.

As midnight approached, he watched them all pile into Hannah's car and off they went. About 45 minutes later, the doorbell went and Hannah was back at his door.

"If this carries on, I'll have to get you a parking permit!"

Jimmy always hated New Years' Eve parties. They were always such an anti-climax. Everyone hung around, waited for midnight, sang a song and then either got hammered or started fighting. The staff from other venues could also be great fun to deal with as they finished around 1am, made their way to the clubs and proceeded to drink at breakneck speed for a few hours as they attempted to catch up with the revellers who had been partying all night.

As the midnight hour approached this year, everything had been relatively tame. Mostly people just enjoying themselves, they had refused a few people who had timed their run for the midnight celebrations a bit early and tanked out.

The internal doors opened and Lee appeared.

"Andy is ready for the countdown; everything is set and he's just wanting to check that you want all the balloons to be dropped at midnight."

"Yes, please, and remind him to announce that the bar shuts from 11:55 to 12:05 so the staff can see in the New Year as well."

Jimmy stopped pacing up and down in the foyer and relaxed for a second.

"No problem."

Lee ducked back into the building. Jimmy listened as the announcement was made again. Just a few minutes later, he was listening to the New Years' countdown from in the foyer, he could hear everyone joining in, "Ten, nine, eight…two, one. Happy new year!" And then the sound of balloons blowing up. The bells continued over the sound system.

Jimmy had worked out a long time ago back in Parker's that Hell's Bells by AC/DC had the same timings as the bell on the New Years' Eve broadcasts, so it fed lovely into being the first song of the year. He insisted on very little from the DJ regarding the makeup of the music but that was the only thing he demanded every year.

Almost as soon as a few staff and revellers had begun shaking hands, Jimmy heard the city radio go off. It was the Ferrers just up the road, as Jimmy stepped out into the street, he could hear the commotion up the road. He couldn't quite see what was happening but it did not sound good.

"SEB, LEE. Front door quick."

Jimmy yelled over the club radio and immediately started running up the road towards the Ferrers.

"On our way."

As he got closer, he could see several people fighting including the landlord, Bobby Atkins. There was glass all over the pavement outside and it was not a pretty sight. He heard a loud bang as he watched a lad punch his hand through one of the ornate windowpanes at the front of the pub. Jimmy dove in and began separating people. He glanced back down the road and saw Lee and Seb weren't far off joining in.

Jimmy grabbed the lad who had smashed the window before he could do anymore damage. They hit the deck and Jimmy was pretty glad he was stone cold sober as this muppet could brawl.

Jimmy got him locked down and held him tight, he wasn't not letting him get back up until the police arrived. It was New Year's Eve so Jimmy was shocked that they arrived within 3 minutes. As Jimmy lay on the floor, he could see the melee was slowing down greatly. Seb and Lee were keeping the main protagonists far apart.

"You ok, Jim?"

"Yeah, I'm ok."

Jimmy was trying his best to reassure his guys he was fine and to keep separating the others who were trying to fight.

"Let fucking go."

"Not a chance, pal, struggling will make it worse."

Two officers ran to Jimmy who was still struggling away on the floor.

"You got him?"

Jimmy was relieved as he handed over the man to the custody of the police. Having given his details to an officer so he could give a proper statement later on, he looked around to check everyone was ok. Sebastian had handing over someone to the police and Lee stood chatting with an officer.

"Thank you, Jimmy, that was getting crazy."

"Bobby, what was that about?"

The landlord of the Ferrers, Bobby Atkins, had made a bee line for Jimmy as soon as the police were on the scene.

"Four or five lads without tickets trying to get in. What happened to you?"

Jimmy looked down at his suit and could see why Bobby was looking at him in such a way. His suit was covered in blood, as were his hands. Apart from that, he had come out unscathed somehow even though he was rolling around on the road. Luckily, it was a dry night so he wasn't soaked as well.

"It was the prick who put the window through. He must have cut himself on the pane getting his arm out."

Jimmy gathered his team and headed back to the club. They all needed a bit of a breather after that.

"You can't wear that inside, Jim."

Lee was referring to Jimmy's blood caked attire.

"It wouldn't be the best look on the door. I've got some spare clothes out the back. You can borrow those."

Half an hour later, after cleaning up and getting changed, Jimmy reappeared from the office. Whilst grateful for the clothes, Jimmy now felt horribly under dressed. Gone was his lovely suit and in its place were a pair of jogging bottoms and white t-shirt that were massively too big for him. He looked like a very bad Eminem impersonator.

"Happy New Year."

Hannah came over and gave him a kiss on the cheek and a hug.

"I couldn't find you at New Year's and then I heard what happened. Are you ok?"

"I'm fine but think I might hide at a table for the rest of the night."

"I'll grab you a drink and bring it over."

"Get one for yourself and join me. I've just got a say happy new year to a few people so give me 10 minutes."

Jimmy wandered off into the throbbing mass of the club and she could see him shaking hands with people; quite a few were pointing out his attire to him, it was unusual to not see him in a suit of some kind. She watched him mingling and making sure everyone was having a good time. *How can he just flip a switch and do that?* she wondered. She took herself off to the bar to get some drinks for them.

After sorting a few issues on the bar and making sure everyone had enough change, Hannah went and found Jimmy. He had finished his tour of duty around the building and gone and sat at his usual table. She was pleased to be spending time with him even if he still insisted that at work they must give the impression of just being friends.

The staff Christmas party was always fun. It was always held in the first few weeks of January as it was just easier for everyone to come as the club could be shut for a couple of days to allow everyone to come and everyone who came had the chance to recover the next day. This time, Jimmy had organised go karting for them followed by a meal.

As they all walked into Mega Kart, the receptionist did a double take. They ranged from small and petite to massive and enormous. She knew that they were in for an interesting afternoon. After they'd done the briefings, the duty manager approached Jimmy.

"Good afternoon, Mr Harris. I don't believe I'm going to have race suits to fit some of the bigger members of your party. Will they sign disclaimers and race in just their normal clothes?"

"We had anticipated that and yes, they will."

"Also some of your party might be better getting their suits from the children's section."

Having made sure everyone had watched the instructional video and handed over all relevant disclaimers, he showed everyone through to the changing rooms.

By the time everyone was into their karts, it did resemble the start line of Mario Kart. Jimmy was still pushing Lee and Sebastian down into their karts when the duty manager approached him.

"Are they in ok?"

"They're in fine but it's getting them out I'm worried about."

Jimmy left the lads, put his own helmet on, and made his way over to his kart. He was laughing so hard he steamed up his own visor.

As Jimmy zoomed around in his kart, trying his hardest not to embarrass himself, he could see who was who by the speed of their kart. The power to weight ratio was affecting some of the lads as their karts were easily accelerated past by some of the others who were a lot lighter. He came up behind Sebastian and decided to go round the outside heading into a corner.

Jimmy had totally misjudged how much speed Seb was carrying, and just how brave Seb actually was. As they went through the corner, Seb's kart simply couldn't grip the surface and within a second, the two of them were well and truly wedged in the tyre wall on the outside of the corner.

The two of them were stuck in their karts and couldn't do a thing as the rest of the staff drove by offering all sorts of hand signals and words of support. They waved back as politely as they could.

The marshals eventually arrived and freed the pair of them but Jimmy was suffering from a shooting pain in his right wrist. He informed one of the marshals and his kart was pulled safe from the track as he walked back to the medical room. Once there, it became immediately apparent that Jimmy had broken his arm and his wrist was screwed.

By the time the rest of the staff had finished racing and got changed, Jimmy had made his way into the foyer to meet them. His right arm was heavily strapped up. The duty manager was walking with him.

"Jimmy, you have to go to A and E."

For the umpteenth time, the duty manager was insisting Jimmy took further medical treatment. Jimmy was having none of it.

"I will later but I've looked forward to this day for a long time and I'm not going to miss it. Don't worry, your medical care has been superb. I won't being suing you."

"I saw you weren't on track. What the hell have you done?"

George asked staring at Jimmy's arm.

"He's broken his arm."

"I'm fine, a few beers and I won't feel a thing, plus I've already paid for the meal."

It was clear to all that he would not be heading to hospital anytime soon so it was just much easier to let him get on with it. At different points, they'd all seen him patch himself up and refuse medical treatment for various ailments, at least this time he wasn't sewing a wound up.

Sat in accident and emergency the next morning with a throbbing arm and a massively swollen hand, Jimmy really did feel that this year had not started exactly as he had planned. Still he was soon straightened out, plastered up and sent on his way. Six weeks in a cast when he had so much to be getting on with was not ideal.

That afternoon, he dropped his suit from New Years' Eve off at the dry cleaners. Hopefully, they could get all the blood out otherwise he'd have to get a new one. He dropped it in and made his way to the Anchor for a pint, he'd arranged to bump into Hannah there sometime after 7pm. These clandestine meetings were quite exciting he thought as he admired his new arm accessory.

He was also trying to get used to having his watch on his left wrist. It felt most unusual but he was sure he would be used to it in a few days.

Jimmy got himself a pint in the Anchor and went and sat outside. Isabelle was there as well with some friends. He gave her a wave and she reciprocated. Hannah came and joined him as did TJ.

"I heard you fucked up go karting, you ok?"

"Yes, I'm fine."

"He wouldn't go hospital though, TJ. He insisted that he stay out all night and he only went the next day as it had swelled up."

TJ gave a wry smile at Hannah.

"Many years ago, we went paint balling and you may have noticed he's slightly competitive. Well, somehow in the one game, he shattered his jaw. He wouldn't go then either, spent the whole night drinking through a straw just so he wouldn't miss out."

"You are an idiot sometimes."

Jimmy flushed a slight shade of red but he knew it was all true.

Chapter 13
Suits You, Sir!

Jimmy was lying in bed with Hannah when his phone rang. It was from a private number and he normally ignored those calls but this time, he didn't. Something told him he should answer it.

"Good morning, Jimmy here."

"Good morning. Is that Mr Jimmy Harris?"

It was a lady on the other end of the phone and Jimmy didn't recognise her voice at all.

"Yes, yes, it is. How can I help you?"

"Mr Harris, this PC Green from West Mercia police. Could you hand yourself into the local station preferably today please? We have a few questions we would like to ask you as a matter of urgency."

"Yes, of course. What is this about please?"

"Hand yourself in today and we can discuss the matter when you get here."

"Should I bring a lawyer?"

Jimmy was starting to get a bit nervous about how the phone call was unfolding. He couldn't think of anything specific he had done to warrant having to go to the police station. Normally, he knew if he had messed up but this had caught him completely off guard.

"That is up to you, Sir, when you get here present yourself at the desk and ask for myself."

With that, PC Green had hung up, leaving Jimmy to scratch his head.

"What was that about?"

"You know as much as I do, Hannah. It was the police asking me to hand myself in. Suppose I'd best get up and go and find out."

Jimmy dressed smart but casually and walked into the city. He declined Hannah's offer a lift down to the city as he figured the walk might help him figure out what exactly was going on.

He arrived at the police station and lit a cigarette whilst he stood outside. He knew these things could take a while and he wasn't sure when his next opportunity would be for a cigarette; he suppressed the idea of having two in case he managed to flare his cough up. He didn't want to be coughing all the way through an interview. He made his way in and up to the counter. The desk sergeant immediately engaged with him.

"How can I help you, Sir?"

"Morning, I'm Jimmy Harris. PC Green has asked to see me."

"Take a seat, Sir. I'll let her know that you're here."

The desk sergeant made a few notes and he picked up the telephone nearest him.

Jimmy took a seat in the waiting area. He knew he could never prove it but he had always been quite sure that the police were trained to leave you waiting for a long time so you would get nervous. Unlike in casinos, in here there were clocks everywhere to constantly remind you how slowly time was passing. The first few times he had fallen into that trap. Now he was very aware of the game and actively practised staying cool, calm and collected. Just ride it out and they'd get to you soon enough.

The door to police reception area opened and a young PC stood there. She looked straight at Jimmy.

"Mr Harris?"

"Yes, I am."

"Good, thank you for coming in so swiftly. Follow me please."

"Am I under arrest?"

"Not yet, Mr Harris."

PC Green held the door open to the inner sanctum of the police station for him and showed him into an interview room. Jimmy noticed she flicked the sign to show the room was now in use.

"Please take a seat and I will be back in 2 minutes."

Jimmy sat in the interview room still none the wiser as to why he was there. He figured he'd be put out of his misery soon enough. *What a sterile room*, he thought as he observed his new surroundings. The door to the room opened and

PC Green returned clutching a large brown paper bag. She sat down opposite Jimmy, put the bag by her feet, and turned the interview recording machine on.

"It is 11:25am, 5 January 2016. PC Harris interviewing Jimmy Harris. Mr Harris is not under caution but has been made aware of his rights."

Jimmy thought that was interesting at least. He wasn't sure why he was there and hadn't been informed of any rights.

"Mr Harris, did you take a suit to be dry cleaned recently at SpeedyCo Dry Cleaners in High Town?"

"Yes, I did."

The PC reached down into the paper bag and produced Jimmy's suit which was now sealed in a plastic bag and had an evidence label on it.

"Is this that suit?"

Jimmy looked carefully at the suit and concluded that it most definitely was his.

"Yes, it is."

Jimmy was eyeing up his suit up in the bag. In fact he couldn't take his eyes of it. Had he confiscated drugs that night and inadvertently left them in a pocket? He soon dismissed that idea adamant he hadn't.

"Right, we were contacted by the dry cleaners who informed us that this suit has an extraordinary amount of blood on it. We have taken a sample from two areas of the suit jacket and one from the trousers. Our forensics team have confirmed that it is blood and that it is human blood. How do you explain the presence of such an amount of blood?"

PC Green placed the suit in the middle of the interview table and Jimmy breathed a sigh of relief. Suddenly, he had some context for this situation. It finally made sense.

"Are you telling me you have cut holes in my suit?"

Jimmy went to pick up the evidence bag to have a closer look at his suit but he was quickly admonished for such an act.

"Don't touch the evidence, Sir. And could you answer the question please?"

"Very simply. As the dry cleaners were aware, there was a fight at the Ferrers on New Years' Eve. I, along with my door team, restrained the aggressors until the police arrived and arrested them."

"And how do you explain the blood? Mr Harris, the suit is drenched in human blood."

PC Green was really trying to press the point about the blood.

"Certainly. The one idiot, who I ended up restraining, decided in his infinite wisdom to punch one of the pub's windows. He put his arm straight through the front window and in the process lacerated it. Then he managed to get his claret all over my nice suit as I restrained him. How do I go about getting compensation for you ruining my suit?"

PC Green was now nowhere near as comfortable as she had been earlier. She looked at Jimmy, then at the suit, she then stood up.

"Interview suspended at 11:30am. Excuse me, Mr Harris, for a couple of minutes. I'm just going to talk to my superior officer. Don't touch the suit."

With that, she exited the room. Jimmy sat looking at his suit in the bag. *What an absolute faff,* he thought to himself and a waste of a good suit. He couldn't believe this was all caused because he'd done a good deed.

After what seemed an eternity, PC Green returned to the interview room although now she was accompanied by Inspector Thomas.

"Jimmy, how are you?"

Inspector Thomas greeted Jimmy as if he was long lost friend as he entered the room. He put his hand out to shake Jimmy's hand. Jimmy showed him the cast and shook the inspector's hand with his left one instead.

"What happened to your arm?"

The inspector looked at the cast protruding from Jimmy's coat sleeve and covering most of his hand.

"Went go karting and got run over by a giant."

"That sounds painful. I believe there's been a few unfortunate mistakes and you have found yourself here. A communication breakdown, Jim, is what this is."

"You've cut holes in my suit, Inspector. A simple phone call and this could've been prevented."

The inspector went into his jacket pocket.

"I've got a compensation form here, Jim. If you fill it in, we will reimburse you for the suit. You just need to drop it into the desk sometime soon."

He handed Jimmy the compensation forms which ran to several pages.

"Thank you, Inspector. Is this matter concluded, can I go?"

Jimmy have had quite enough of dealing with the police for one day.

"Of course, Jimmy, make sure you fill that form in and get it back to me ASAP. As soon as it arrives on my desk, I will deal with it. PC Green will show you out, and thanks for coming in so swiftly today."

Everyone stood up and the inspector held the door open for everyone. Jimmy followed PC Green down the corridor.

"I'm really sorry, Mr Harris, I was only following orders."

PC Green looked mortified at what had transpired.

"That is why you shouldn't follow orders blindly. Many people in this building have hidden agendas. Agendas for which they will throw people, like you, happily under the bus for until they get the result they want. Goodbye, PC Green."

Jimmy strode out into the winter's sunshine. He lit a cigarette and headed into the city to get a coffee, it felt like he had properly earned one.

Jimmy found the six weeks he was in a cast pretty annoying and frustrating. It seemed to hinder him in everything he wanted to do and he was grateful when it was finally removed. Although, his arm ached for a few days afterwards, it soon eased and he could resume his normal duties. He detested having to ask for favours but there had been no real other option. Now he was back and fighting fit, he spent the next few days giving the club a complete deep clean and making himself feel that everything ship shape.

To be honest, the whole team had pulled together and done an amazing job. Lee had even come in and helped Jimmy with the deliveries and the line cleaning. As a team, he was very proud of all of them. What could've been a major headache of nearly seven weeks and had turned into Jimmy getting to know them all a little more. It was an insight he wouldn't have had without the broken arm.

"You've always been absolutely useless at delegating, Jim, you're like a control freak who can't let go."

Jimmy had only popped into the Anchor for a few beers and a chance to relax not to receive a lecture off TJ. There was a time and place for lectures and this was not it.

"I'm not that bad. I give everyone plenty to do and let them get on with it."

"Bollocks, you give everyone plenty to do as you stand there, looking over their shoulder, checking they've done everything right. Or your version of right."

TJ was right to a point. Jimmy did like everything done to his standards. He knew he could be quite exacting and a bit of a nit-picker but that's because he set the standards and he expected everyone else to adhere to those standards.

"It's not always a bad thing, Jim, but you could help instil more confidence in them sometimes by leaving them to their own devices. Let them use their initiatives."

Jimmy took another swig of his beer as he contemplated his friend's advice. He spotted Hannah walking through the pub and she gave him a little wave. TJ also spotted Hannah as he followed Jimmy's line of sight to see who he waved at.

"You're meeting that girl again then. That's about the fourth or fifth time now."

"She's been helping me with a lot recently, I've had to delegate."

"I'll bet she has. What have I always told you about getting involved with members of staff?"

"It's not like that. It's ever since I've had a broken arm, she's been a real help."

Jimmy felt like he was pleading his case to the Judge, Jury, and Executioner.

"Broken arm, broken heart, what's the difference, eh lad?"

TJ stood up and pressed the button to turn the outside heater back on for their table.

"Do you want another pint?"

"Hannah's got me one, she's getting you one too."

"How helpful."

TJ sat back down and eyed his friend as a wry smile crept across his face.

A few weeks later, Jimmy was sat in his office just passing the time of day when he received an email. He had always been aware that the police licensing department had a vendetta against him. Combined with the council licensing departments efforts to thwart him, he knew he quite often walked a tight rope line and his situation was precarious at best. The email he had received was simply marked REVIEW. *Here we go again*, thought Jimmy.

The email contained a very brief statement.

Jumping Jacks is to have its premises licence reviewed. This has been brought about by an accumulation of incidents. These incidents ended with a mass fight in Fourth Street. All details are in the attached documents. This review is being conducted on the grounds of the prevention of crime and disorder.

It was signed off by both Mr Lewis and Mr Scott.

Jimmy read through all the documents. Somehow they had 43 incidents, including the Fourth Street one, between Jan 2016 and March 2016 logged against the club. Having digested all the information, he wrote down his thoughts and called Mr Scott.

"Hello, Mr Scott here."

"Good afternoon, Mr Scott, It's Jimmy Harris here."

"Ah, Mr Harris, I've been expecting your call. Before you go off at me, let me just say that this review is being led by the police and we at the council are just supporting their application. If you resolve it with them, then you will resolve it with us too."

"So you actually have nothing against the club, you just backed them up to make it look like it's a weightier document than it actually is?"

"As I said, Mr Harris, we are just supporting the police. Please direct any questions to Mr Lewis or Inspector Thomas."

"Thank you for your time, Mr Scott."

Jimmy ended the phone call. That had partly helped as he now knew what and who he was facing. On the other hand, it had made the situation a lot worse. Mr Lewis and Inspector Thomas hated him. There was no two ways about that. They had waited quite a while to try and get their revenge but when they had they had fired both barrels and left nothing in the chamber.

Next, Jimmy phoned Inspector Thomas.

"Good afternoon, Jimmy. I assume you have seen the review notice?"

"Yes, Inspector. I was hoping we could get together and talk about the matter."

"Jimmy, this is such a complex situation, we feel it would be much better all round to deal with this in committee."

"So you're not willing to talk about it?"

"We will in committee."

With that, the inspector rang off. This was turning into a nightmare. How could he negotiate his way through it if he couldn't talk about it with them? He sent Mr Lewis an email requesting a meeting and very promptly received one back saying 'see you in committee'. Well at least he had a few weeks to prepare his defence for the ensuing onslaught in committee.

The weeks ticked by and Jimmy started to sort his response out to the accusations. The Forth Street one was easy but it was the other 42 incidents that were his issue. There hadn't been that many incidents at the club in the time scale prescribed by the police in the review documents. What were they about? All they said were police logged incident.

Jimmy had written out all the dates and times of the incidents that the police were claiming had happened, and for the life of him, couldn't match anything to his incident sheets apart from two. Hannah walked into the office and he showed the problem to her. She too couldn't match them to any incident.

She studied the documents and times, she too went through the same incident logs. Jimmy went through to the kitchen and started making them both a cup of coffee. He suddenly heard Hannah call out form the office.

"I've got it."

Hannah suddenly jumped up from the leather chair she had been sat in and reached for a different box file off the shelf. She started rummaging through it. Jimmy hurried back into the office to see what was causing her to be so animated.

"That's the ID register."

"Bear with me."

Hannah spent about 5 minutes cross referencing the incidents with those logged in the ID register and then shot Jimmy the biggest smile.

"It's refusals for no ID or false ID"

"What?"

Jimmy had spent nearly three weeks pouring over this trying to make head nor tail of it and got nowhere.

"The 40 incidents are all refusals. They've obviously logged it against us for crime and disorder."

Jimmy was absolutely stunned but she was right. The times and dates all matched up. What were they playing at? Refusing people for no ID should've been a good thing. He cross referenced them all himself just to be sure. She was, however, spot on. Every detail matched up.

"Don't tell anyone about this. We're going to have to hit them cold with this so they can't cook anything up."

True to form, not a word was said to anyone. He very much appreciated Hannah's candour in this matter. She kept completely quiet. All Jimmy would tell people was we'll deal with it on the day of committee. He had worked out a plan and he was going to stick to it.

Isabelle came by the Sunday before the review to drop the children off. It was unusual for her to come in. She normally just watched them go into Jimmy's home from the car but tonight was different. She came to the door with the children. She was carrying a bag with some of his things in and used this as the pretence to gain admittance to Jimmy's flat.

"I thought you might like these bits. They're all yours."

"Thank you, that's very thoughtful of you."

"Are you set for the review?"

"As set as I'm ever going to be. I've gone through it all and think I'll be able to defend it."

"Word on the street is you're going to lose your personal licence and that the club will be closed."

"What have I told you about listening to the jungle grapevine? Anyway you're not here to talk shop. What can I do for you?"

"Can we go in the kitchen. It's not for the boys' ears."

They left the boys playing on their X-Box and went into the kitchen. Jimmy shut the door behind them. Unlike their other houses which they had shared, the kitchen in the flat was quite small and with the door shut it felt a bit weird. Almost claustrophobic but at least it was private.

"Fire away."

"I wanted you to hear it from me rather than off the street."

Jimmy could see Isabelle was very nervous and he sort to put her at ease.

"Come on, it's me, relax. Whatever it is, I'm sure I can deal with it."

"Ok, I've started seeing someone."

Jimmy wasn't sure why but it oddly felt like a proper gut punch. That really did signal they were over. He had convinced himself that he didn't care what she did but his reaction meant something inside him still did. He tried to remain composed.

"Good for you. Thank you for telling me. It's very thoughtful of you."

Jimmy was now operating on auto-pilot. He thought about telling her about Hannah but made the choice that it wasn't the right moment. Not in a confined kitchen with someone with known temper issues. Isabelle soon left Jimmy alone with his thoughts. He was pleased she was moving on and that she would now be someone else's problem but it did feel like the end of an era.

Tuesday morning came round very fast and soon Jimmy found himself sat back in Hockington House in the same committee room that he and Isabelle had previously sat together in. The only difference was this time he was sat on his own. The proceedings began in exactly the same format as the last time. Sir David invited Mr Lewis to state the polices reasons for the hearing and why they felt it serious enough to be brought before him.

"Mr Lewis, I must first ask did you try and engage with Mr Harris before commencing the licence review?"

"Yes, Sir David, we did."

"I object."

Sir David noticed Jimmy was standing up already. Sir David had an immediate sense of déjà vu. He couldn't help but feel that this had a very familiar feeling to the last time the authorities had dragged Mr Harris here. He just hoped and prayed Mr Lewis had done his homework better than Mr Scott had previously.

"On what grounds are you objecting, Mr Harris?"

"Sir David, I have an email here from Mr Lewis stating that instead of meeting, he would rather see me in committee. This was after I attempted to engage with the police to resolve the matter via a phone call."

"I'd like to see that email please."

Jimmy gave a copy to the clerk who in turn handed in to Sir David. Sir David read the email studying it very carefully.

"Mr Lewis, it quite clearly says here that you refused to meet with Mr Harris. This is against procedure, please explain yourself."

"Well, Sir David, Inspector Thomas and I decided that the gravitas of the situation required your expert opinions and advice. There are 43 incidents to be taken into consideration."

"Very well, Mr Lewis, objection overruled."

One nil to Mr Lewis, thought Jimmy. This was not going to plan at all. Mr Lewis then explained that within the time frame he had set out in the review outline, there were 43 incidents logged on InnKeeper, a police database of trouble hotspots and problems. All these incidents were attributed to Mr Harris' club. The sheer volume of incidents triggered a response from the police.

After what seemed like an eternity, Jimmy was given the right of rebuttal. He had objected no further to what Mr Lewis was saying and bided his time.

"Thank you, Sir David. Firstly, I wish to address the 42 incidents excluding the Fourth Street incident. I don't wish to teach anyone to suck eggs so I must start with a question for the committee. Do you know how InnKeeper works?"

There was some murmuring and some off mic discussions with the panel before Sir David replied.

"We understand that it is for logging incidents that occur in the city and that they are attributed to the relevant licensed premises which they come from or are nearest too."

"That's good. Does the committee know that InnKeeper does not differentiate between positive incidents and negative incidents?"

"Objection."

It was now Mr Lewis' turn to be standing and objecting. *At least his suit fits*, thought Jimmy to himself.

"On what grounds are you objecting, Mr Lewis?"

"The purpose of InnKeeper is to record incidents. InnKeeper is designed to record all incidents indiscriminately."

"I'm going to let Mr Harris explain his position, Mr Lewis, before I rule on it. Mr Harris?"

"There are two types of incidents in licensing: positive and negative. Negative is fighting, drug dealing, and things of that ilk. What Mr Lewis has not divulged is that there are also positive incidents being recorded. These include refusing entry to underage people that are then radioed through on the city radio to make other venues aware of such situations."

"Is that correct, Mr Lewis?"

Mr Lewis stood up and Jimmy could visibly see him trying to concoct an answer that would appease the committee. Jimmy took this moment to sit down and have a glass of water.

"As I stated earlier, all incidents are recorded on InnKeeper. If the licensed premises weren't there, then there would be no incidents logged. It is, therefore, the position of the police that all incidents are negative."

"You both have made strong cases; I can see both sides of the issue. We shall proceed as we are and let the facts come to light. Mr Harris, please continue."

"Thank you, Mr Chair. So as Mr Lewis has said 43 incidents in 13 weeks of which the club was open 78 days. Two of these incidents were fights. Not surprising really, we give people booze and some people react badly or have a bad night. However, one fight every month and a half isn't bad.

"40 incidents, that I will refer to as positive incidents are where myself or my team have ID'd people who have turned out not to have ID or been carrying false ID. We have been penalised for showing due diligence and upholding the licensing code."

"Is that correct, Mr Lewis?"

"As I have said, the police view all incidents as negative."

"But 40 were for IDing people who were underage?"

"I don't have the exact figure to hand."

Whilst Mr Lewis was battling with Sir David to retain any dignity he had left, Jimmy took the time to get his laptop out and line up a video he had prepared earlier on it. Eventually, after the back and forth, it was Jimmy's turn to continue his case.

"Thank you, Sir David. As I have already insinuated, the police have been underhand in their whole phrasing of this case against myself and my club. To prove how much, I wish to show you the CCTV from the night of the mass brawl in Fourth Street that Mr Lewis and Inspector Thomas are pinning on myself and my premises. May I show you this video? It's set up to show one minute in the club every second and runs from 7pm until 2am."

"Of course, Mr Harris."

Jimmy approached the bench and positioned the laptop so all on the committee could see. He hit play and sat down.

The panel sat eagerly watching the video. A series of four camera angles, three showing inside the club and one showing the road outside of the front of the club. All in grayscale as the lights in the club were off.

After the panel had watched through the first 3 minutes, or three hours where nothing happened at all except the odd car or person walking by on the street camera boredom had set in.

"Mr Harris, nothing has happened. Have you brought the correct CCTV?"

Jimmy rose to his feet and adjusted his suit, his new suit. He took a long look at Mr Lewis and Inspector Thomas before he looked squarely at the panel.

"Sir David, this is the correct CCTV, the date stamp in the corner corresponds with the date of the mass brawl in Fourth Street. This is the video and this is all it shows. A point that Mr Lewis has forgot to inform the panel of, but he has hung his whole case against me on, is we were shut that night. We don't open on Mondays. He can blame me as much as he wishes for the fight but I cannot alter or change the very simple fact that we were shut."

Jimmy could see the panel staring at him in complete amazement. He could see Mr Lewis sat to his right simmering with anger. He paused for a while to add a sense of gravitas to his argument before he continued.

"So just so the panel are really clear on the police's case against the club. 40 cases of stopping people entering the club due to being underage or carrying false ID and one case of a fight which happened in Fourth Street on a day when we were closed."

Jimmy returned to his seat and poured yet another glass of water, although he longed for something much stronger. He felt he'd given the best account of himself he possibly could. If they hung him out to dry now, then so be it. Sir

David told the room there would now be a recess whilst the committee retired and made its decision.

Jimmy didn't get up. He had no one with him so he couldn't see a point in loitering outside with people he didn't know, or people he could quite happily smack into next week.

Soon enough, the committee retuned. The room filled back up and everyone waited with bated breath for the verdict. No one more so than Jimmy who was trying everything to remain nonplussed by it all. Sir David stood at the bench. *Here we go*, thought Jimmy.

"The committee has concluded that Jumping Jacks has no case to answer. No licensed premises should be penalised for showing due diligence. We have also concluded to write to the chief inspector so that the role, and uses of InnKeeper, are more transparent. Furthermore, we will be writing to West Mercia to ensure that due diligence is shown in their work as trying to assign a fight to a club that is shut is scandalous. Committee is now in recess until the next case at 1pm."

With that, Sir David exited the room followed by the rest of the panel. Everyone else got up to leave but Jimmy remained seated. It seemed like such an anti-climax. All that effort and work, the time he'd put into defending himself and the club and for what? He thought to himself. The licensing officers would head back to their cosy jobs with no recriminations. He, however, would just wait for their next assault on his livelihood.

Jimmy was really thinking quite seriously about whether he could be bothered to carry on. He eventually gathered his things and went to go home.

As he got to his car in the car park, Mr Lewis crossed from his car to talk with him. Jimmy placed all his files in the boot of his car and turned to face him.

"Mr Harris, well played."

"Thank you."

"You realise you'll make a mistake eventually. In time you will run out of luck."

"Mr Lewis, with the upmost respect, and after your treatment of myself you're not actually due that much, eventually you will be forced to retire and when you do, I hope West Mercia police have an interview process in place which has a greater degree of due diligence than when you snuck in the job."

With that, Jimmy got into his car and drove away to enjoy the rest of his day.

Chapter 14
Men at Work

"Jimmy, can you come to the front door please?"

This was an unwelcome interruption to Jimmy's evening. Excusing himself from his friends and his brother's family, Jimmy made his way to the door. He had specifically asked not to be interrupted. *This had better be good*, he thought as he made his way through the crowd to the front doors.

"What's up?"

"Halfway down the queue. Right hand side, you can't miss it."

Lee had his heckles up so something was wrong. Jimmy stuck his head out of the door and lit a cigarette so his appearance at the front would appear to be innocuous. He looked down the queue and there she was. Isabelle queuing up for entry with her father and new boyfriend. Jimmy took a few drags and disposed of his cigarette.

"If they haven't got wristbands, let them in on my tab. I do want them shadowed wherever she goes though."

Lee nodded in approval and Jimmy headed back inside. It was a bit of an affront to be coming in but he was no longer involved. They were all just punters to him now. He gave the bar staff a heads up and headed back to his friends.

"Can I get you a drink?"

Isabelle startled Jimmy. He was utterly flummoxed by this turn of events. She'd never bought him a drink in her life.

"I'm good but thank you for offering."

"Thank you for letting us in."

"Not a problem, enjoy your evening."

Jimmy figured that Isabelle wanted a further conversation but at that moment, he had other things to do and conversations he'd much rather be involved in. Isabelle looked quite crestfallen as she walked away. Jimmy wasn't sure what the plan she had for that evening was but he just knew he wasn't becoming a part of it. He'd managed to avoid all the silliness for months and he fully intended to keep on doing so.

Hannah clocked off at 2am that evening. George could handle the final two hours and it would be good experience for him. It wasn't the busiest of nights and help was not far away should he need it.

"You did the right thing letting them in."

"I couldn't see an easier option."

"It was strange though, Jim. She has only drunk orange juice and lemonade all night."

"That is strange. She wanted to chat earlier but I was preoccupied. I wonder if she's pregnant? Come on, sit down, take a load off and tell me how your evening has been."

Hannah felt proud that Jimmy had tried to act magnanimously towards a distinct breach of decorum. However, she had other things she wished to discuss with him and now most of his friends and his brother had left it was the opportune moment. It was time to get certain things off her chest.

"You might be right. Guess we'll find out in time."

"That we will."

"We have to talk. I want more from this relationship. I'm not happy being a bit part as and when it suits you. All the clandestine meetings and hiding us from everyone, it's not for me. Where do you see us heading?"

"That's a bit full on when I've had a drink. I'm not sure, I thought we were just taking everything one day at a time. I'm not sure I can give more than that at the moment. We're having fun and enjoy each other's company, don't we?"

Hannah reached into her trouser pocket and handed Jimmy a letter addressed to himself.

"What's this?"

"Read it and find out. You're a great guy, Jimmy, and when you think you can *give more,* please let me know."

"I don't like games."

Hannah got out of her seat, finished her drink, and set the glass down.

"Neither do I, Jimmy, neither do I. Sometimes you just have to do what feels right for you."

With that, she walked out. Jimmy opened the envelope. She had resigned. She had also worked out that she had two weeks of holiday so she was done. It was another gut punch. Jimmy finished his drink and thought for a moment. He hadn't expected this but he also wasn't bowing to pressure, he was quite prepared to walk away.

He could feel a mixture of sadness and anger welling up inside him. He took his phone out of his pocket to message her but it was too late. She had already blocked him on every format. Jimmy figured she meant business. As he sat there in a slight daze, Isabelle came over and wished him good night, she and her entourage were off home.

"Are you ok?"

"I'm fine, Isabelle, you are unusually sober. Are you ok?"

"I am fine, Jimmy, just pregnant. I was going to tell you earlier but well…anyway now you know."

"Congratulations, I hope you and the baby are both staying healthy."

He gave her a kiss on the cheek and they shared a hug. Jimmy was finding this whole evening a little bit overwhelming. *Guess it never rains but it pours*, he thought to himself.

Jimmy resorted to what he did best in these situations, he wholeheartedly threw himself into his work and ignored it all. He knew no different than to bury his head and find other ways to occupy his time, it was his coping mechanism.

The Euro 2016 football championship was coming up and he was intending to maximise his extra TVs and make a quick killing on this. He put the adverts up. Special prices during the games. The club wasn't a sports bar but Jimmy hoped with a bit of luck, he could capitalise on other premises being oversubscribed and make a few quid. He'd checked a few times but Hannah still wasn't in the mood for talking as he was still blocked.

The day before England's first game, he was made aware of a problem. Big yellow road closed overnight signs were erected outside the club. The enforcement was overnight from 6pm to 7am for essential road works. The day of the first game, Jimmy might as well have thrown the towel in. The council dug up the road. The noise was horrendous with jack hammers and assorted heavy machinery going up and down right outside the front doors.

As the tournament progressed, it got no easier. The whole road was dug up, the ironworks exposed, and then the tarmac was re-laid. The smell was unbelievable. Jimmy even shut the doors some nights to avoid the smell becoming ingrained in the club. The whole time this was going on, Jimmy had radio silence from Hannah.

A month had passed and he had hoped she would perhaps see the error of her ways and contact him but there was nothing. After five weeks, he received a request for a reference from another bar in the city for her.

Sunday came and Isabelle dropped the boys off. Jimmy sat at his desk and wrote Hannah a fantastic reference. He double checked WhatsApp but she still had him blocked. *C'est la vie*, he told himself, not believing a word of it. The Euros had not been good. Not only had the council thwarted his attempt to earn a few extra quid with their road replacement but England had got knocked out nice and early so only the hardcore fans were out for the games. Although, the road outside the club was now absolutely lovely.

It was very apparent to everyone in the club what a loss Hannah was to Jimmy's operation. He tried repeatedly to downplay the situation but everyone knew. The spark wasn't there. Jimmy knew it and the staff knew it. The elixir of life wasn't part of it anymore. Jimmy knew which bar she was working at but he avoided it like the plague.

In truth, he had avoided going out at all in case he bumped into her. A couple of times he had seen her car but he had pretended that he hadn't, deliberately looking in different directions.

September came and with it came Zoya. Jimmy showed her through to the club's office. *Had it really been 2 years?* Jimmy thought to himself. Jimmy settled in his chair with Zoya sat opposite.

"Good afternoon, Jimmy, how are you?"

"I'm good, thank you, how are you?"

"I'm fine, thank you. Thought we should catch up and see what we're going to do going forward."

Jimmy had been caught slightly on the hop so he was having to wing this whole meeting. He knew that not announcing that she was coming was part of the plan. It gave her the edge.

"Fire away then. What are you asking?"

Zoya went into her side bag and produced a large brown A4 envelope that wasn't sealed. From that envelope, she took out the proposed contract and handed it to Jimmy. Jimmy could see all the rental amounts had been highlighted in yellow. They were more than the prices she had quoted 2 years previously. He took a moment to absorb what he was seeing.

"How did you come to these prices?"

"Fair market value, Jimmy. This time it is non-negotiable."

"Zoya, over half the building is still empty, these prices are Jackanory! If you had got more tenants in, if you had continued tidying up the building, then maybe I would consider it. As it stands, it's not worth it."

"Jimmy, I could easily get someone in to take over and run a club here."

"Getting someone in and making it work are two different things. I will not pay more than I am now. It would be financial suicide."

"Jimmy, I like you but this is business and they are the prices. You have until 31 December to let me know, otherwise I will expect you to vacate your unit by 15 January as per your current lease."

"I do love how you distance yourself from the premises and the businesses by referring to them as units."

Jimmy was slightly surprised how hard Zoya was playing. She had a game plan and was sticking to it. He wasn't going to fall out with her as she was just doing her job but he did get the impression that she thought he needed the building more than he really did.

"Thank you, Zoya. I will take these home and study them."

Zoya started gathering her things together and preparing to leave.

"Jimmy, I'd like you to stay but you must understand I have a business to run. This is the latest licensed club in the city. That alone means the rent should be more."

"Not a problem, Zoya. I'll see you out."

They walked towards the front doors and Jimmy held them open for her. The rain outside was thundering down, a real autumnal shower.

"I hope to hear from you soon, Jimmy."

"Zoya, I think you should be aware that the licence on this building is my licence. It's not yours, it's not belonging to the building, it is mine. Therefore, if I decide not to continue, I will offer to transfer the licence to you at a fair market price and if you don't agree, I will surrender it to the authorities and there will be no licence. As you have already pointed out, it is the latest licence in the city and adds value to the rentable value."

"Jimmy, there is no need to be like that."

"You fired the first shots. I will come back to you in due course with my offer."

With that, Jimmy shut the doors. He stayed by the front doors. He was struck by the magnitude of the threat he had just made and couldn't physically move. He felt sick to the core. Had he just helped or hindered the whole situation? Should he have said a damn thing? His mind was swarming with ideas.

Jimmy didn't talk to anyone about the proposed rent increase and the options on the table. He waited a week and sent an email to Zoya stating he would be willing to stay for 3 more years but the maximum he would pay would be the original amount she requested 2 years ago. He didn't hold out much hope she would agree and the lack of response did feel a bit ominous to him.

The doorbell rang one Tuesday evening. George was running the club for him so he could work on some advertising. Jimmy ignored the first three or four rings but then figured he'd better answer before it upset the other residents. Jimmy answered the door in his dressing gown and pyjamas. He stood there looking at Lee and Sebastian.

"Come on, get dressed, boss, we're going out."

Jimmy didn't want to leave the sanctuary of his flat but he knew he had no option. This was a demand not a request. He'd avoided anything since June if he was honest and it was now September. They had quite clearly made the choice that enough was enough. Jimmy made himself perfectly clear that he was not going to the bar she worked in. She had a job to do and he wasn't going to impinge on that.

He got himself changed and they headed into the city. Both of them had got quite a head start on Jimmy, clearly part of the reason they had turned up. A bit of Dutch courage first before kidnapping the boss.

As they arrived at their second destination, Lee enthusiastically ordered shots. Jimmy was fully aware that although they were bigger than him, he could drink them into submission. He took the shots Lee ordered and settled down into a sofa.

"What's the game plan, boys? Drink me into submission and go from there?"

"Jim, this is all so silly. We all know about you and her."

"Do I look like I give a fuck? I have certain barriers, push them and you're gone! Anyhow, this was her choice not mine and, to be perfectly frank, guys, it's none of your business."

Jimmy was taking no prisoners, although his two assailants were bearing the brunt of it. They were hammered. Jimmy knew this and he now had to protect them from their own stupidity. They had been drunk at his door and now they had passed the point of no return. It had got to such a point that he knew only Hannah could actually dig him out of this mess. There was no way a taxi would take them and she would have her car at work.

Jimmy now had two options. One, ditch the idiots who had dragged him out or head to Juice where Hannah now worked and politely ask if she could help him get them home. He couldn't leave his mates so realistically he had only one option.

As he walked them down Forth Street, he felt like he was babysitting two giants who couldn't walk in straight line if you paid them. He eventually managed to get them into Juice. Hannah was behind the bar.

She spotted him before he spotted her. This was an unexpected intrusion into her night but she was pleased to see Jimmy.

"Good evening."

"Mr Harris, good evening. How are you?"

"I'm ok, thank you for asking"

Jimmy was standing at the bar and he couldn't take his eyes off Hannah. She looked amazing. Her beautiful brunette hair cascading over her shoulders, her greeny blue eyes sparkling brighter than the sun itself. God how he had missed her.

"I should've come to see you sooner. I'm sorry."

"You're here now. I've missed you, Jimmy. I really have. I'm sorry it all ended the way it did. It just all got on top of me and I had to get away."

"It's ok. You look like you're currently thriving. I'll be honest, I had intended to drop these two here and run away."

"Well, I'm glad you didn't. I assume you want help getting chuckle one and chuckle two home."

"Yes, that would be good. I figured that I had no hope carrying them home and that a taxi was out the question."

"I've got a few things to finish up and then I shall assist you in your quest."

"That would be much appreciated. Could I possibly get a drink please? This poor knight is parched from his said quest."

Hannah smiled at him and got him his usual vodka and red bull.

Soon enough, they'd managed to get Lee and Seb into Hannah's car. They dropped Seb off first and Jimmy helped him in through his front door. Next was Lee who only lived 100 yards from Jimmy. Jimmy got him out of the car and lent him up against his front wall. Jimmy popped his head back inside the car.

"I can walk from here, Hannah, save you waiting around whilst I get him inside. It will probably take a while."

"I don't mind waiting for you."

"It's ok. I'll probably be a quite some time getting him sorted."

"Jim, will you call me this week?"

"You'll have to unblock me and then I'll see what I can do."

"If I unblock you, then you best call me."

"Goodnight, Hannah."

Jimmy turned round and got Lee standing up. He heard Hannah's car make its way along the road and out of earshot. He'd have liked to have taken her up on the offer of waiting but had no intention of over playing his hand.

"We knew you should come out."

"Come on, you, let's get you inside."

"You love her."

"If you say one more word, I'll leave you here."

He draped one of his giant arms around Jimmy's neck and together they made their way to his front door. After 2-3 minutes, Lee eventually found his keys and undid the latch. As the door shut and Jimmy started making his way back down the garden path, he was sure he heard a giant thud that he assumed was Lee falling over. He was inside warm and dry so Jimmy figured he had done all he could for him. He made his way home and back to the sanctuary of his flat.

Just over half an hour later, his phone went off. It was a text from Hannah and just simply said, 'Testing, testing. Good night, Mr Harris'.

As the week progressed, they exchanged quite a few messages back and forth. The banter was still there, the fun was still there and he knew how he felt. Jimmy was pleased they were talking but wanted to take this one day at a time. Jimmy was surprised he found himself checking his phone first thing in the morning to see if she had messaged him, and when she had, he was ecstatic. He was happy meeting for a coffee once or twice a week but soon they were meeting almost every day for a coffee or a walk. Any excuse to see her really.

As they walked arm in arm through Cherry Blossom Wood taking in the autumnal colours, it just felt right. A peace had descended over him and he knew in his heart he was with his soulmate.

"So, Mr Harris, this lovely dance we have been having has gone on for nearly a month now, and as much as this girl loves dancing, she does need to know if she needs a backup dance partner or if this current one can give her all she needs."

"This boy will dance all night for you and will do his upmost best to give you everything she needs, desires, and requires."

"And this boy will he hold this girl's hand in public and be proud to be seen with her?"

"If this girl will hold his hand in public, then he will go everywhere with her."

Together, they strolled on through the woods only now they were hand in hand, their fingers tightly entwinned together keeping each other warm and happy.

October was roaring along. The time disappearing with not enough time every day to do what he set out to achieve. Jimmy was trying very hard to make a conscious effort to make time for Hannah, he wasn't going to blow this situation for a second time. He was also busy plotting his biggest Halloween party ever. He had smoke machines but he had ordered quite a few floor smokers to go around the building and some animatronics to be placed strategically around the club.

The posters were done, the Halloween pub crawl was all organised, and now it was just a case of waiting for the day to arrive.

Jimmy could barely contain his excitement as he fired everything up on the night of his Halloween party. The whole club was decorated from top to bottom. All doors had decals on them, the ceiling was covered in hanging bats and witches, the walls were adorned with cobwebs and cut outs of Dracula, ghosts and assorted horror scenes. The animatronics were situated at the front and on the bars.

All the smoke machines were full and the timers were set so they would go off automatically. Jimmy had even sourced some decals for the mirrors in the bathroom and the exploding balloons were all loaded and ready to go off in the ceiling. There was very little more that Jimmy could do.

This year, he'd made the decision to let George lead the procession around the city. He took himself off to Juice to see Hannah. The pub crawl would be going in there right before it headed to the club so he wouldn't miss the fun at the club. Hannah was quite busy so he got himself a drink and went and sat outside the front to watch the world go by. It was about 9pm when she finally got a break and came to see him. She brought the city radio with her.

"Why, Frankenstein, you do scrub up well!"

"Thank you. You look pretty awesome too, Miss Harley Quinn."

As they sat there, the radio went off.

"Jumping Jacks, can you hear us?"

"Loud and clear, Echo Alpha. Is everything ok?"

"We were going to ask you the same thing, there's a lot of smoke coming out of your building."

"One of our smoke machines has gone a bit nuts, we're sorting it."

"Better safe than sorry, we're sending a fire engine down to check on things."

Jimmy sighed, stood up and looked at Hannah.

"I would give you a kiss but I'm worried our make-up would stick together. I'd best go and see what's going on. I'll see you later."

"I'll be down as soon as I finish. Don't forget stay in character on your walk over. Just imagine Michael Jackson's *Thriller* playing in your ears."

Jimmy walked as quickly as he could to the club and he was there in less than 5 minutes but the fire engine still beat him to the door. It was quite a bizarre sight with fire officers running around in breathing apparatus and a whole group of people dressed as Jack Sparrow and his pirate colleagues trying to get into the club. Jimmy slipped in and put all the extractor fans on. As he did so, he came face to face with a fire officer telling him he had to evacuate.

"Give it 2 minutes, I've put the extractors on. They'll soon shift the smoke."

"I must insist you follow me, Sir."

Jimmy was having none of it and proceeded to go round turning off smoke machines. The fire officer followed him round the building as he did so. When the last one was off, it was already apparent the smoke was clearing. Jimmy made his way to the front door. The fire officer in charge was not impressed.

"You will be hearing about this Monday. I'm going straight to the chief with it."

"Oh come on, it was a technical issue, there was no real harm."

It was too late though, the damage was done. Jimmy resigned himself to an impending problem to deal with on Monday.

The rest of the evening was a tremendous success. It was the largest Halloween pub crawl yet and George hadn't lost anyone. Jimmy was sat near the bar when Hannah came in.

"So I hear you're now quite popular with the local fire brigade!"

"Yes, I am. I am top of their Christmas card list. What a palaver! It's the least of my worries though."

He then talked Hannah through his current lease issues as they shared a few drinks. It felt cathartic for Jimmy to get it all off his chest. The weight was lifted and he was able to share his dilemma. He hoped that by sharing Hannah would see just how much he trusted her and valued her opinion.

"Ok, I get it's a lot of money but what will you do if you don't run the club? Have you got a plan?"

"I haven't given that much thought at all. I've got a few quid put by so I'll be alright for a few months. Plus if I sell everything, I'll make a few bob."

"Well, whatever you choose, I will be right by you. It'll work out for the best. Who knows they might accept your counteroffer."

Monday rolled around and Jimmy found himself sat at the bar with Oliver Andrews, the Chief Fire Officer in the city. Jimmy made them both a coffee, although it had been made very clear that this was no social visit.

"Mr Harris, what occurred was a disgrace! We should not have to send an engine and whole unit out to deal with you on a Saturday for a self-inflicted act."

"Mr Andrews, I have apologised. As soon as I was made aware of the issue, I came and fixed it within 10 minutes. Short of flogging myself, I'm not sure what more I can do."

"Mr Harris, I had both the police and council licensing officers phone me earlier. Both would be supportive of me putting your club in review."

"I'll bet they would."

"I, however, have decided to offer you another option. I want to borrow your club for a training exercise. It seems you can provide my officers with a live situation to practise search and rescue. It says on your website you are shut on Mondays which is one of our quieter nights so this would fit well with ourselves."

"I would be happy to help."

"We would need some people to be in the building to be rescued. Could you arrange that?"

"I can get some staff in and I do a lot of youth mentoring. I'm sure a few of those guys and girls would be up for it."

"Well, then it seems we have come to an arrangement that all parties find acceptable. Two weeks today at 7pm sharp. I will inform the city CCTV what is going on so there is no confusion."

He picked up his hat and notes signalling their meeting was at an end.

Thus, it came to pass that two weeks later on a cold Monday night in November, Jimmy cranked the speakers up, set the lights off, and let the smoke machines go off at maximum capacity. The teenagers and staff were all in different places around the building and Jimmy was in the DJ box. Jimmy couldn't help but liken it to a giant game of hide and seek. He could see how beneficial it was for the fire brigade.

When the exercise had been thoroughly completed and the chief was happy, he came and sort Jimmy out.

"That went incredibly well, Mr Harris. My officers have learnt much and gained experience."

"Not a problem, Mr Andrews."

"Mr Harris, this has been your get out of jail card tonight. However going forward, could I ask what you would think of doing this more regularly?"

"Mr Andrews, I have no issue but the kit I have in there is transferrable to the other pubs and clubs. I think it would be helpful all round if we included them. I know how much I have learnt tonight. It could be invaluable for every other venue to be involved."

"That is a very good idea. I will call a meeting after Christmas is over and get everyone together to discuss the matter. Good night, Mr Harris."

The fire engines disappeared into the night. Jimmy thanked everyone for coming and shut the club down. It was unusual for him to be out on a Monday after 11pm. He just hoped his mum had managed to get the boys to bed in a timely fashion as they had school the next day.

Chapter 15
Deal or No Deal

An email came through from Zoya at the start of December. She had made a counteroffer to Jimmy's counteroffer. The timescale was the same. It would start at the rate he offered and then go up in increments to get to what she was after for the final year. This was unexpected and Jimmy wasn't really sure how he felt about it.

He knew both Hannah and TJ were unsure what he would do without his club. Jimmy had acknowledged to both of them he would miss it but was sure he would find something to occupy himself and pay the bills. It was a lot of food for thought. Unfortunately with it coming up to Christmas, he didn't have much spare time to think about it all. He had Christmas parties to organise, stock to sort and staff to deal with.

Jimmy was sat at the bar in Juice one Wednesday night two weeks before Christmas staring into space.

"Penny for your thoughts."

"Not sure they're worth that much."

Jimmy smiled at Hannah. She was all too aware what he was thinking about. He'd been sitting there for an hour with the same drink so she was sure he was thinking about the club again. She had tried to remain impartial on the matter. Offering her thoughts but making no actual recommendations.

"I've said to you a few times that you have to do what is right for you. No one else can answer that question. Has Zoya contacted you?"

"Yes, she has. She wants an answer. I said I'd let her know by next Monday. I'm edging towards signing it. 3 more years and that gives me time to plan my out. Perhaps get on a course or two at the college. Maybe get a proper job. Mum has been on to me for years to do so."

"That's not a bad idea. It would at least buy you time."

That evening when they got home from Juice, Jimmy brought Hannah a cup of tea. She looked at him and pointed at the giant box in the front room.

"Oh yes, that. That was supposed to be surprise for you but I haven't got round to building it."

"What is it?"

"It's a wardrobe and draws thing for you to keep your clothes in. You're here most nights, I just figured it would make your life easier."

"That's very kind of you."

"No problem at all. I mean let's be honest, you basically you do live here. I do half your washing, I just have nowhere to put the clothes. You might as well live here!"

"Mr Harris, are you insinuating you want me to live here?"

"Why not? You basically do. Think of the money you'll save on fuel!"

Jimmy sat down and she hugged him almost spilling the cup of tea she hadn't spotted he was holding on his lap.

"I take it that's a yes then."

Inside, Hannah was thrilled. She knew what a big step this was for Jimmy and with everything he had going on, he had still taken the time to think about her needs. It meant the world to her. In her mind, she was already planning what bits she was going to bring from her mum and dad's house. This would definitely not look like a bachelor pad come the New Year.

"Before you tell anyone or officially move in, I will need to let Isabelle know. She did that courtesy for me; it wouldn't be right otherwise."

"Ok, Jim, I understand. I'll bring a couple of bits each time and we'll aim to get it all sorted in January. How does that sound?"

"Perfect, just perfect."

The next morning, Jimmy wrote an email to Zoya asking for the paperwork to be sent over so he could double check it before signing it. He had made his mind up; 3 more years. He was half tempted to offer Hannah her job back at the club but had thought better of it. They were going to living together, working together might be too much.

Thursday night, Jimmy was working in the club when he got a call from Hannah.

"Evening, Jim, any chance you could come and get George out of here. He's being a dick."

"What is he doing?"

"He's had a row with his girlfriend, she's walked out and he's now acting like Billy Big Bollocks."

"Fuck's sake, give me a few minutes and I'll be there."

Jimmy explained to the guys what was going on; leaving Lee in charge he headed straight for Juice. This was the last thing he needed. At least it was early in the evening. He arrived at Juice, stopped at the door, prepped himself and walked in. As he pushed the heavy oak front door open, he could hear George.

"Answer your phone, you bitch!"

Jimmy stood just inside the front door and looked square at George. He'd had a skin full and could barely stand. Hannah looked over at Jimmy. Jimmy remained expressionless and eventually, George turned round to see him.

"JIMMY! What are you doing here? Come have a drink with me!"

"I think you've had enough, George. I think it's home time."

The door staff employed at Juice were shirt fillers at best and they, although watching the situation, were grateful to see Jimmy. Jimmy remained impassive, he acknowledged them and walked towards his employee. George was oblivious to how angry Jimmy was.

"Drink up, George, you're going home."

"Jimmy, I'm ok. I'll be fine."

"George, I'm not asking, I'm telling! It's game over tonight."

"Ahh, come on, Jimmy, be reasonable!"

"I am, George, that's why I'm saying drink up. Don't you dare be embarrassing me in here."

Before Jimmy could even start escorting him out, George had gone to fly at the first member of door staff he saw. His anger towards his girlfriend manifesting itself as anger towards the door staff. Jimmy wrapped him up in a heartbeat and dragged him out. He was a strong lad and sessions at the gym with Lee had clearly helped his core strength.

Jimmy was battle hardened and that saw him get the edge. Jimmy had him tight though. As they flew into the street, Jimmy ended up sat on top of him.

Jim sat there knowing George would blow himself out in due course. Hannah came out of the front door and saw the sight of Jimmy sat on George's back. She carefully placed his baseball cap back on his head as a police van was driving by. The van stopped and the officers got out. They approached the scene.

"It's ok, officers, I'll get him home. He's just had a bad night."

"Jimmy, we're gonna have to see him making his way home."

"You hear that, George? Get up."

Jimmy stood him up, George was standing with Jimmy gripping his elbow. He'd seen Jimmy do it a hundred times to customers being ejected but now it was happening to him. He'd never worked out quite how he did it but just that simple grip turned whoever he was dealing with, regardless of size, into a toy.

"Walk!"

Jimmy frog marched him down Forth Street and off into the night. George lived by the local park and so Jimmy knew it wouldn't take long to march him home to his mother. After about 150 yards, Jimmy let go of his arm.

"Seriously, mate, what are you playing at?"

Even in his state of inebriation, George could tell Jimmy was angry, very angry. George snuck his phone out of his pocket again and went to ring his girlfriend.

"Are you sure you want to do that? Angry words can't be taken back or undone."

They walked on with Jimmy half chaperoning him, half holding him up. As they passed the local lake that led to the park George's house, his girlfriend answered the phone. Jimmy felt empathy for George but also knew, from his own inabilities to control his drunken temper in his youth, that this was a mistake. Within 30 seconds, he was proven right as a drunken George totally lost his temper.

"Fuck you, fuck you, it's over."

With that, he threw his phone in the lake. *What a waste*, Jimmy thought as he watched the phone hit the water. George was now incandescent with rage. Jimmy was also aware that the police had followed them at a distance to this point. George in his drunken mindset decided he needed to retrieve the phone from the lake and went to climb the small fence that surrounded the lake. Jimmy successfully managed to man handle him back to the pavement.

Jimmy could hear the boots hit the floor, running towards him before George did. Jimmy knew it was too late. It was Christmas and the police had better things to do than babysit people. They slammed George against the nearest fencepost and unleashed the handcuffs on him.

"You tried, Jim."

Jimmy was of clear conscience that he had tried for his friend, and his employee, but it was of little consolation as he was dragged away in handcuffs.

"We'll take him, get him to sleep it off and read him the riot act in the morning."

"Thank you."

That was all Jimmy could muster in response as the back of the van was slammed shut. Jimmy dusted himself off and started walking back to the club. His phone pinged with a message. It was Hannah.

"Thanks, Jim, is he home safe?"

"Don't ask and nope."

Jimmy finished his text, wrapped his coat around himself tightly, and headed back to his club. He really was starting to hate Christmas. At least it wasn't snowing he told himself.

The Friday night that followed didn't do anything to really appease his dislike of Christmas. George was so contrite it got annoying, constantly checking if he was ok or if he needed a drink. He dealt with morons trying to climb the Christmas trees in the club, drunk staff parties not grasping that some people in their parties were too drunk to come in and a lot of silly domestics. Christmas was very stressful and a lot of people had trouble handling the stress.

The Saturday night was much better and Jimmy almost felt like it was the lull before the storm. He had geared himself up for a full-on crazy night and bugger all happened. It was a total anti-climax. *Sometimes you have to take the rough with the smooth*, Jimmy thought to himself as George brought him another drink.

Sunday night, Jimmy had said to Hannah to come round after 7pm. He knew Isabelle would be dropping the boys off to him and he wanted the conversation without anyone watching or eavesdropping. He watched attentively at the front window for her car to pull up. It did so and he bounded out of the door.

"Good evening, boys. Good evening, Isabelle."

He looked at her new partner, Keith, and gave him a nod of approval.

"Have you got a few minutes. I just need a quick chat."

"Of course, Jim."

Isabelle parked up her car in the car park. He couldn't believe she was seven and a half months pregnant and was still driving. They all made their way into Jimmy's flat. Jimmy had already set the X-Box up for the boys so they dove straight into that. Jimmy asked Isabelle to join him in the claustrophobic kitchen and shut the door. Jimmy didn't care that he had put Keith's nose out of joint with this scenario. By the same token, he hadn't asked Isabelle to leave him in the car, but she had.

"I am repaying your favour to myself. I have asked Hannah to move in with me."

Isabelle reached out and gave Jimmy a big hug even though her massive bump was in the way.

"I'm happy for you, Jimmy. She's a great girl and the boys adore her. I have a question to ask you, well moreover, Keith and I have a question to ask you."

Isabelle waddled out of the kitchen, went into the car park and brought Keith into the fold.

"We are expecting a little girl and we were wondering, Jimmy…"

She looking at Keith for support and solidarity, he gave her the nod of approval.

"Will you be her godfather?"

Jimmy didn't know how to respond to this request, he felt an amazing number of conflicting emotions. He could see their reasons. It was a reaffirmation that as a big giant inclusive family they were all on the same hymn page. He felt it would ease Isabelle's conscience more than assist the child. *Look at the big picture*, he told himself, *they could end up being one big friendly dysfunctional functioning family.*

"I would be absolutely honoured."

Keith was immediately shaking his hand, like for the first time since the party at the big house when he thought Jimmy was going to stab the shit out of him. Isabelle waited and gave him another hug.

"Thank you."

She whispered that in his ear so only he could hear. Isabelle knew Jimmy was all about the peace and quiet in life. The kitchen door opened and there was their youngest.

"I want a milkshake please."

"I'll bring it out to you."

As he left the kitchen and returned to the X-Box, there was a collective sigh of relief. They might not have been the perfect family but at least they were trying. Jimmy felt like they had reached a level of understanding that meant they could go forward. He knew he hadn't been perfect throughout this situation and thus he would not be the one to start throwing stones. *Life was too short for that sort of bullshit*, he thought to himself.

Isabelle and Keith bade their goodbyes and set off into the night and Jimmy sat down awaiting Hannah's arrival so he could recant her with how everything had gone down.

This Christmas week was going to be very different as Christmas Eve was a Saturday and thus, everyday would be fundamentally different to normal. Jimmy had decided way before that from Wednesday onwards, he was going to throw the kitchen sink at it. Pretend everyday was a Saturday. As the week progressed, he was proven right to do so. It was chaos.

On the Wednesday, he received all the details from Zoya but it was too late to get a lawyer to witness any signatures, they'd all signed off until the New Year. Jimmy phoned Zoya and her let know that it was a problem, but it would be dealt within the New Year. There was still time and Zoya had no issues with the delay.

It's amazing what can change in such a short space of time. Feelings, emotions and plans. By the time Jimmy and the team had reached 23 December, everyone was ready to admit enough was enough. It had been idiot central and everyone had a guts full. As they started the penultimate night before Christmas, there wasn't one member of the door team not nursing an injury of some sort.

Jimmy was at the front door pleasantly surprised how quiet the night was thus far as the city radio crackled into life.

"All premises stand by for transmission...all premises stand by for transmission."

Jimmy knew this had to be serious. They rarely did a BOLO to all but they had decided to.

"Everyone is to be made aware that the charity Santa run has gone rogue."

What does that mean? Jimmy thought to himself. The charity Santa run ran every year raising £1000s for charity how the hell had that gone rogue?

"They've been directing traffic and causing mayhem. Please radio through any Santa Clauses coming to your front door! The police are very keen to talk with them."

If they hadn't sounded so serious, Jimmy would've sworn that they were taking the piss. However, this was as serious on the radio as it got and within 15 minutes, Jimmy found himself stopping a group of 12 Santas entering the building. All he could do was pray that the police were going to be reasonable and proportionate in their response. That was a great plan in theory.

The PCSOs who turned up managed to make a mountain out of a mole hill and within 20 minutes since their original interaction, Jimmy found he was trying to stop the PCSOs getting the shoeing of their life. This was going down as an absolute bloody disaster. The police vans rolled up at the front containing proper police officers. As funny as it was seeing 12 Santas loaded into the back of the vans, Jimmy was acutely aware he had taken several huge blows.

Most notably to his right eye. A haymaker he hadn't seen coming had destroyed his glasses and pumped straight into his eye. He couldn't even describe who had hit him as they all looked like fucking Santa Claus!

Jimmy went to his office and spent half an hour trying to stem the flow of blood and limit the damage to his eye. His glasses were screwed beyond redemption but he had a spare pair at home.

"They said you were in here. You ok?"

Quite literally what a sight for sore eyes, or sore eye, Hannah was.

"Ah, what a shit storm it's been. You're early? I wasn't expecting you until 1am or 2am?"

"Been one of those nights, shut early to get out of the firing line."

"It's quite amazing, isn't it, it's like a pack mentality. It's not a full moon, is it?"

Jimmy stood and took stock of the situation. It wasn't even midnight and everything was going wrong. He walked with Hannah to the bar. The decorations looked amazing, the inside of the club was pure harmony, they were successfully keeping all the muppets out. This was what was needed, this was what people paid their money for. Jimmy got himself and Hannah a drink and headed for a table. Hannah knew he would be off to the front door any second.

True to form, he set his drink down and headed to the door. The front was a riot. Jimmy looked at the melees ensuing all over the street and declared that the door was now shut to new customers. He sent all door staff inside to keep tabs on the customers they had inside. He, himself, remained bolted to the door. Jimmy stood there refusing innumerate people on the grounds of being of full. Jimmy surveyed the street. Heading towards him was TJ and five members of his staff.

"Lee, open the rear fire doors for TJ please."

Jimmy radioed through and directed TJ to the back door. It was easier than sending them through the front door, it could've caused a riot with the current crop of idiots he was dealing with.

"They're in, bossman."

Jimmy was pleased they were in but he knew he still had two hours refusing people on the door. The door behind him opened a few inches.

"Where do you keep the hi vis jackets?"

"On the back hangers in the cloak room."

TJ appeared a few seconds later putting one of the jackets on.

"Can I get you a drink?"

"No, I'm all good but thank you. You are also really early. What's going on?"

"Dickheads everywhere. We shut early. I thought to myself why should you have all the fun and so here I am."

"Thank you. You planning on rolling back the years, are you?"

Together, they stood on the front door refusing people. It was like a throwback to Parker's. Jimmy knew his friend could be inside partying with his other friends and TJ knew Jimmy would stand out here on his own taking on all comers. It wasn't bravado, it was the job and TJ knew he'd instilled that discipline in him over the years. Never ask anyone to do something you wouldn't do and lead by example. As he looked at Jimmy staring down and refusing group after group, he couldn't help but feel he'd created a machine.

Jimmy and TJ successfully navigated their way through the remaining few hours of the penultimate night through Christmas. Hannah kept them fully libated in beverages and TJ couldn't help but comment that Jimmy had got a good girl there and perhaps, she needed her head read being with him. As the night ended, Jimmy informed the staff that they weren't opening Christmas Eve. Go and enjoy some family time.

As Jimmy sat down on his sofa in his flat, after what had been a tough Friday, even for Christmas it was exceptionally brutal. He felt his eye sting where he taken that thundering right hand. He got up and went into his kitchen and retrieved his spare set of glasses. On the side lay the new terms of his lease extension. He picked them up and reread them.

Another 3 years. More rent, more regulations and he knew the world was changing. Nightclubs were no longer the mecca they once were. He poured himself a drink and went and sat back down.

He knew Isabelle had the pool hall and she had extended her lease but there was something in his gut, a niggling feeling that it would be better to call time on his own terms rather than when he couldn't pay the bills. He took his phone from his pocket. There were a few messages on Facebook from people who had lost items that evening but he decided to ignore those until the morning came; wasn't like he could do anything about it at that precise moment.

Jumping Jacks' last night will be New Years Eve Monday, 31 December. Thank you all for your support over the years. #Mammajammaskeen #Nightclub #independent #NewYearsEve, he typed into Twitter. He stared at it for a long time, he looked around his flat at some of the mementos from over the years and that brought a smile to his face. Jimmy finished his drink. The timing felt right. He was very much at peace with the decision. He knew as soon as he sent the tweet, his phone would blow up with messages but it was ok.

He opened up WhatsApp and clicked on the club group. 'Guys, New Years Eve will be our last night. I wanted you all to know first before I made it public'. He sent that to the group and then clicking back on Twitter, he sent the tweet.

And just like that, with one simple tweet, he brought the curtain down on 20 years of working in nightclubs. He turned off notifications on his phone and went to bed. He slept well that night for the first time in a long time.

He woke up and turned his phone notifications on. He dismissed almost everyone. Except one. He looked at it hard and long. He sat up in bed and reread it five times.

"So I understand you're about to be an unemployed bum. I can offer you a job as a glass collector?"

Jimmy laughed as he sat up in bed. He had laid out his situation for everyone. He had umm and ahhed enough about what he was going to do but this Christmas has made it very clear, enough was enough.

He enjoyed his Christmas Eve. He took the time away from work to make sure everyone's presents were as they needed to be. He was crap at wrapping presents but at least he had tried. He realised the biggest difference would be time. He would actually have some.

As Christmas Eve's go, he spent the time deflecting away suggestions he should come out; the staff were obviously out enjoying themselves. He fully intended to wake up Christmas day fully refreshed and without any new injuries or lethargy caused by alcohol.

The doorbell went at about 7:30pm and he thought about ignoring it but ultimately decided not to, it was Christmas after all. When he opened the door, Hannah stood there. She didn't say a word, just handed him a present. It was beautifully wrapped. He looked at her and she put a finger to his lips.

"I'll see you tomorrow night."

He gave her a kiss and she walked away slowly. He knew she had family things planned in the day but he would see her soon enough.

Jimmy woke early on Christmas day. He knew he had no one to wake up with but he also knew by teatime, he'd have a flat full of people. He had to get the food cooking so no one would go hungry. He couldn't remember who he had invited to tea, he thought it was everyone. It was probably easier to work out who wasn't invited. He knew Isabelle was dropping the kids off at 2pm and he was greatly looking forward to that.

Jimmy stood there in his kitchen; it wasn't the size he had grown accustomed to over the years but he felt complete in it. Somehow by losing everything, he had gained a sense of self-worth. By deciding to end the club, he had gained a sense of self purpose. Stood alone in his kitchen, waiting for his real friends to arrive and his family, he had a sense that although for the second time in his life he was unemployed, everything was going to be just fine.